Empire Builders

Francis Lynde

Illustrated by Jay Hambidge

EMPIRE BUILDERS

FRANCIS LYNDE

EMPIRE BUILDERS
By
FRANCIS LYNDE
Author of

TheQuickening,TheGrafters
A Fool for Love, etc.

With Illustrations by

JAY HAMBIDGE

INDIANAPOLIS

THE BOBBS-MERRILL COMPANY

PUBLISHERS

1907

CONTENTS

I.   A MASTER OF MEN

II.   A SPIKED SWITCH

III.   LOSS AND DAMAGE

IV.   COLD STORAGE

V.   WANTED: THIRTY-FIVE MILLIONS

VI.   THE AWAKENING OF CHARLES EDWARD

VII.   HAMMER AND TONGS

VIII.   THE AUTOMATIC AIR

IX.   THE RACE TO THE SLOW

X.   THE SINEWS OF WAR

XI.   HURRY ORDERS

XII.   THE ENTERING WEDGE

XIII.   THE BARBARIANS

XIV.   THE DRAW-BAR PULL

XV.   AN UNWILLING HOST

XVI.   THE TRUTHFUL ALTITUDES

XVII.   A NIGHT OF ALARMS

XVIII. THE MORNING AFTER

XIX.   THE RELUCTANT WHEELS

XX.   THE CONSPIRATORS

XXI.   THE MILLS OF THE GODS

XXII.   THE MAN ON HORSEBACK

XXIII. THE DEADLOCK

XXIV.   RUIZ GREGORIO

XXV.   THE SIEGE OF THE NADIA

XXVI.   THE STAR OF EMPIRE

"I wont attempt to apologise—it's beyond all that"

I.
A MASTER OF MEN

Engine Number 206, narrow gauge, was pushing, or rather failing to push, the old-fashioned box-plow through the crusted drifts on the uptilted shoulder of Plug Mountain, at altitude ten thousand feet, with the mercury at twelve below zero. There was a wind—the winter day above timber-line without its wind is as rare as a thawing Christmas—and it cut like knives through any garmenting lighter than fur or leather. The cab of the 206 was old and weather-shaken, and Ford pulled the collar of his buffalo coat about his ears when the grunting of the exhaust and the shrilling of the wheels on the snow-shod rails stopped abruptly.

"Gar-r-r!" snarled Gallagher, the red-headed Irish engineer, shutting off the steam in impotent rage. "The power is not in this dommed ould camp-kittle sewin' machine! 'Tis heaven's pity they wouldn't be givin' us wan man-sized, fightin' lokimotive on this ind of the line, Misther Foord."

Ford, superintendent and general autocrat of the Plug Mountain branch of the Pacific Southwestern, climbed down from his cramped seat on the fireman's box and stood scowling at the retracting index of the steam-gauge. When he was on his feet beside the little Irishman, you saw that he was a young man, well-built, square-shouldered and athletic under the muffling of the shapeless fur greatcoat; also, that in spite of the scowl, his clean-shaven face was strong and manly and good to look upon.

"Power!" he retorted. "That's only one of the hundred things they don't give us, Mike. Look at that steam-gauge—freezing right where she stands!"

"'Tis so," assented Gallagher. "She'd be dead and shtiff in tin minutes be the clock if we'd lave her be in this drift."

Ford motioned the engineer aside and took the throttle himself. It was the third day out from Cherubusco, the station at the foot of the mountain; and in the eight-and-forty hours the engine, plow and crew of twenty shovelers had, by labor of the cruelest, opened eleven of the thirteen blockaded miles isolating Saint's Rest, the mining-camp end-of-track in the high basin at the head of the pass.

The throttle opened with a jerk under the superintendent's hand. There was a snow-choked drumming of the exhaust, and the driving-wheels spun wildly in the flurry beneath. But there was no inch of forward motion, and Ford gave it up.

"We're against it," he admitted. "Back her down and we'll put the shovelers at it again while you're nursing her up and getting more steam. We're going to make it to Saint's Rest to-day if the Two-six has to go in on three legs."

Gallagher pulled the reversing lever into the back gear and sent the failing steam whistling into the chilled cylinders with cautious little jerks at the throttle. The box-plow came out of the clutch of its snow vise with shrillings as of a soul in torment, and the bucking outfit screeched coldly down over the snowy rails to the "let-up," where the shovelers' box-car had been uncoupled.

Ford swung off to turn out the shoveling squad; and presently the laborers, muffled to the eyes, were filing past the 206 to break a path for the plow. Gallagher was on the running-board with his flare torch, thawing out an injector. He marked the cheerful swing of the men and gave credit where it was due.

"'Tis a full-grown man, that," he commented, meaning Ford. "Manny's the wan would be huggin' the warm boiler-head these times, and shtickin' his head out of the windy to holler, 'G'wan, boys; pitch it out lively now, and be dommed to yez!' But Misther Foord ain't built the like o' that. He'll be as deep in that freezin' purgatory up yander in th' drift as the foremist wan of thim."

The Irishman's praise was not unmerited. Whatever his failings, and he groaned under his fair human share of them, Stuart Ford had the gift of leadership. Before he had been a month on the branch as its "old man" and autocrat, he had won the good-will and loyalty of the rank and file, from the office men in the headquarters to the pick-and-shovel contingent on the sections. Even the blockade-breaking laborers—temporary helpers as they were—stood by him manfully in the sustained battle with the snow. Ford spared them when he could, and they knew it.

"Warm it up, boys!" he called cheerily, climbing to the top of the frozen drift to direct the attack. "It's been a long fight, but we're in sight of home now. Come up here with your shovels, Olsen, and break it down from the top. It's the crust that plugs Mike's wedge."

He looked the fighting leader, standing at the top of the wind-swept drift and crying on his shovelers. It was the part he had chosen for himself in the game of life, and he quarreled only when the stake was small, as in this present man-killing struggle with the snowdrifts. The Plug Mountain branch was the sore spot in the Pacific Southwestern system; the bad investment at which the directors shook their heads, and upon which the management turned the coldest of shoulders. It barely paid its own operating expenses in summer, and the costly snow blockades in winter went to the wrong side of the profit and loss account.

This was why Ford had been scheming and planning for a year and more to find a way of escape; not for himself, but for the discredited Plug Mountain line. It was proving a knotty problem, not to say an insoluble one. Ford had attacked it with his eyes open, as he did most things; and he was not without a suspicion that President Colbrith, of the Pacific Southwestern, had known to the full the hopelessness of the mountain line when he dictated the letter which had cost one of the great Granger roads its assistant engineer in charge of construction, transferring an energetic young man with ambitions from the bald plains of the Dakotas to the snow-capped shoulders of the Rockies.

Originally the narrow gauge had been projected and partly built by a syndicate of Denver capitalists, who were under the hallucination, then prevalent, that any railroad penetrating the mountains in any direction, and having Denver for its starting point, must necessarily become at once a dividend-paying carrier for the mines, actual or to be discovered.

Failing to tap their bonanza freight-producer on the route up Blue Canyon, the projectors—small fish in the great money-pool—had talked vaguely of future extensions to Salt Lake, to San Francisco, to Puget Sound, or to some other of the far-beyonds, and had even gone the length of surveying a line over Plug Pass and down the valley of the Pannikin, on the Pacific slope of the range. But they had prudently stopped building; and the pause continued until the day of the great silver strike at Saint's Rest.

The new carbonate beds chanced to lie within easy rifle-shot of the summit of Plug Pass; in other words, they were precisely on the line of the extension survey of the narrow gauge. The discovery was a piece of sheer luck for the amateur railroad builders. For a time, as all the world knows, Saint's Rest headed the mining news column in all the dailies, and the rush for the new camp fairly swamped the meager carrying facilities of the incomplete line and the stages connecting its track-end with the high-mountain Mecca of the treasure-seekers.

Then, indeed, the Denver syndicate saw its long deferred opportunity and grasped it. Long purses might be lacking, but not shrewd heads. The unfinished Plug Mountain was immediately bonded for more than it ever promised to be worth, and in the hottest heat of the forwarding strife it was extended at the rate of a mile a day until the welcome screech of its locomotive whistles was added to the perfervid clamor of the new camp in the Plug Pass basin.

The goal reached, the Denver folk took a fresh leaf out of the book of shrewdness. Holding the completed line only long enough to skim the cream of the rush earnings, they sold their stock at a sound premium to the Pacific Southwestern, pocketed their winnings cannily, and escaped a short half-year before the slump in silver, and the consequent collapse of Saint's Rest, came to establish the future Waterloo for Napoleonic young superintendents in the Southwestern's service.

This was all ancient history when Ford left the Granger road to climb, at President Colbrith's behest, into the Plug Mountain saddle; and a round half-dozen of the young Napoleons had been broken before he put foot in stirrup for the mounting. While his attacking of the problem had been open-eyed, he had not stopped to specialize in the ancient history of the Plug Mountain branch. When he did specialize, his point of view was pretty clearly defined in a letter to Mr. Richard Frisbie, of St. Paul, written after he had been for six months the master of the Plug Mountain destinies.

"I'm up against it, good and solid," was the way he phrased it to Frisbie. "My hundred and fifty miles of 'two streaks of rust and a right-of-way' has never paid a net dollar since the boom broke at Saint's Rest, and under present conditions it never will. If I had known the history of the road when President Colbrith went fishing for me—as I didn't—I wouldn't have touched the job with a ten-foot pole.

"But now I'm here, I'm going to do something with my two streaks of rust to make them pay—make a spoon or spoil a horn. Just what shall be done I haven't decided fully, but I have a notion in the back part of my head, and if it works out, I shall need you first of all. Will you come?

"Have I told you in any of my earlier letters that I have personally earned the ill-will of General Manager North? I have, and it is distinct from and in addition to his hostility for the unearning branch for which I am responsible. I'm sorry for it, because I may need his good word for my inchoate scheme later on. It came up over some maintenance-of-way charges. He is as shrewd as he is unscrupulous, and he knows well how to pile the sins of the congregation on the back of the poor scapegoat. To make a better showing for the main line, and at the same time to show what a swilling pig the Plug Mountain is, he had the branch charged up with a lot of material we didn't get. Naturally, I protested—and was curtly told to mind my own business, which had no ramifications reaching into the accounting department. Then I threatened to carry it over his head to President Colbrith; whereupon I gained my point temporarily, and lost a possible stepping-stone to success.

"None the less, I am going to win out if it costs me the best year of my life. I'm going to swing to this thing till I make something out of it, if I have to put in some more winters like the one I have just come through—which was Sheol, with ice and snow in the place of the traditional fire and brimstone. If I have one good quality—as I sometimes doubt—it's the inability to know when I am satisfactorily and permanently licked."

Stuart Ford was shivering through the second of the winters on the gray, needle-winded day when he stood on the crusted drift, heartening his men who were breaking the way for further rammings of the scrap-heap 206 and her box-plow. During the summer which lay behind the pitiless storms and the blockading snows he had explored and planned, studied and schemed; and now a month of good weather would put the finishing touches preparatory upon the "notion" hinted at in the letter to Frisbie.

"That'll do, boys; we'll let Gallagher hit it a few times now," he sang out, when he saw that the weaker ones among the shovelers were stumbling numbly and throwing wild. "Get back to the car and thaw yourselves out."

The safety-valve of the 206 was stuttering under a gratifying increase of steam pressure when the superintendent climbed to the canvas-shrouded cab.

"Ha! two hundred and fifty pounds! That looks a little more like it, Michael. Now get all the run you can and hit her straight from the shoulder," he ordered, mounting to his seat on the fireman's box, and bracing himself for what should come.

Gallagher released the driver-brakes and let the 206 and the plow drift down the grade until his tender drawhead touched the laborers' car. Then the reversing lever went forward with a clang, and the steam squealed shrilly in the dry-pipe. For a thunderous second or two the driving-wheels slipped and whirled futilely on the snowy rails. Gallagher pounced upon the sand lever, whereat the tires suddenly bit and held and a long-drawn, fire-tearing exhaust sobbed from the stack.

"You've got her!" shouted Ford. "Now hit it—hit it hard!"

Swiftly the huge mass of engine and plow gathered headway, the pounding exhausts quickening until they blended in a continuous roar. The little Irishman stayed himself with a foot against the boiler brace; the fireman ducked under the canvas curtain and clung to the coal bulkhead; and Ford held on as he could.

The shock came like the crashing blow of a collision. The box-plow buckled and groaned with fine cracklings as of hard-strained timbers, and an avalanche of snow thrown up from its inclined plane buried engine and cab and tender in a smothering drift. Ford slid his window and looked out.

"Good work, Michael; good work! You gained a full car-length that time. Try it again."

Gallagher backed the plow carefully out of the cutting, and the fireman opened the blower and nursed his fire. Again and again the wheeled projectile was hurled into the obstruction, and Ford watched the steadily retrograding finger of the steam-gauge anxiously. Would the pressure suffice for the final dash which should clear the cutting? Or would they have to stop and turn out the wretched shovelmen again?

The answer came with the fourth drive into the stubborn barrier. There was the same nerve-racking shock of impact; but now the recoil was followed by a second forward plunge, and Gallagher yelled his triumph when the 206 burst through the remaining lesser drifts and shot away on the clear track beyond.

Ford drew a long breath of relief, and the engineer checked the speed of the runaway, stopped, and started back to couple on the car-load of laborers.

Ford swung around and put his back to the open window.

"Let's hope that is the worst of it and the last of it for this winter, Mike," he said, speaking as man to man. "I believe the weather will break before we have any more snow; and next year—"

The pause was so long that Gallagher took his chance of filling it.

"Don't be tellin' me the big boss has promised us a rotary for next winter, Misther Foord. That'd be too good to be thrue, I'm thinking."

"No; but next winter you'll be doing one of two things, Michael. You will be pulling your train through steel snow-sheds on Plug Mountain—or you'll be working for another boss. Break her loose, and let's get to camp as soon as we can. Those poor devils back in the box-car are about dead for sleep and a square meal."

II
A SPIKED SWITCH

Ford's hopeful prophecy that the snow battles were over for the season proved true. A few weeks later a warm wind blew up from the west, the mountain foot-trails became first packed ice-paths and then slippery ridges to trap the unwary; the great drifts began to settle and melt, and the spring music of the swollen mountain torrents was abroad in the land.

At the blowing of the warm wind Ford aimed the opening gun in his campaign against fate—the fate which seemed to be bent upon adding his name to the list of failures on the Plug Mountain branch. The gun-aiming was a summons to Frisbie, at the moment a draftsman in the engineering office of the Great Northern at St. Paul, and pining, like the Plug Mountain superintendent, for something bigger.

"I have been waiting until I could offer you something with a bread-and-meat attachment in the way of day pay," wrote Ford, "and the chance has come. Kennedy, my track supervisor, has quit, and the place is yours if you will take it. If you are willing to tie up to the most harebrained scheme you ever heard of, with about one chance in a thousand of coming out on top and of growing up with a brand new country of unlimited possibilities, just gather up your dunnage and come."

This letter was written on a Friday. Frisbie got it out of the carriers' delivery on the Sunday morning; and Sunday night saw him racing westward, with the high mountains of Colorado as his goal. Not that the destination made any difference, for Frisbie would have gone quite as willingly to the ends of the earth at the crooking of Ford's finger.

It was the brightest of May days when the new supervisor of track debarked from the mountain-climbing train at Saint's Rest, stretched his legs gratefully on *terra firma*, had his first deep lungful of the ozonic air of the high peaks, and found his welcome awaiting him. Ford would have no talk of business until he had taken Frisbie across to the little shack "hotel," and had filled him up on a dinner fresh from the tin; nor, indeed, afterward, until they were smoking comfortably in the boxed-off den in the station building which served as the superintendent's office.

"I've been counting on you, Dick, as you know, ever since this thing threatened to take shape in my head," Ford began. "First, let me ask you: do you happen to know where you could lay hands on three or four good constructing engineers—men you could turn loose absolutely and trust implicitly? I'm putting this up to you because the Plug Mountain exile has taken me a bit out of touch."

"Why—yes," said Frisbie, taking time to call the mental roll. "There are Major Benson and his son Jack—you know 'em both—just in off their job in the Selkirks. Then there is Roy Brissac; he'd be a pretty good man in the field; and Chauncey Leckhard, of my class,—he's got a job in Winnipeg, but he'll come if I ask him to, and he is the best office man I know. But what on top of earth are you driving at, Stuart?"

Ford cleared his pipe of the ash and refilled it.

"I'll go into the details with you a little later. We shall have plenty of time during the next month or six weeks, and, incidentally, a good bit more privacy. The thing I'm trying to figure out will burst like a bubble if it gets itself made public too soon, and"—lowering his voice—"I can't trust my office force here. *Savez?*"

"I *savez* nothing as yet," laughed the new supervisor, "but perhaps I shall if you'll tell me what is going to happen in the next month or six weeks."

"I'm coming to that, right now. How would you like to take a hunting trip over on the wilderness side of the range? There are big woods and big game."

Frisbie grinned. He was a little man, with sharp black eyes shaded by the heaviest of black brows, and it was his notion to trim his mustaches and beard after the fashion set by the third Napoleon and imitated faithfully by those who sing the part of Mephistopheles in *Faust*. Hence, his grin was handsomely diabolic.

"You needn't ask me what I'd like; you just tell me what you want me to do," he rejoined, with clansman loyalty.

"So I will," said Ford, taking the reins of authority. "We leave here to-morrow morning for a trip over the Pass and down the Pannikin on the other side, and if anybody asks you why, you can say that we expect to kill a deer or two, and possibly a bear. Your part of the outsetting, however, is to pack your surveying instruments on the burro saddles so they'll pass for grub-boxes, tent-poles, and the like."

"Call it done," said Frisbie. "But why all this stage play? Can't you anticipate that much without endangering your bubble?"

Ford lowered his voice again.

"I gave you the hint. Penfield, my chief clerk—his desk is just on the other side of that partition—is an ex-main-line man, shoved upon me when I didn't want him. He was General Manager North's stenographer. For reasons which will be apparent to you a little later on, I want to blow my bubble in my own way; or, to change the figure, I'd like to fire the first volley myself."

Frisbie's grin was rather more than less diabolic.

"Then I'd begin by firing Mr. Penfield, himself," he remarked.

"No, you wouldn't," said Ford. "There are going to be obstacles enough in the way without slapping Mr. North in the face as a preliminary. Under the circumstances, he'd take it that way; Penfield would make sure that he took it that way."

It was at this point in the low-toned conference that the ingenious young man in the outer office put down the desk telephone ear-piece long enough to smite with his fist at some air-drawn antagonist. Curiosity was this young man's capital weakness, and he had tinkered the wires of the private telephone system so that the flicking of a switch made him an auditor at any conversation carried on in the private office. He was listening intently and eagerly again when Ford said, still in the same guarded tone:

"No, I can't fire Penfield, and I don't particularly want to. He is a good office man, and loyal to his salt: it's my misfortune that it is Mr. North's salt-cellar, and not mine, that he dips into. Besides, I'd have trouble in replacing him. Saint's Rest isn't exactly the paradise its name implies—for a clean-cut, well-mannered young fellow with social leanings."

"Now, what in the mischief does all that mean?" mused the chief clerk, when Ford and his new track man had gone out. "A month's hunting trip over the range, with the surveying instruments taken along. And last summer Mr. Ford spent a good part of his time over there—also hunting, so he said. Confound it all! I wish I could get into that private drawer of his in the safe. That would tell the story. I wonder if Pacheco couldn't make himself an errand over the Pass in the morning? By George!" slapping his thigh and apostrophizing the superintendent, "I'll just go you once, Mr. Ford, if I lose!"

Now the fruit, of which this little soliloquy was the opening blossom, matured on the second day after Ford and Frisbie had started out on the mysterious hunting trip across the range. Pacheco, the half-breed Mexican who freighted provisions by jack train to the mining-camps on the head waters of the Pannikin, came in to report to the chief clerk.

"Well, 'Checo, what did you find out?" was the curt inquiry.

The half-breed spread his palms.

"W'at I see, I know. Dey'll not gone for hunt much. One day out, dey'll make-a da camp and go for squint t'rough spy-glass, so" — making an imaginary transit telescope of his hands. "Den dey'll measure h-on da groun' and squint some more, so."

Penfield nodded and a gold piece changed hands silently.

"That's all, 'Checo; much obliged. Don't say anything about this over in the camp. Mr. Ford said he was going hunting, and that's what we'll say, if anybody asks us."

That night the chief clerk sent a brief cipher telegram to the general manager at Denver.

> Ford and his new track supervisor, who is really a high-priced constructing engineer, gone over the range for a month's absence. Gave it out here that they were going after big game, but they took a transit and are picking up the line of the old S.L. & W. extension in the upper Pannikin.

It was late in the month of June when Ford and Frisbie, tanned, weathered and as gaunt as pioneers, returned to Saint's Rest; and for those who were curious enough to be interested, there were a couple of bear-skins and one of a mountain lion to make good the ostensible object of the absence.

But the most important trophies of the excursion were two engineers' note-books, well filled with memoranda; and these they did not exhibit. On the contrary, they became a part of the collection of maps, statistics, estimates and private correspondence which Chief Clerk Penfield was so anxious to examine, and which Ford kept under lock and key when he and Frisbie were not poring over some portion of it in the seclusion of the private office.

None the less, Penfield kept his eyes and ears open, and before long he had another detail to report by cipher telegram to the general manager. Ford was evidently preparing for another absence, and from what the chief clerk could overhear, he was led to believe that the pseudo supervisor of track would be left in charge of Plug Mountain affairs.

It was on the day before Ford's departure for Denver that a letter came from General Manager North. Ford read it with a scowl of disapproval and tossed it across the double desk to Frisbie.

"A polite invitation for me to stay at home and to attend to my business," he commented.

"Had you written him that you were going away?" inquired Frisbie.

"No; but evidently somebody else has."

Frisbie read the letter again.

"'So that all heads of departments may be on duty when the president makes his annual inspection trip over the lines,'" he quoted. "Is Mr. Colbrith coming out this early in the summer?"

"No, of course not. He never comes before August."

"Then this is only a trumped-up excuse to make you stay here?"

"That's all," Ford replied laconically.

Mr. Richard Frisbie got up and walked twice the length of the little room before he said:

"This Denver gentleman is going to knock your little scheme into a cocked hat, if he can, Stuart."

"I am very much afraid we'll have to reckon upon that. As a matter of fact, I've been reckoning upon it, all along."

"How much of a pull has he with the New York money-people?"

"I don't know that: I wish I did. It would simplify matters somewhat."

Frisbie took another turn up and down the room, with his head down and his hands in his pockets.

"Stuart, I believe, if I were in your place, I'd enlist Mr. North, if I had to make it an object for him," he said, at length.

"Certainly, I mean to go to him first," said Ford. "That is his due. But I am counting upon opposition rather than help. Wait a minute"—he jerked the door open suddenly and made sure that the chief clerk's chair was unoccupied. "The worst of it is that I don't trust North," he went on. "He is a grafter in small ways, and he'd sell me out in a minute if he felt like it and could see any chance of making capital for himself."

"Then don't go to him with your scheme," urged Frisbie. "If you enlist him, you won't be sure of him; and if you don't, you'll merely leave an active opponent behind you instead of a passive one."

"I guess you're right, Dick; but I'll have to be governed by conditions as I find them. Aside from North's influence with Mr. Colbrith, which is considerable, I believe, he can't do much to help. But he can do a tremendous lot to hinder. I think I shall try to choke him with butter, if I can."

Notwithstanding the general manager's letter, Ford took the train for Denver the following morning, and the chief clerk remarked that he checked a small steamer trunk in addition to his hand baggage.

"Going to be gone some time, Mr. Ford?" he asked, when he brought the night mail down for the superintendent to look over.

"Yes," said Ford absently.

"You'll let me know where to reach you from time to time, I suppose?" ventured Penfield.

Ford looked up quickly.

"It won't be necessary. You can handle the office work, as you have heretofore, and Mr. Frisbie will have full charge out of doors."

Penfield looked a little crestfallen.

"Am I to take orders from Mr. Frisbie?" he asked, as one determined to know the worst.

"Just the same as you would from me," said the superintendent, swinging up to the step of the moving car. And the chief clerk went back to his office busily concocting another cipher message to the general manager.

On the way down the canyon Ford was saying to himself that he was now fairly committed to the scheme over which he had spent so many toilful days and sleepless nights, and that he would have it out with Mr. North to a fighting conclusion before he slept.

But a freight wreck got in the way while the down passenger train was measuring the final third of the distance, and it was long after office hours in the Pacific Southwestern headquarters when Ford reached Denver.

By consequence, the crucial interview with the general manager had to be postponed; and the enthusiast was chafing at his ill luck when he went to his hotel—chafing and saying hard words, for the waiting had been long, and now that the psychologic moment had arrived, delays were intolerable.

Now it sometimes happens that seeming misfortunes are only blessings in disguise. When Ford entered the hotel café to eat his belated dinner, he saw Evans, the P. S-W. auditor, sitting alone at a table-for-two. He crossed the room quickly and shook hands with the man he had meant to interview either before or after the meeting with North.

It was after they had chatted comfortably through to the coffee that the auditor said, blandly: "What are you down for, Ford?—anything special?"

"Yes. I am down to get leave of absence to go East," said Ford warily.

"But that isn't all," was the quiet rejoinder. "In fact, it's only the non-committal item that you'd give to a *Rocky Mountain News* reporter."

Ford was impatient of diplomatic methods when there was no occasion for them.

"Give it a name," he said bluntly. "What do you think you know, Evans?"

The auditor smiled.

"There is a leak in your office up at Saint's Rest, I'm afraid. What sort of a bombshell are you fixing to fire at Mr. North?"

Ford grew interested at once.

"Tell me what you know, and perhaps I can piece it out for you."

"I'll tell you what Mr. North knows—which will be more to the purpose, perhaps. For a year or more you have been figuring on some kind of a scheme to pull the company's financial leg in behalf of your good-for-nothing narrow gauge. A month ago, for example, you went all over the old survey on the other side of the mountains and verified the original S.L. & W. preliminaries and rights-of-way on its proposed extension."

Ford's eyes narrowed. He was thinking of the warning letter he would have to write to Frisbie. But what he said was:

"I'd like to know how the dickens you guessed all that. But no matter; supposing I did?"

"It's no good," said the auditor, shaking his head. "I'm talking as a friend. North doesn't like you, personally; and if he did, you couldn't persuade him to recommend anything in the way of an experiment on the Plug Mountain. So far from extending your two-by-four branch—if that is what you have in mind—he'd be much more likely to counsel its abandonment, if the charter didn't require us to keep it going."

Ford found a cigar for the auditor, and lighted one for himself.

"From all of which I infer that the semiannual report of the Pacific Southwestern is going to be a pretty bad one," he said, with carefully assumed indifference.

Evans regarded him shrewdly.

"Are you guessing at that? Or is there a leak at our end of the line as well as at yours?"

"Oh, it's a guess," laughed Ford. "Call it that, anyhow. At least, I haven't any of your confidential clerks in my pay. But just how bad is the report going to be?"

The auditor shook his head.

"Worse than the last one. Perhaps you have noticed that the stock has dropped six points in the past week. You're one of the official family: I don't mind telling you that we are in the nine-hole, Ford."

"Of course we are," said Ford, with calm conviction. "That much is pretty evident to a man who merely reads the Wall Street news bulletins. What is the matter with us—specifically, I mean?"

Evans shrugged.

"Are you a division superintendent on the system and don't know?" he demanded. "We are too short at both ends. With our eastern terminal only half-way to Chicago, we can't control the east-bound grain which grows on our own line; and with the other end stopping short here at Denver, we can't bid for west-bound transcontinental business. It's as simple as twice two. Our competitors catch us going and coming."

"Precisely. And if we don't get relief?"

The auditor smiled grimly.

"As I've said, you're one of us, Ford, and I don't mind speaking freely to you. A receivership is looming in the distance, and the not very dim distance, for the P. S-W."

"I thought so. How near is it?"

"I don't know—nobody knows definitely. If we had a man of resources at the head of things—as we have not—it might be stood off for another six months."

"I'm on the way to stand it off permanently, if I can get any backing," said Ford quietly.

"You!" was the astonished reply.

"Yes, I. Listen, Evans. For two years I have been buried up yonder in the hills, with not enough to do in the summer season to keep me out of mischief. I am rather fond of mathematics, and I am telling you I have this thing figured out to the fourth decimal. If President Colbrith and his associates can be made to see that the multiplication of two by two gives an invariable resultant of four, there will be no receivership for the P. S-W. this year, or next."

"Show me," said the auditor.

Ford hesitated for a moment. Then he took a packet of papers, estimates, exhibits and fine-lined engineer's maps from his pocket and tossed it across the table.

"That is for you, personally—for David Evans; not the P. S-W. auditor. You've got to keep it to yourself."

The auditor went through the papers carefully, shifting his cigar slowly from one corner of his mouth to the other as he read and examined. When he handed them back he was shaking his head, almost mournfully.

"It's a big thing, Ford; the biggest kind of a thing. And it is beautifully worked out. But I know our people, here and in New York. They will simply give you the cold stare and say that you are crazy."

"Because it can't be financed?"

"Because it doesn't come from Hill or Harriman or Morgan, or some other one of the big captains. You'll never be able to stand it upon its feet by your single-handed lonesome."

Ford set his teeth, and his clean-cut face seemed to grow suddenly older and harder as the man in him came to the fore.

"By heavens! if I put my back under it, it's got to stand upon its feet! I'm not going into it with the idea that there is any such thing in the book as failure."

The auditor looked darkly into the cool gray eyes of the man facing him.

"Then let me give you a word of advice before you start in. Skip North, absolutely; don't breathe a word of it to him. Don't ask me why; but do as I say. And another thing: drop into my office to-morrow before you leave. I'll show you some figures that may help you to stir things up properly at the New York end. Do you go direct from here?"

"No; I shall have to stop over a few days in Chicago. I know pretty well where to put my hands on what I need; I have laid the foundations from the bottom up by correspondence. But I want to go over the situation on the ground before I make my grand-stand play before Mr. Colbrith and the board of directors."

"Well, come in and get the figures, anyway: come to the private door of my office and rap three times. It will be just as well if it isn't generally known that you are confabbing with me. Our semiannual report will probably be in New York ahead of you, but it won't hurt if you have the information to work with." Evans was pushing his chair from the table when he added: "By the way, you happened upon the exact psychological moment to make your raid; the report coming out, and things going to the dogs generally."

Ford's laugh was genially shrewd.

"Perhaps it wasn't so much of a happening as it appears. Didn't I tell you that I had figured this thing out to the fourth decimal place? Psychological moments are bigger arguments than dollars and cents, sometimes."

The auditor had taken his hat from the waiter and was shaking hands with his dinner companion.

"I'd like to believe you're a winner, Ford; you deserve to be. Come and see me—and make your call upon Mr. North as brief as possible. He'll probe you if you don't."

This was how it came about that the next morning, when Ford went to call upon the sallow, heavy-faced, big-bodied man who sat behind the glass door lettered "General Manager, Private,"—this after half an hour spent in Auditor Evans' private office,—it was only to ask for leave of absence to go East—on business of a personal nature, he explained, when Mr. North was curious enough to ask his object.

III
LOSS AND DAMAGE

At this period of his existence, Stuart Ford troubled himself as little as any anchorite of the desert about the eternal feminine.

It was not that he was more or less than a man, or in any sense that anomalous and impossible thing called a woman-hater. On the contrary, his attitude toward women in the mass was distinctly and at times boyishly sentimental. But when a young man is honestly in love with his calling, and is fully convinced of its importance to himself and to a restlessly progressive world, single-heartedness becomes his watchword, and what sentiment there is in him will be apt to lie comfortably dormant.

For six full working-days Ford had been immersed to the eyes in the intricacies of his railway problem, acquiring in Chicago a valiseful of documentary data that demanded to be classified and thoroughly digested before he reached New York and the battle-field actual. This was why he was able to ride all day in studious abstraction in his section of the Chicago-New York Pullman, without so much as a glance for the young woman in the modest gray traveling coat directly across the aisle.

She was well worth the glance, as he admitted willingly enough afterward. She was the dainty type, with fluffy bright brown hair, eyes the color of wood violets, a nose tilted to the precise angle of bewitching piquancy, and the adorable mouth and chin familiarized to two continents by the artistic pen of the Apostle of the American Girl. How he could have ridden within arm's reach of her through all the daylight hours of a long summer day remained as one of Ford's unanswered enigmas; but it required an accident and a most embarrassing *contretemps* to make him aware of her existence.

The accident was one of the absurd sort. The call for dinner in the dining-car had been given, and Ford was just behind the young woman in the rear of the procession which filed forward out of the

Pullman. The train had at that moment left a way station, and the right-hand vestibule door was still open and swinging disjointedly across the narrow passage. Ford reached an arm past the young woman to fold the two-leaved door out of her way. As he did it, the door-knob hooked itself mischievously in the loop of her belt chatelaine, snatched it loose, and flung it out into the backward-rushing night.

Whereupon: "Oh!—my purse!" with a little gasp of sudden bereavement, and a quick turning to face the would-be helper.

Ford was honestly aghast when the situation fully enveloped him.

"Heavens and earth! Did you ever see such idiotic clumsiness!" he ejaculated. And then, in deepest contrition: "I won't attempt to apologize—it's beyond all that. But you must let me make your loss good."

In all the pin-pricking embarrassment of the moment, he did not fail to remark that she quickly recovered the serenity which belongs to the well-bred. She was even smiling, rather ruefully, when she said:

"Fortunately, the conductor has my passes. But really"—and now she laughed outright—"I am afraid I shall have to go hungry if I can't borrow enough to pay for my dinner."

Another man, a man less purposefully lost in the purely practical labyrinth of professional work, would have found something fitting to say. But Ford, having discovered a thing to do, did it painstakingly and in solemn silence. There was an unoccupied table for two in the dining-car; he seated her, gave her his purse, called a waiter, and would have betaken himself forthwith to another table if she had not detained him.

"No," she said decisively, with a charming little uptilt of the adorable chin. "I do not forget that you were trying to do me a kindness. Please sit down here and take your purse. I'm sure I don't want it."

He obeyed, still in somber silence, gave his dinner order after she had given hers, and was wondering if he might venture to bury himself in a bundle of the data papers, when she spoke again.

"Are you provoked with yourself, or with me?" she asked—rather mockingly, he thought.

"Neither," he said promptly. "I was merely saying to myself that my wretched awkwardness didn't give me an excuse for boring you."

"It was an accident—nothing more or less," she rejoined, with an air of dismissing finally the purse-snatching episode. Then she added: "I am the one who ought to be embarrassed."

"But you are not," he returned quickly. "You are quite the mistress of yourself—which is more than most women would be, under the circumstances."

"Is that a compliment?" she asked, with latent mockery in the violet eyes. "Because if it is, I think you must be out of the West; the—the unfettered West: isn't that what it is called?"

"I am," Ford acknowledged. "But why do you say that? Was I rude? I beg you to believe that I didn't mean to be."

"Oh, no; not rude—merely sincere. We are not sincere any more, I think; except on the frontier edges of us. Are we?"

Ford took exceptions to the charge for the sheer pleasure of hearing her talk.

"I'd be sorry to believe that," he protested. "The conventions account for something, of course; and I suppose the polite lie which deceives no one has to have standing-room. But every now and then one is surprised into telling the truth, don't you think?"

"If I can't fully agree with you, I can at least admire your point of view," she said amiably. "Is it Western—or merely human?"

He laughed.

"Shall we assume that the one implies the other? That would be in accordance with your point of view, wouldn't it?"

"Yes; but it would be a distinct reversal of yours. Truth belongs to another and simpler time than ours. We are conventional first and everything else afterward."

"Are we?" he queried. "Some few hundreds or thousands of us may be; but for the remainder of our eighty-odd millions the conventions are things to be put on and off like Sunday garments. And even the chosen few of us brush them aside upon occasion; ignore them utterly, as we two are ignoring them at this moment."

She proved his assertion by continuing to talk to him, and the dining-car was emptying itself when they realized that there is an end even to a most leisurely dinner. Ford paid the steward as they left the car, but in the Pullman he went back to first principles and insisted upon some kind of a definite accounting for the lost purse.

"Now you will tell me now much I threw away for you, and I'll pay my debt," he said, when she had hospitably made room for him in the opposing seat of her section.

"Indeed, you will do nothing of the kind!" she asserted. "You will give me your card—we're going back to the conventions now—and when we reach the city you may lend me enough money to take me up-town. And to-morrow morning my brother will pay you back."

He gave in because he had to.

"You are much more lenient than I deserve. Really, you ought to stick me good and hard for my awkwardness. It would serve me right."

"I am considering the motive," she said almost wistfully, he fancied. "We have drifted very far from all those quiet anchorages of courtesy and helpfulness. If we lived simpler lives—"

He smiled at the turn she was giving it.

"Are you, too, bitten with the fad of the moment, 'the simple life'?" he asked. "Let me assure you that it is beautiful only when you can look down upon it from the safe altitude of a comfortable income. I know, because I've been living it for the past two years."

She looked as if she were sorry for him.

"That is rank heresy!" she declared. "Our forefathers had the better of us in many ways, and their simpler manner of living was one of them. They had time for all the little courtesies and kindnesses that make life truly worth living."

Ford's laugh was boyishly derisive.

"Yes; they certainly had plenty of time; but they didn't have much else. Why, just think, for a moment, of what our own America would be if merely one of the modern civilizers, the railroads, had never existed. There simply wouldn't be any America, as we know it now."

"How can you say that?"

"Because it is so. For nearly two centuries we stood still, because there were no means of locomotion—which is another word for progress and civilization. But in less than fifty years after the first railroad was built we had become a great nation."

She was silenced, if not wholly convinced; and a few minutes later the train drew into the Forty-second Street Station. When the parting time came, Ford dutifully gathered her belongings, said good-by, and put her on a north-bound subway; all this without remembering that he did not know her name. The recollection came, however, when the subway train shot away into the tunnel.

"Of all the blockheads!" he growled, apostrophizing his own unreadiness. "But I'll find her again. She said she'd send her brother to the hotel with the dinner money, and when I get hold of him it will go hard with me if I don't manage some way to get an introduction."

This was what was in his mind when he sought the down-town hotel whose name he had written on his card for her; it was his latest waking thought when he went to sleep that night, and his earliest when he awoke the following morning.

But when he went to the clerk's desk, after a leisurely breakfast, to get his mail, he found that the sure thread of identification had broken in his fingers. There was a square envelope among the other letters in his key-box containing the exact amount of the young woman's indebtedness to him; this, with a brief note of thanks—unsigned.

IV

COLD STORAGE

If courage, of the kind fitted to lead forlorn hopes, or marchings undaunted up to the muzzles of loaded cannon, be a matter of gifts and temperament, it is also in some degree a matter of environment.

Stuart Ford was Western born and bred; a product of the wider breathing spaces. Given his proper battle-field, where the obstacles were elemental and the foes to be overcome were mere men of flesh and blood fighting freely in the open, he was a match for the lustiest. But New York, with its submerging, jostling multitudes, its thickly crowding human vastness, and, more than all, its atmosphere of dollar-chasing, apparent and oppressive even to the transient passer-by, disheartened him curiously.

It was not that he was more provincial than he had to be; for that matter, there is no provincialism so rampant as that of the thronging, striving, self-sufficient city. But isolation in any sort is a thing to be reckoned with. The two pioneering years in the Rockies had done their work,—of narrowing, as well as of broadening,—and the plunge into the chilling sea of the money-mad metropolis made him shiver and wish he were out.

This feeling was really at the bottom of the late rising and the leisurely breakfast, making him temporize where he had meant to be prompt, energetic and vigorously aggressive. Having pocketed the young woman's unsigned note, he glanced at his watch and decided that it was still too early to go in search of President Colbrith.

"I don't suppose he'll be in his office for an hour yet," he mused reflectively; "and anyway, I guess I'd better go over the papers again, so I can be sure to speak my piece right end to. By Jove! I didn't suppose a couple of thousand miles of easting would take the heart out of things the way it does. If I didn't know better, I should think I'd come here to float the biggest kind of a fake, instead of a life-boat for the shipwrecked people in the Pacific Southwestern. It is beginning to look that way in spite of all I can do."

Going once again over his carefully tabulated argument did not help matters greatly. He was beginning to realize now how vastly, antipodally different the New York point of view might be from his own. It came to him with the benumbing effect of a blow that his own ambitions had persistently looked beyond the mere money-making results of his scheme. Also, that President Colbrith and his fellow-investors might very easily refuse to consider any other phase of the revolutionary proposition he was about to lay before them.

By ten o'clock postponement was no longer a tenable city of refuge: the plunge had to be taken. Accordingly, he fared forth to present himself at the Broadway address given in the Pacific Southwestern printed matter as the New York headquarters of the company.

The number proved to be a ground floor, with the business office of the eastern traffic representative in front, and three or four private desk-rooms in the rear, one of them labeled "President" in inconspicuous gilt lettering. Entering, with less assurance than if he had been the humblest of place-seekers out of a job, Ford was almost relieved to find only a closed desk, and a young man absently scanning a morning paper.

Inquiry developed a few facts, tersely stated but none the less enlightening. Mr. Colbrith was not in: the office was merely his nominal headquarters in the city and he occupied it only occasionally. His residence? It was in the Borough of the Bronx, pretty well up toward Yonkers—locality and means of access obligingly written out on a card for the caller by the clerk. Was Mr. Ford's business of a routine nature? If so, perhaps, Mr. Ten Eyck, the general agent, could attend to it. Ford said it was not of a routine nature, and made his escape to inquire his way to the nearest subway station. To pause now was to lose the precious impetus of the start.

It was worth something to be whirled away blindly out of the stifling human vortex of the lower city; but Ford's first glimpse of the Colbrith mansion depressed him again. The huge, formal house had once been the country residence of a retired dry-goods merchant. It fronted the river brazenly, and the fine old trees of a ten-acre park shamed its architectural stiffness. Ford knew the president a little by family repute and more particularly as a young subordinate knows the general in command. It struck him forcibly that the aspect of the house fitted the man. With the broad river and the distant Palisades to be dwelt upon, its outlook windows were narrow. With the sloping park and the great trees to give it dignity, it seemed to assume an artificial, plumb-line dignity of its own, impressive only as the product of rigid measurements and mechanical uprightness.

From the boulevard there was a gravelled driveway with a stone portal. The iron gates were thrown wide, and at his entrance Ford stood aside to let an outgoing auto-car have the right of way. Being full of his errand, and of the abstraction of a depressed soul, Ford merely remarked that there were two persons in the car; a young man driving, and a young woman, veiled and dust-coated, in the mechanician's seat beside him. None the less, there floated out of the mist of abstraction an instantly vanishing phantom of half-recognition for the Westerner. Something in the pose of the young woman, the way she leaned forward and held her hat with the tips of her gloved fingers, was, for the fleeting moment, almost reminiscent.

If Ford had wished to speculate upon abstruse problems of identity, there was neither time nor the mental aptitude. A little later he had given his card to the servant at the door and was waiting in a darkened and most depressive library for the coming of the master of the house. The five minutes of waiting nearly finished him. As the absurdly formal clock between the book-cases ticked off the leaden-winged seconds, his plan for the rescue of Pacific Southwestern took the form of a crass impertinence, and only the grim determination to see a lost cause decently coffined and buried kept the enthusiast with his face to the front.

After all, the beginning of the interview with the tall, thin, gray-haired and hatchet-faced old man, who presently stalked into the library and gave his hand with carefully adjusted cordiality to the son of one of his college classmates, was only a little more depressing: it was not mortal. Ford had been born in Illinois; and so, something better than a third of a century earlier, had the president. Moreover, Mr. Colbrith had, in the hey-day of his youth, shared rooms with the elder Ford in the fresh-water university which had later numbered the younger Ford among its alumni. These things count for somewhat, even when the gap to be bridged is that between the president of a railroad and one of his minor officials.

But when the revolutionary project was introduced, the president's guarded cordiality faded like a photographic proof-print in the sunlight, and the air of the darkened library grew coldly inclement.

"So you came to talk business, did you?" said the high, rasping voice out of the depths of the easy-chair opposite; and Ford raged inwardly at the thought that he had clearly placed himself at a disadvantage by becoming even constructively the guest of the president. "As a rule, I positively refuse to discuss such matters outside of their proper environment; but I'll make an exception for Douglas Ford's son. Your plan is simply impossible. I can understand how it may appear possible, and even attractive, to a young man, and especially to the young man who has invented it. But as an investment for capital—my dear young sir, go back to your division, and strive by faithful service to rise in the accepted and time-honored way. You are wasting your time in New York."

Curiously enough, Ford found his evaporated courage recrystallizing under opposition.

"I can not believe that I have made the plan, and the present condition of the system, sufficiently clear to you," he insisted; whereupon he went patiently and good-naturedly over the argument again, emphasizing the desperate straits to which the Pacific Southwestern was reduced.

"We know all that, Mr. Ford," was the unyielding reply. "But granting it to be the fact, don't you see the absolute futility of asking for thirty-five millions additional capital at such a crisis?"

"No, I don't," said Ford stubbornly. "I know—as I can not explain to you in detail in a half-hour interview—that this plan of mine can be made successful. For two years, Mr. Colbrith, I have been the man on the ground: no word that I am saying to you is speculative. Every clause of the proposition has a carefully established fact behind it."

"No doubt it seems so to you," came the rasping voice from the chair-depths. "But thirty-five millions!"—with a quavering gasp. "And at a time when our earnings are falling off steadily and the stock is going down day by day. It's—it's simply preposterous! I must really decline to discuss it any further."

Ford had his packet of data in hand.

"I have all the exhibits here, carefully tabulated and condensed. Won't you reconsider far enough to examine them, Mr. Colbrith?"

A thin white hand of negation and protest waved out of the depths of the engulfing easy-chair.

"I am sorry to disappoint you, Mr. Ford. I knew your father, and we were great friends. You are like him," he added reminiscently. "He might have died rich if he had gone into corn-buying with me when we were graduated, as I wanted him to. But he was too enthusiastic. He wanted to turn the world upside down—just as you do, my dear young man; just as you do."

Ford got upon his feet. The time had arrived for the firing of the shot of last resort, and he aimed it deliberately.

"I came first to you, Mr. Colbrith, because it was my duty as a subordinate, and your own appointee, and because you were my father's friend so many years ago. I may say, frankly, that I did it against good advice. Men who profess to know you have counseled me to appeal directly to the board. What I wish to know now is if you are willing to take the entire responsibility of turning this plan of mine down. Will it not relieve you of all responsibility if you will call a meeting of the directors, and let me lay this absurd proposal of mine before it? You can surely have no fears for the result."

The shot told. The president struggled to his feet and took a nervous turn up and down the long room. When he replied, it was with the indecisive man's reluctance to commitment of any sort.

"If I call the meeting, I shall be ridiculed; and if I don't call it, I suppose you'll go to Brewster and Magnus and tell them I've muzzled you. Have it your own way. I'll issue the call for ten o'clock, the day after to-morrow, in McVeigh and Mackie's offices in Broad Street. But I warn you in advance, Mr. Ford, I shall not be able to help you in the least. And I may add this: that when you reach that part of your proposal where you call for thirty-five millions additional capital, you may as well put on your hat and go home. That will be the end of it."

"And of me," laughed the enthusiast. But in spite of the cold comfort, and of the still colder promise of opposition, he took his leave with a lighter heart, refusing Mr. Colbrith's rather perfunctory invitation to stay to luncheon.

And on the gravelled drive, where he again had to make way for the auto-car purring in on its return, he did not so much as look up at the pair in the driving-seat.

V

WANTED: THIRTY-FIVE MILLIONS

The offices of McVeigh and Mackie, brokers and financial agents, are in Broad Street, and the windows of the room used for board meetings look down upon the angle where beats the money pulse of the nation.

Ford had successfully resisted the temptation to lobby for his scheme during the one-day interval between his conference with Mr. Colbrith and the date of the called meeting of the directors. It was not any mistaken sense of loyalty to the president that restrained him; on the contrary, he decided that Mr. Colbrith's declaration of war left him free to fight as he would. But upon due consideration he concluded to set the advantage of an assault *en masse* over against the dubious gain of an advanced skirmish line, and when he turned out of Broadway into Wall Street on the morning of destiny the men whom he was to meet and convince were still no more to him than a list of names in the *Poor's Manual*, consulted within the hour for the purpose.

He was early on the battle-ground; much too early, he thought, when a clerk ushered him into the board room in the rear of the brokers' offices. As yet there was only one person present—a young man who was lounging in the easiest of the leather-covered chairs and yawning dismally. At the first glance the face seemed oddly and strikingly familiar; but when the young man marked the new-comer's entrance, the small hand-bag in which the amateur promoter carried his papers, and got up to shake hands, Ford found the suggestive gropings baffled.

"My name is Adair," said the lounger genially; "and I suppose you are the Mr. Ford Uncle Sidney has been telling us about. Pull up a chair and sit by the window. It's the only amusement you'll have until the clan gathers."

Ford looked at his watch.

"I seem to be ahead of time," he remarked. "I understood Mr. Colbrith to say that the meeting would be called for ten o'clock."

"Oh, that's all right; and so he did," rejoined the other cheerfully. "But that means anything up to noon for a directors' meeting in New York." Then, after a pause: "Do you know any of us personally, Mr. Ford?"

Ford was rummaging in his memory again. "I ought to know you, Mr. Adair. It isn't very decent to drag in resemblances, but—"

"The resemblance is the real thing, this time," said Adair. "You saw me day before yesterday, driving out of the Overlook grounds as you were going in."

Ford shook his head.

"No; it goes back of that; sometime I'll remember how and where. But to answer your question: I know Mr. Colbrith slightly, but I've never met any of the directors."

"Well, you are meeting one at this moment," laughed the young man, crossing his legs comfortably. "But I am the easiest mark of the lot," he added. "I inherited my holdings in Pacific Southwestern."

Ford was crucially anxious to find out how the battle was likely to go, and his companion seemed amiably communicative.

"Since you call Mr. Colbrith 'Uncle Sidney,' I infer that you know what I am here for, Mr. Adair. How do you think my proposition is likely to strike the board?"

Again the young man laughed.

"Fancy your asking me!" he said. "I haven't talked with any one but Uncle Sidney; and the most I could get out of him was that you wanted thirty-five million dollars to spend."

"Well," said the Westerner anxiously, "am I going to get it?"

"You can search me," was the good-natured rejoinder. "But from my knowledge of the men you are going presently to wrestle with, I should say 'no' and italicize it."

"Perhaps it might help me a little if I could know in advance the particular reason for the italics," Ford suggested.

"Oh, sure. The principal reason is that your name isn't Hill or Harriman or Morgan or Gates. Money is ridiculously sheepish. It will follow a known leader blindly, idiotically. But if it doesn't hear the familiar tinkle of the leader's bell, it is mighty apt to huddle and run back."

Ford's smile was grim.

"I don't mind saying to you, Mr. Adair, that this is one of the times when it will be much safer to huddle and run forward. Have you seen the half-yearly report?"

"I? Heaven forbid! I have never seen anything out of the Pacific Southwestern—not even a dividend."

Ford would very willingly have tried to share his enthusiasm with the care-free young man, whose face was still vaguely but persistently remindful of some impression antedating the automobile passing; but now the other members of the board were dropping in by twos and threes, and privacy was at an end.

Just before President Colbrith took his place at the head of the long table to call the meeting to order, Adair leaned forward to say in low tones: "I couldn't give you the tip you wanted, Mr. Ford, but I can give you another which may serve as well. If your good word doesn't win out, scare 'em—scare 'em stiff! I don't know but you could frighten half a million or so out of me if you should try."

"Thank you," said Ford. "I may take you at your word,"—and just then Mr. Colbrith rose in his place, fingering his thin white beard rather nervously, Ford thought, and rapping on the table for silence.

It was admitted on all hands that the president of the Pacific Southwestern was a careful man and a thrifty. It was these qualities which had first determined his election. There were many small stock-holders in the company, and it is the foible of small stock-holders to believe that rigid economy counts for more than adventurous outreachings in the larger field.

"Gentlemen," he began, his high, raucous voice rasping the silence like the filing of a saw, "this meeting is called, as you have probably been informed, for the purpose of considering a plan for betterments submitted by Mr. Stuart Ford, who is at the present time superintendent of our Plug Mountain Division.

"In making this unusual innovation, and in introducing Mr. Ford, I desire to say that I have been actuated by that motive of prudence which, while it stands firmly upon its own feet, is willing to consider suggestions from without, even when these suggestions appear to be totally at variance with a policy of careful and judicious financiering.

"In presenting Mr. Ford as the son of an old friend, long since gone to his reward, I wish it distinctly understood that I am in no sense committed to his plan. The policy of this company under the present administration has been uniformly cautious and prudent: Mr. Ford would throw caution and prudence to the winds. Our best efforts have been directed toward the saving of the ultimate dollar of expense: Mr. Ford urges us to spend millions. We have been trying to dispose of some of our non-paying branches: Mr. Ford would have us acquire others and build new lines."

While Mr. Colbrith was speaking, Adair was rapidly characterizing the members for Ford, checking them off upon his fingers.

"The little man at Uncle Sidney's right is Mackie, and the miserly looking one next to him is McVeigh," he whispered. "One of them will furnish your coffin, and the other will drive the nails into it. The big man with the beard is Brewster—a multimillionaire; and the one who looks like Senator Bailey is Magnus, president of the Mohican National. Connolly, the fat Irishman, is a politician—wads of money, but not much interest in the game. The other three—"

But now the president had made an end and was beckoning to Ford.

The young engineer rose, feeling much as if a bucket of ice-water had been suddenly emptied down the back of his neck. But one of his saving qualities was the spring-like resilience which responds instantly to a shock. Spreading his papers on the table, he began with a little apology.

"I didn't come here this morning prepared to make a promoter's speech; and perhaps it is just as well, since my gift, if I have one, lies in doing things rather than in talking about them. But I can lay a few facts before you which you may deem worthy of consideration."

From this as a beginning he went on swiftly and incisively. The Pacific Southwestern, in its present condition, was a failure. It was an incomplete line, trying vainly to hold its own against great and powerful systems overlapping it at either end. The remedy lay in extension. The acquisition of a controlling interest in three short roads, which, pieced together, would bridge the gap between the Missouri River and Chicago, would place the Pacific Southwestern upon an equal footing with its competitors as a grain carrier. By standardizing the Plug Mountain narrow gauge and extending it to Salt Lake and beyond, the line would secure a western outlet, and would be in a position to demand its share of transcontinental business.

To finance these two extensions a capital of thirty-five million dollars would be needed; five million dollars for the purchase of the majority stock in the three short roads, and the remainder for the western outlet. These assertions were not guesses: by referring to exhibits marked "a" "b" and "f," his hearers would find accurate estimates of cost, not only of construction, but also of stock purchases.

As to the manner of providing the capital, he had only a suggestion to offer. The five million dollars necessary for the acquirement of a controlling interest in the three short roads would be a fair investment. It could be covered immediately by a reissue—share for share—of the reorganization stock of the P. S-W., which would amply secure the investors, since the stock of the most prosperous of the three local roads was listed at twenty-eight, ten points lower than the present market quotation of P. S-W.

The thirty million dollar extension fund might be raised by issuing second mortgage bonds upon the entire system, or the new line itself could be bonded mile for mile under a separate charter. Ford modestly disclaimed any intention of dictating the financial policy; this was not in his line. But again he would submit facts. The grain crop in the West was phenomenally large in prospect. With its own eastern terminal in Chicago, the Pacific Southwestern could control the grain shipments in its own territory. With the moving of the grain, the depressed P. S-W. stock would inevitably recover, and on a rising market the new issue of bonds could doubtless be floated.

The enthusiast closed his argument with a hasty summing-up of the benefits which must, in the nature of things, accrue. From being an alien link in the great transcontinental chain, the Pacific Southwestern would rise at a bound to the dignity of a great railway system; a power to be reckoned with among the other great systems gridironing the West. Its earnings would be enhanced at every point; cross lines which now fed its competitors would become its allies; the local lines to be welded into the eastern end of the system would share at once in the prosperity of a strong through line.

For the western extension he could speak from personal knowledge of the region to be penetrated. Apart from the new line's prime object—that of providing an outlet for the system—there was a goodly heritage of local business awaiting the first railroad to reach the untapped territory. Mines, valueless now for the lack of transportation facilities, would become abundant producers; and there were many fertile valleys and mesas to attract the ranchman, who would find on the western slopes of the mountains an unfailing water supply for his reservoirs and ditches. Ford did not hesitate to predict that within a short time the extension would earn more, mile for mile, than the grain-belt portion of the system.

When he sat down he felt that his cause was lost. There was no enthusiasm, no approval, in the faces of his auditors. After a short and informal discussion, in which the engineer was called on to explain his plans and estimates in detail to one and another of the members, Magnus, the bank president, sufficiently summed up the sense of the meeting when he said:

"There is no question about the ingenuity of your plan, Mr. Ford. You must have given a great deal of time and thought to it. But it is rather too large for us, I'm afraid, and there are too many contingencies. Your province, I understand, is the building and operating of railroads, and it is nothing to your discredit that you are unfamiliar with the difficulties of financing an undertaking as vast as this proposal of yours."

"I don't deny the difficulties," said Ford. "But they wouldn't seem to be insuperable."

"Not from your point of view," rejoined the banker suavely. "But you will admit that they are very considerable. The opposition on the part of the competing systems would be something tremendous. No stone would be left unturned in the effort to dismount us. To go no further into the matter than the proposed purchase of the majority stocks in the three short roads: at the first signal in that field you would find those stocks flying skyward in ten-point advances, and your five millions wouldn't be a drop in the bucket. In view of the difficulties, I think I voice the conviction of the board when I say that the plan is too hazardous."

The nods of assent were too numerous to leave Ford any hope of turning the tide in his favor. He rose, gathered up his papers, and reached for his hat.

"It is very pointedly your own funeral, gentlemen," he said curtly. "'Nothing venture, nothing have' is an old proverb, but it is as true now as it was when it was coined. With P. S-W. stock at thirty-eight and steadily declining; with another dividend about to be passed; and with the certainty that the July interest on the bonds will have to be defaulted unless some compromise can be effected with the bondholders—"

"What's that you're saying?" broke in Mackie, whose P. S-W. holdings were large.

Ford drew a folded paper from his pocket and laid it on the table.

"I was merely quoting from the auditor's semiannual report, of which that is a summary," he said, indicating the folded paper. "The report itself will doubtless reach you in a day or two. It would seem to an unprejudiced observer that the present condition spells something like a receivership, unless you have the bondholders with you."

"One moment, Mr. Ford," interposed the banker member; but Ford was working up to his climax and refused to be side-tracked.

"Of course, as an officer of the company, I have felt in duty bound to bring my grist first to the company's mill. But if you gentlemen don't wish to grind it, it will be ground, notwithstanding. I could very easily have found a market for my proposal without coming to New York."

With which parting shot, and a word of apology for having taken the time of the board to no good purpose, he bowed himself out, closing the door upon a second attempt on the part of the banker member to renew the argument.

VI
THE AWAKENING OF CHARLES EDWARD

Ford went directly to his hotel from the meeting in the Broad Street board room, paid his bill, and had himself shot up to the fifth floor to prepare for a swift retreat from the scene of his humiliating defeat. It was hardly in keeping with his boast of persistence that he should suffer himself to be thus routed by a single reverse, however crushing. But in a world where every problem contains its human factor, red wrath accounts for much that is otherwise unaccountable.

Ford was thoroughly and unreasoningly angry and disgusted when he began to fling his belongings into the small steamer trunk, and it was only natural that he should turn with a little brow-wrinkling of resentment when, a little later, Mr. Charles Edward Adair, following his card up to the fifth floor front, lounged good-naturedly into the room.

"Beg pardon, I'm sure," said the intruder easily. "Didn't know you were busy. I thought maybe you'd like to know the effect of your little double-headed bombshell, and I couldn't be sure Uncle Sidney would take the trouble to tell you."

Ford made no effort to conceal his contempt for the financial gods.

"I don't imagine it will take you very long to tell it," he retorted. "Nothing short of a combined earthquake and volcanic eruption would have any effect upon that crowd."

"Oh, but you're wrong!" protested Adair. "That shot of yours with the semiannual summary for a projectile stirred 'em up good. It seems that Uncle Sidney and Hertford and Morelock—they're the executive committee, you know—have had the auditor's figures for some days, but they hadn't thought it necessary to harrow the feelings of the other members of the board with the cataclysmic details. So there was a jolly row. Magnus wanted to know, top-loftily, why a small official from the farther end of the system should be the first to bring the news; and Mackie was so wrathy that he inadvertently put the hot end of his cigar in his mouth. Even Connolly woke up enough to say that it was blanked bad politics."

"But nothing came of it?" said Ford, hope rising in spite of the negative query.

"No; nothing but a general hand-out of pretty sharp talk. What was needed right then was a unifier—somebody who could take command and coax or bully the scrapping factions into line. Magnus tried it, but he's too smooth. Brewster was the man, but he has too many other and bigger irons in the fire to care much about P. S-W. Connolly could have done it if the scrap had been a political split, but he was out of his element."

"Humph!" growled Ford. "It didn't occur to me that there were any differences of opinion to be reconciled. The entire board sat on my proposition—as a unit."

Adair laughed with imperturbable good-humor.

"The factions were there, just the same. You see, it's like this: Brewster and Magnus and two or three more are pretty well-to-do, and their holdings in P. S-W. don't cut much of a figure with them, one way or another. The others have more stock in the company, and fewer millions. When the jangle came, Brewster and the heavy men said, 'Oh, let it go; it isn't worth bothering with.' Naturally, the little fellows, with more to lose and less money-nerve, said, 'No.'"

"It spells the same word for me, in any event," Ford commented, and went on pitching things into his steamer trunk.

Adair got upon his feet and strolled away to the window.

When he turned again to face the beaten one he said:

"If I wasn't so infernally lazy, Mr. Ford, I more than half believe that I could pull this thing off for you, myself. But that is the curse of being born with too much money. I can take a plunge into business now and then—I've done it. But my best friend couldn't bet on me two days in succession."

Ford looked up quickly.

"Then don't put your hand to this plow, Mr. Adair. I'll be frank with you. I can fit the mechanical parts of this scheme of mine together, so that they will run true and do business. But I, or any man in my place, would have to have solid backing here in New York; a board that would be as aggressive as a handful of rebels fighting for life, and every man of it determined to win out or smash something. Mr. Magnus spoke of the opposition we should encounter from our competitors. He might have said more. What the Transcontinental, for example, wouldn't do to obliterate us needn't be catalogued. How do you suppose the present P. S-W. board would fare in such a fight?"

The youngest member of the flouted board laughed again.

"You mustn't say in your wrath that all men are liars—or cowards. There is plenty of fight in our crowd; and plenty of money, too, if you could only get it sufficiently scared."

"I've done my best," said Ford, slamming the lid of the trunk and buckling the straps vigorously. "The next time I'll find my market first and build my scheme afterward."

"Well, if I can say it without offense, I'm honestly sorry for you, Mr. Ford; you've been butchered to make a Broad Street holiday," said Adair, lounging toward the door. "You are going back to the West, I suppose?"

"Yes."

"What line?"

"Pennsylvania; five-ten this afternoon."

"That is a long time between drinks. Suppose you come up to the club and have luncheon with me?"

Ford hesitated, watch in hand.

"I was about to lie to you, Mr. Adair, and plead business; but I shan't. I'll tell you the plain truth. I'm too sore just now to be any good fellow's good company."

"Which is precisely the reason why I asked you," laughed the golden youth. "Come on; let's go now. You can take it out on me as much as you like, you know. I shan't mind."

But the club luncheon ignored the business affair completely, as Adair intended it should. Ford came out of the shell of disappointment with the salad course, and by way of reparation for his former attitude talked rather more freely of himself than he was wont to do on such short acquaintance with any one. The young millionaire met him quite half-way on this road to a better understanding, contrasting with mild envy Ford's well-filled, busy life with his own erratic efforts at time-killing.

"You make me half sorry for myself," he said, when they went to the smoking-room to light their cigars. "It's no less than a piteous misfortune when a fellow's father has beaten all the covers of accomplishment for him."

Ford could laugh now without being bitter.

"The game isn't all corralled, even for you, Mr. Adair. There was excellent good shooting for you in that directors' meeting this morning, but you wouldn't take the trouble."

"That's the fact," was the easy-going rejoinder. "That is just what my sister is always telling me—that I won't take the trouble. And yet I do take the trouble to begin a lot of things; only they never seem worth while after a few days' dip into them."

"Pick out bigger ones," suggested Ford. "My trouble is just the other way about; I am always tackling things that are worlds too big for me—just as I have this time."

"It isn't too big for you, Mr. Ford. It was too big for Colbrith, Magnus, *et al.* And, besides, you're not going to give it up. You'll drop off in Chicago, hunt up some meat-packer or other Cr[oe]sus, and land your new railroad independently of the P. S-W."

It was a measure of the sincerity of Ford's liking for his host when he said: "That little shot of mine at your colleagues was merely a long bluff. If my scheme can't be worked with the P. S-W., it can't well be worked without it. We are lacking the two end-links in the chain—which I could forge. But my two end-links without the middle one wouldn't attract anybody."

It was quite late in the afternoon when they left the club, and Ford had no more than time to check his luggage and get to his train. He wondered a little when Adair went with him to the ferry, and was not ungrateful for the hospitality which seemed to be directed toward a lightening of the burden of failure. But Adair's word of leave-taking, flung across the barrier when the chains of the landing-stage were rattling to their rise, was singularly irrelevant.

"By the way, Mr. Ford; what time did you say your train would reach Chicago?"

"At eight forty-five to-morrow evening," replied the beaten one; and then the boat swung out of its slip and the retreat without honor was begun.

VII
HAMMER AND TONGS

It was raining dismally the evening of the following day when Ford saw from his Pullman window the dull sky-glow of the metropolis of the Middle West. It had been a dispiriting day throughout. When a man has flung himself at his best into a long battle which ends finally in unqualified loss, the heavens are as brass, and the future is apt to reflect only the pale light of the past failure.

It was after the train had entered the suburbs of Chicago that a blue-coated messenger boy came through the Pullman, with the car conductor for his guide. Ford saw himself pointed out, and a moment later was reading a telegram, with a tumult, not of the drumming car wheels, roaring in his ears.

Had a talk with my sister and made up my mind to see you through—if I don't get tired and quit, as usual. Secure options on that short-road stock quick, and wire me care McV. & M. Funds to your credit in Algonquin National, Chicago. Another directors' meeting to-day, and things look a little less chaotic. Answer.   ADAIR.

For some time Ford could only read and re-read the exciting telegram, scarcely trusting the evidence of his senses. That the coldly indifferent members of the P. S-W. board, with a man like President Colbrith at their head, could be swung into line in the short space of a single day by a young fellow who seemed to be little more than a spoiled son of fortune, was blankly incredible.

But he was not long in realizing that the cherished scheme for which he had studied and struggled was actually beginning to stagger to its feet; or in reaching the equally stirring conclusion that his part in the suddenly reopened game called instantly for shrewd blows and the swiftest possible action.

The stock-holders in the three local roads which were to be united to bridge the Chicago-Missouri River gap were scattered all over the Middle West. To secure the necessary options on working majorities of the stock would be a task for a financial diplomat, and one who could break the haste-making record by being in a dozen different places at one and the same moment. Moreover, secrecy became a prime factor in the problem. If the opposition, and particularly the Transcontinental people, should get wind of the move, it would take fifteen millions to do the work of five, as Banker Magnus had intimated.

Notwithstanding the thickly marshaled obstacles, Ford had his plan of campaign pretty well thought out by the time his train was slowing into the Union Station. Before going to New York he had painstakingly "located" the required holdings of the three stocks. Some of them were in Chicago, but the greater number of the men to be bargained with were local capitalists living in the smaller cities along the lines of the three short railroads.

In his bag was a carefully compiled list of these stock-holders, with their addresses and the amounts of their respective holdings. At the worst, he concluded, it should mean nothing more formidable than a deal of quick traveling, some anxious bargaining, perhaps, and a little finesse to keep his object in securing the options safely in the background.

This was how it appeared in the prospect; and the young engineer had yet to learn that the securing of options is a trade by itself—a trade by no means to be caught up in passing, even by the most gifted of tyros.

Hence, it was extremely fortunate for this particular tyro—more fortunate than he could possibly know at the moment—that his telephone message sent from the first telephone he could reach after his train stopped in the Union Station, caught Kenneth at the Green Bag Club. It was a mere chance that he knew that Kenneth, the senior member of the firm of attorneys having general oversight of the Pacific Southwestern's legal department, was at the moment in

Chicago; a chance hanging upon the fact that he had met Kenneth as he was passing through on his way eastward. But it was not by chance that the first familiar face he saw on entering the rotunda of the Grand Pacific Hotel was that of Kenneth. The sight was merely the logical result of Ford's urgent request telephoned to the lawyer's club.

"By Jove, Kenneth; this comes within two inches of being a miracle!—my catching you here before you had started West," Ford ejaculated. And then: "When are you going back?"

"I am supposed to be on the way now," was the lawyer's reply. "I had made all my arrangements to start back to-night on the slow train, but I dined with some friends on the North Side and made a miss. Where have you been?"

"I'm just in from New York. Let me register and get a room; and you put away any lingering notion you may have of heading westward to-night. I've got to have your ear for a few hours to begin with, and the whole of you for the next few days. No; don't probe me here. Wait, and I'll unload on you gradually. You won't be sorry you missed your train."

Fifteen minutes later Ford had his adviser safely behind a closed door, and had put him succinctly in possession of the world-subverting facts, as far as they went. When he concluded, the lawyer was shaking his head dubiously, just as Auditor Evans had done.

"Ford, have you any adequate idea of what a tremendous proposition you are up against?" he asked quietly, helping himself to a cigar out of the engineer's freshly opened box.

"I don't believe I have underrated the difficulties, any of them," said Ford, matching the attorney's gravity. "There are bones all the way along, but I think I have struck the biggest of them just here. I ought to be in a dozen places at once, and not later than to-morrow noon. That's something I can't quite compass."

"Getting these options, you mean? That is very true; but it isn't all of it, by long odds. There are the thousand and one mechanical details to be worked out: the coupling up of these three local lines at their connecting points, the securing of proper trackage or trackage rights at these junctions, the general ordering of things so that a through line may be opened immediately when the stock is secured. If there were ten of you, you couldn't get things licked into shape in time to get in on the grain carrying this season."

Ford had relighted his cigar, which had gone out in the explanatory interval, and was blowing smoke-rings toward the ceiling.

"I may be the biggest ass this side of the jack trails, and the most conceited, Kenneth; but you're over on my side of the ring when you talk about the mechanical obstacles. What I'm worrying about now is the fact that I can't do two things at once. The options must be secured before we can make the fifth part of a move in the other field; and the Lord only knows how long that will take. To hurry is to lose out."

The lawyer nodded. "And not to hurry is to lose out, too," he qualified. Then he smoked in thoughtful silence for five full minutes before he said, abruptly: "Give me your list of stock-holders and turn the option business over to the legal department, where it properly belongs. That will leave you foot-loose to go after the mechanical matter. How does that suit you?"

Ford sprang to his feet.

"By Jove, Kenneth, you're a man and a brother; I'm not forgetting that you are taking this entire fairy tale on my personal say-so; and I shan't forget it, either. It's what I wanted to ask—and was afraid to ask, after I got you safely jailed up here."

The attorney's smile was grim but friendly.

"I'm not forgetting how you took a sick man over into the Pannikin wilderness on a two-months hunting trip last fall and made a well man of him, Ford," he said. "Any man who can shoot as straight as you do wouldn't be sitting here telling me lies about a trifling little matter involving the expenditure of a beggarly thirty-five millions. But to come down to earth again: you haven't shifted any considerable part of the burden, you know. I can do this bit of routine work; but the main thing is up to you, just as it was before I said yes."

Ford rose, stretching himself like a man who has just been relieved of a burden whose true weight was appreciable only in its lifting.

"I know," he said cheerfully. "It has been up to me, all along. In the morning we'll go around to the Algonquin National, and I'll put you into the financial saddle. Then I'll get out on the line, and by the time you have the stock corralled, we'll be practically ready to pull through freight—if not passengers—from Denver to Chicago. Oh, I know what I am talking about," he added, when the general counsel smiled his incredulity. "This is no affair of yesterday with me. I have every mile of these three short roads mapped and cross-sectioned; I have copies of all their terminal and junction-point contracts. I know exactly what we can do, and what we can't do."

The lawyer's comment was frankly praiseful, not to say flattering.

"You're a wonder, Ford—and that's no figure of speech. How on earth did you manage to do it all at such long range?"

Ford's smile was reminiscent of the obstacles.

"It would take me all night to tell you in detail, Kenneth. But I did it. It's no mere brag to say that I could walk into the Chicago, Peoria & Davenport general offices here to-morrow morning and organize a through service over the P. S-W. and the three stub lines within twenty-four hours, if I had to."

"Well, that part of it is far enough beyond me," said the attorney. "The stock-chasing is more in my line. I hope we can keep quiet enough about it so that the opposition won't guess what we are trying to do. You're sure it won't be given away from the New York end?"

It was the engineer's turn to shake his head and to look dubious.

"Now you are shouting, Kenneth. I can't tell anything about it. You'll remember that when I left New York the board had turned the plan down, definitely and permanently, as I supposed. I should say that our only safety lies in lightning speed. When you get the options on those controlling stock majorities snugly on deposit in the Algonquin National, we can draw our first long breath. Isn't that about the way it strikes you?"

"It is, precisely," agreed the general counsel, rising and finding his hat. "And because it does strike me that way, I think I'll go down and do a little telegraphing to-night."

"Hold on a minute," said Ford, "and I'll give you a message to take down, if you don't mind. I must answer Adair, and it won't do any harm to prod him a little—on the secrecy side."

Kenneth waited, with his hand on the door-knob, as it chanced. Hence the opening of the door a minute or two later was quite without any preliminary stir of warning in the room of conference. That was possibly the reason why the lawyer almost fell over a man crouching in the corridor.

"Hello, there!" said Kenneth; "I beg your pardon."

The man got upon his feet, exhibiting all the signs of intoxication.

"Beg yoursh, I'm sure," he mumbled, and was lurching crookedly away when the lawyer suddenly came to his senses and grabbed at him. The clutching hand fell short, and there was an agile foot-race down the corridor, fruitless for Kenneth, since the fugitive suddenly developed sobriety enough to run like a deer. Beaten in the foot-race, Kenneth went back for a word with Ford.

"The battle is on," was the form the word took. "There was a man here, listening at the key-hole, when I opened the door. How much he overheard we'll be likely to find out to-morrow when we begin to pull the strings. Thought I'd give you the pointer. Good night, again."

VIII
THE AUTOMATIC AIR

Set out in cold type, Ford's itinerary for the four days following his conference with Kenneth would read like the abbreviated diary of a man dodging the sheriff. His "ticker" memorandum for that period is still in existence, but the notes are the hurried strokes of the pen of haste, intelligible, we may say, only to the man who made them. To quote:

"Thursday, nine A.M., Peoria—see Sedgwick; ten—make trackage contract with T.P. & W.; eleven A.M., Davenport—inventory motive power—see chief despatcher—get profiles and maps—get copies of yard contracts—get crossing rights—get total tonnage of grain cars. Three P.M., Hannibal—see Berdan and whip him into line—inspect shops—get contracts—get—"

But the string of "gets" fills the page, and is vital now to no living soul of man, least of all to us who are interested only in finding out if our young captain of industry actually did make good his boast of flogging the three short roads into some semblance of a through line in the brief interval at his disposal; and this without advertising to the railroad world at large who he represented and what he was doing.

He did it, and without a slip for which he could be held responsible. It was a wire from the chief office of the Transcontinental in New York, a telegram inspired by sundry leakages from Pacific Southwestern sources, that gave him a silent and observant follower in all of his dodgings. Of this, however, he was in blissful ignorance. Twice, indeed, he sat in the same Pullman section with his "shadow," quite without suspecting it; and once he was saved from disaster—also without suspecting it.

It was at a way station in Missouri, and the section-sharing traveling companion, who had paid only for an hour's ride in the Pullman, was leaving the train. His hand-bag chanced to be the exact

54

counterpart of Ford's: what more natural than that he should make the mistake of taking the wrong one? Ford caught him in the vestibule, and there was a reëxchange, accompanied by grateful acknowledgments and profuse apologies from the debarking one. Ford, immersed fathoms deep in his problems, thought nothing of it; but a moment lost would have been a cause lost, if he had guessed it. For the mistake was no mistake, and the hand-bag rescued contained documents for which the Transcontinental Company would have paid a month's salary of its board of vice-presidents, charging the amount, not to profit and loss, but rather to salvage.

It was on the fourth day of the campaign, while Ford was working his way on an inspection trip over the third link in the short-lines chain, that two telegrams overtook him.

One was from Adair, announcing the tardy, but now certain triumph of the expansionist faction in the board of P.S-W. directors, and begging pathetically for news of the option-getting. The other was signed "K," and Ford had a sharp attack of joy when he read it. The attorney had been successful at all points. The necessary stock majorities were secured and the certificates were safely on deposit in the Algonquin National Bank, in Chicago. What remained was only a matter of routine, provided the P. S-W. bidders would furnish the capital for the purchases.

Ford swamped the local operator at the next way station with a thick sheaf of "rush" telegrams, left the west-bound train at the first cross-road junction, and caught a night express on a fast line for Chicago. Kenneth was waiting for him at the hotel; and after breakfast there was another telegram from Adair. Matters were still progressing favorably, and President Colbrith, traveling in his private car, "Nadia," *via* the Lake Shore, would be in Chicago the following morning to take final action in the stock purchases.

Ford gave the message to Kenneth, and the attorney drummed softly on the table with his finger-tips when he read the announcement.

"We are in for it now," he said with a grimace of dismay. "If Mr. Colbrith doesn't manage to queer the whole deal, it will be because he has suffered a complete change of heart."

Ford answered the grimace with a scowl, and the masterful side of him came uppermost.

"What in the name of common sense were they thinking of to send him out here?" he gritted.

The general counsel laughed.

"You don't know Mr. Colbrith as well as I do, I fancy," he suggested. "He is rather hard to suppress. He'll be president until his successor is elected — or he'll know all the reasons why."

"Well, I hope you've got everything straight in the option business," said Ford. "If there is so much as a hair displaced, he will be sure to find it."

"It is all straight enough," was the confident rejoinder. "Only I had to bid five points over the market on odd lots of the stock. I'm not sure, but I think the Transcontinental people got wind of us during the last day or two and bid against us."

"But you have safe majorities?"

"Oh, yes; we are all in."

"Good," said Ford. "That puts it up to Mr. Colbrith, at all events. And now, while we have a clear day before us, I want to go over these C.P. & D. terminal contracts with you. Right here in Chicago is where the Transcontinental will try hardest to balk us. The C. P. & D. has trackage rights to the elevators; but I want to be sure that the contracts will hold water under a transfer of ownership."

Subjected to legal scrutiny, the contracts promised to be defensible, and Ford came through the day with his apprehensive burdens considerably lightened. After dinner he took his papers to Kenneth's room, and together they went carefully over all the legal points involved in the welding of the three local lines into the Pacific Southwestern system, Ford furnishing the data gathered by him during the four days.

Kenneth was shrewdly inquisitive, as his responsibilities constrained him to be, and it was deep in the small hours when Ford made his escape and went to bed. By consequence, he was scarcely more than half awake the next morning, when he dressed hurriedly and hastened over to the Van Buren Street station to see if the president's car had arrived.

The Nadia was in and side-tracked, with a sleepy porter on guard. Ford climbed to the platform and asked for the president.

"Yas, suh; dis is Mr. Colbrith's cyar; but he don't see no newspapuh men—no, suh. Besides, dey's just gettin' up," was the rebuff; but Ford ignored it.

"'They?' Then Mr. Colbrith isn't alone?"

"No, suh; got a pahty 'long with him—a young gentleman and two ladies; yes, suh. Mr. Colbrith nebber goes nowhah's 'dout he teks a pahty in de cyar."

"Heavens!" groaned Ford, under his breath; "as if the thing wasn't complicated enough without making a picnic of it!" Then aloud. "I wish to go in. My name is Ford, and Mr. Colbrith is expecting me."

"Sho' you isn't a newspapuh man?"

"Of course not," said Ford shortly.

"All right, suh," said the negro; and he made way and opened the door.

The Nadia was a commodious hotel on wheels, with a kitchen and buffet forward, four state-rooms opening upon a narrow side vestibule, and a large dining and lounging room looking out through full-length windows upon a deep, "umbrella-roofed" platform at the rear.

There was no one in the large compartment when Ford reached it; but a moment later a door opened and closed in the vestibule, and Adair made his appearance. Ford drew a breath of relief and shook hands with his backer.

"I'm glad it's you, Mr. Adair. I've been scenting all sorts of hindrances since the porter told me there was a party aboard."

The young man without an avocation dropped into the easiest of the wicker chairs and felt in his pockets for his cigarette case.

"Your prophetic soul didn't deceive you any," he laughed. "The hindrances are here in full force. It is one of Uncle Sidney's notions never to travel without a tail like a Highland chieftain's. I had a foreboding that he'd ask somebody, so I took it upon myself to fill up his passenger list with Aunt Hetty, my sister, and my uncle's nephew."

"I understand," said Ford, and would have plunged forthwith into the business pool; but Adair stopped him with a gesture of dismay.

"Not before breakfast, if you love me, my dear fellow!" he protested, with a little grimace that instantly set the reminiscent part of Ford's brain at work. "After I've had something to eat—"

The interruption was the noiseless entrance of a motherly little lady in gray, with kindly eyes and a touch of silver in the fair hair drawn smoothly back from her forehead.

"This is Mr. Stuart Ford, I am sure," she said, giving her hand to the young engineer before Adair could introduce him. "You look enough like your father to make me recognize you at once."

Ford was a little embarrassed by the gratefully informal greeting.

"Ought I to remember you, Mrs. Adair?" he asked ingenuously.

"Oh, no, indeed. I knew your father as a young man before he married and went to the farther West. The Fords and the Colbriths and the Stanbrooks are all from the same little town in central Illinois, you know."

"I didn't know it," said Ford, "though now I recall it, I used often to hear my father speak of Miss Hester Stanbrook." Then he was going on to say that trite thing about the smallness of the world when Adair broke in.

"I'd like to know what is keeping Uncle Sidney and Alicia. *I* haven't had breakfast yet."

As if his protest had evoked her, a young woman drew the portière of the vestibule—a young woman with bright brown hair, eyes like dewy wood violets, and an adorable chin. Ford stared helplessly, and Adair laughed.

"Shocked, aren't you?" he jested. "But you needn't be alarmed. I have persuaded my sister not to prosecute in the case of the snatched purse. Alicia, this is Mr. Stuart Ford, and he desires me to say that he is not often reduced to the necessity of robbing unprotected young women for the sake of scraping an acquaintance."

Ford lost sight of the Pacific Southwestern exigencies for the moment, and surely the lapse was pardonable. If the truth must be told, this young woman, who had been discovered and lost in the same unforgetable evening, had stirred the neglected pool of sentiment in him to its profoundest depths, and thoughts of her had been dividing time pretty evenly with some parts of the strenuous business affair. Indeed, the hopelessness of any effort toward rediscovering her had been one of his reasons for hurrying away from New York. He knew himself—a little—and that quality of unreasoning persistence which other people called his strong point. The search he had been half-minded to make once begun—

"I hope you haven't forgotten me so soon, Mr. Ford," she was saying; and he recovered himself with a start.

"Forgotten you? No, indeed!"—this with almost lover-like emphasis. "I—I think I am just a trifle aghast at my good luck in finding you again. It seemed so utterly hopeless, you know. Don't you think—"

But now the president had stalked in, and his high querulous voice was marshaling the party breakfastward. Ford man[oe]uvered skilfully in the pairing off, and so succeeded in securing Miss Adair for a companion on the short walk across to the Grand Pacific.

"You were about to ask me something when Uncle Sidney interrupted you," she prompted, when they were clear of the throng in the station vestibule.

"Yes; I was going to ask if you don't think it was unnecessarily cruel to send me that note of thanks unsigned."

"Cruel?" she echoed, and her laugh was so exactly a replica of her brother's that Ford wondered why the reminiscent arrow had not gone at once to its mark. "How absurd! What possible difference could it make?"

"It made a lot of difference to me," said Ford, refusing to be brushed aside. "How did you expect I was ever going to be able to find you again, without even your name as a clue?"

She glanced up at him with unfeigned interest. The men of her world were not altogether unappreciative; neither were they so primitively straightforward as this young industry captain out of the West.

"It is not impossible that I never thought of your finding me again," she said, and only the tone saved it from being a small slap in the face.

60

Ford took the rebuff as a part of the day's work.

"Perhaps you didn't," he admitted. "But I mean to go on hoping that you did."

"The idea!" she scoffed; but this time she blunted the keen edge of the rebuke by adding: "I thought, perhaps, we might meet again, sometime. You see, we are all stock-holders in the Pacific Southwestern; my brother, Aunt Hetty and I; and Uncle Sidney had shown us a letter—it was from Mr. North, I think—saying that you were likely to come to New York with some kind of a plan of reorganization. So when you gave me your card, I knew at once who you were."

Ford made an immediate mental note of the bit of information implicating Mr. North, but did not allow himself to be diverted by the business affair.

"Yes, I know; but that didn't help me a little bit," he protested, wishing that the distance to the hotel were twice as far.

"That was just because it happened so; you ran away before my brother had a chance to offer you any hospitality," she explained. Then, before he could say any more straightforward things: "Tell me, Mr. Ford; are you really going to find something to interest brother?—something that will keep him actually and enthusiastically busy for more than a few days at a time?"

Ford laughed. "I fancy he hasn't been bored for the lack of work since I left New York, has he?"

"No; and it has made such a difference! Won't you please try and keep him going?"

"You may rest assured that I shall do what I can. But you see he has quit already."

"By coming to Chicago with us? Oh, no, indeed; you are quite mistaken. He is here to help you to—to 'minimize' Uncle Sidney; I think that is the word he used. He was afraid you had been finding Uncle Sidney rather difficult. Have you?"

"I have, for a fact," said Ford, out of the depths of sincerity. And, again out of a full heart: "Your brother is a brick, Miss Adair."

"Isn't he?" and she laughed in sheer good comradeship. "If you can only manage to make him rise to his capabilities—"

"He'll never be able to live the simple life for a single waking hour," said the engineer, finishing the sentence for her.

"Oh, but that is a mistake!" she objected. "The very first requirement is work; plenty of work of the kind one can do best."

The short walk to the hotel, where Kenneth was waiting to go to breakfast with the president's party, came to an end, and the social amenities died of inanition. For one thing, President Colbrith insisted upon learning the minutest ins and outs of the business matter, making the table-talk his vehicle; and for another, Miss Adair's place was on the opposite side of the table, and two removes from Ford's. Time and again the young engineer tried to side-track business in the interests of something a little less banal to the two women; but the president was implacable and refused to be pulled out of the narrow rut of details; was still running monotonously and raspingly in it when Kenneth glanced at his watch and suggested that the time for action was come.

After breakfast the party separated. Mrs. Adair and Miss Alicia were to spend the day with friends in South Chicago, and Mr. Colbrith carried the attorney off to his room to dig still deeper into the possible legal complications which might arise out of the proposed transfer of the three short roads. Ford and Adair sat in the lobby and smoked while they were waiting for the president and the general counsel to conclude their conference, and the young millionaire gave his companion the story of the fight in the directory.

"We have Brewster to thank for the lift which finally pulled our wheel out of the mud," said the young man, modestly effacing himself in the summing up. "Or rather I should say that we have the enemy to thank for stirring Brewster into action. Brewster's got some copper mines out in Utah that he nurses like a sick child. Just at the critical moment some of the people who control the Transcontinental began to worry his copper stock. In the hot part of it he came to me and said, 'Adair, will that western extension of yours be able to fry any fat out of Transcontinental?' I told him it would, most assuredly; that next to making money for ourselves, and, incidentally, saving the Pacific Southwestern from going smash, our chief object was to give the Transcontinental a wholesome drubbing."

"You are progressing rapidly," said Ford, with a grin of appreciation. "Did that fetch him?"

"It did, for a fact. He looked like one of those old bushy-bearded vikings when he said, 'By thunder, I'm with you, young man! And I'll answer for Scott and Magnus and Harding. Get your board together, and we'll settle it to-day."

Ford looked up quickly. "If Mr. Colbrith wasn't the chief of your family clan, Adair, I could wish that we had this Mr. Brewster at the head of things."

The rejoinder was heartily prompt. "You don't wish it any more fervently than I do, Ford. That is why I am here to-day. The board, in spite of all that our handful of revolutionaries could do, has armed Uncle Sidney with almost dictatorial powers in this stock-purchasing deal; and if he doesn't contrive to strangle things by the slow process, it will be simply and solely because you and Kenneth and I are here to see that he does not. Do you know what the men call him out on the main line? When they see the Nadia trundling in, they say, 'Here comes old Automatic Air-Brakes.' And it fits him."

"But I don't quite understand why he should want to put the brakes on here and now," Ford interposed. "I know he is against the scheme, personally; but he is here as the representative of a majority which has committed itself to the expansion measure, isn't he?"

"Oh, yes; and he has no thought of playing the traitor—you mustn't think that of him. But it isn't in his nature to facilitate things. In the present crisis he will feel that he is personally responsible for the expenditure of five million dollars. He will examine and investigate, and probe and pry, and will want to worry through every pen-scratch which has been made up to date."

"Well, there is one comfort; he can't take much time for his worrying," said Ford. "Some of the options expire to-morrow noon."

Adair sat up as one who suddenly takes notice.

"What?—to-morrow? Land of glory! but you two fellows took short chances! Why, any little hitch—"

"I know," said the engineer evenly. "But we took what we could get—and were thankful. Somebody was bidding against us, and prices began to jump. Incidentally, I may say that Kenneth deserves to be made a vice-president of the new company, at the very least. He has done ten men's work in the last three or four days."

"I don't doubt it. Neither do I suspect you of loafing. For that matter, I've been hustling a few lines, myself, since I sent you that first telegram."

"Do you find it exciting enough to keep you interested, as far as you've gone?" inquired Ford, mindful of Miss Alicia's longings.

"It's the best yet," declared the idler. "Only, you mustn't lean too heavily on me, you know. I'm the most uncertain quantity you ever experienced. But here comes Uncle Sidney, with a cowed and brow-beaten Kenneth in tow—say your prayers, and get ready for the battle royal."

IX
THE RACE TO THE SLOW

Adair's prophecy that President Colbrith would prove himself an obstructor of the stubbornest was amply fulfilled during the short interval which remained for decisive action. Truly, in the battle for business celerity the odds were three to one against Mr. Colbrith; yet the three were as those who buffet the wind. The president must see and feel, know and fully understand; and at the very last moment, when the shortest of the options had no more than an hour to live, he was proposing to summon General Manager North from Denver to make a fifth in the council of discord.

It was Adair who took the bull by the horns when the president's caution was about to turn victory into defeat. What was said or done after the young man drew Mr. Colbrith into the private committee-room at the bank and shut the door, Ford and Kenneth, who were excluded, could only surmise. But whatever was done was well done. When the two, uncle and nephew, came out of the room of privacy, the old man was shaking his head and the young one was smiling serenely. So it came about that between eleven and twelve o'clock, when Ford, grimly battling to the last, fought as one without hope, a few strokes of the pen opened the doors upon the new creation; five million dollars, more or less, changed hands, and the Pacific Southwestern took the long leap eastward from the Missouri River to its new base in Chicago.

"It's you for the hustle now, Ford," said Adair, linking arms with the engineer when the quartet left the bank. "How soon do you think you can get that first train-load of grain in transit?"

"I wish I could tell you," said Ford.

"Why can't you?"

"Because it will depend very largely upon the authority Mr. Colbrith or the board sees fit to give me. At present, you will remember, I am still only a division superintendent—Mr. North's subordinate, in fact, and—"

"Say it out loud," encouraged Adair.

"I don't like to, but I suppose it can't be helped. Up to now I have been acting under special orders, as you may say, in a purely financial transaction. But my commission expired five minutes ago when the stock deal went through. When it comes to issuing orders in the operating and transportation department, I have no authority whatever. Mr. North is general manager, and I suppose his jurisdiction will now be extended to cover the new line, won't it?"

"Not much!" retorted the amateur promoter. "You are going to be given a free hand in this from the word go. From what I can learn, North has been an obstructor, all along, hasn't he?"

"I can't say that," said Ford, just, even to an enemy. "To be right honest about it, I shall have to confess that I slurred him entirely—went over his head."

"For good reasons, no doubt, only you are too charitable to give them. Never mind: as I say, you are going to have a free hand. This is your pie and nobody else is going to cut it for you." And when the party reached the hotel there was another conference of two behind closed doors, in which Ford and the general counsel did not participate.

An hour later, when Adair came down from the president's room, he thrust a sheaf of penciled printers' copy into Ford's hands.

"There you are," he said. "I've done the best I could for you on such short notice—with Uncle Sidney trying his level best to get a cross reference to the board before taking action. Get these circulars through a print shop and into the mails. You'll see that one of them announces your appointment, effective to-day, as Assistant to the President. That was as far as Uncle Sidney could be dragged. It doesn't give you a straight flush; but your hand will beat North's if it comes to a show-down between you. Just the same, I shouldn't quarrel with North, if I were you. Uncle Sidney thinks the sun rises and sets in him."

Ford nodded, and while he was reading hastily through the sheaf of pencilings a boy brought him a telegram. When he opened the envelope, Kenneth had turned away. But Adair was looking on, and he did not fail to remark the startling effect of the few typewritten words upon the engineer.

"Whereabouts does it hit us this time?" he inquired, lighting a fresh cigarette.

"In the neck," said Ford curtly. "The possibility occurred to me yesterday—Pacific Southwestern stock being so badly scattered among small holders. I wired a broker, a good friend of mine, to pick up a few shares on my account. Here is what he says: 'Market bone dry. No offerings of P. S-W. at any price.'"

Adair whistled softly. "That's getting next to us with a vengeance!" he commented. "And it can be done, too. Half a dozen of the small stock-holders have been to me since the fire was lighted, trying to get me to take their stock at market."

"How much do we control—that we are sure of?" Ford asked.

"I don't know—in figures. Not more than two-fifths, I should say. At the last board meeting I proposed that we make a safe majority pool among ourselves, but Uncle Sidney sat on me. Said his own personal constituency among the little people was big enough amply to secure us."

Ford swore pathetically.

"The one single instance when his caution might have steered him straight—and it went to sleep!" he raged.

"Exactly," laughed Adair. "And now the Transcontinental moguls are buying up a majority of their own, meaning to capture the main-line dog and leaving us to wag the extension tail which we have just acquired. Say, Ford; doesn't that appeal to your sense of humor?"

"No, it doesn't," said Ford savagely. To see one's air-castles crumbling at the very moment when they were to be transmuted into solid realities is apt to provoke a reversion to type; and Ford's type was Gothic.

"That's a pity," said Adair, absently rolling his cigarette between his thumb and finger. "Also, it's another pity that I am such a hopeless quitter. I believe I could pull this thing out yet, if I could only get up sufficient steam."

"For heaven's sake, tell me what you burn, and I'll furnish the fuel," said Ford desperately.

"Will you? I guess I need something pretty inflammatory."

"Lord of love! haven't you good and plenty, without calling upon me? Are you going to let these stock-jobbing land-pirates on 'Change gibbet you as a solemn warning to aspiring young promoters?"

Adair paused with the cigarette half way to his lips. "Ah," he said, after a thoughtful moment. "Perhaps that was what I needed. No; they will not gibbet any of us to-day; and possibly not to-morrow." Then, with a sudden dropping of the mask of easy-going indifference: "Give me the key to your room, and find me a swift stenographer. Then go over to the Lake Shore headquarters and ask to have the Nadia coupled to the evening train for New York."

"But the president?" Ford began. "Didn't he say something about going over these new lines on an inspection trip?"

"Never mind Uncle Sidney: on this one occasion he will change his plans and go back to New York with us," said Adair curtly.

"Good," said Ford approvingly. "And how about opening the new through line for business? Do we go on? Or do we hang it up until we find out where we are 'at'?"

"Don't hold it up a single minute. Drive it for all the power you can get behind it. If we have to collide with things, let's do it with the throttle wide open. Now find me that shorthand person quickly, will you?"

By what means the president was persuaded or coerced into doing the thing he had not planned to do, Ford was not to know. But for that matter, after carrying out Adair's instructions the engineer plunged at once into his own Herculean task of reorganization, emerging only when he made a tardy sixth at the president's dinner table in the hotel café in the evening.

The dinner, which the young engineer had been fondly counting upon as a momentary relaxation from the heart-breaking business strain, was a dismal failure on its social side. President Colbrith, as yet, it appeared, in blissful ignorance of the latest news from New York, had reserved the seat of honor for his new assistant, and the half-hour was filled to overflowing with minute and cautionary definitions of the assistant's powers and duties.

Ford listened with a blank ear on that side. There was work to do, and one man to do it. He did not care particularly to hear instructions which he would probably have to disregard at the first experimental dash into the new field. He meant to hold himself rigidly to account for results; more than this he thought not even Mr. Colbrith had a right to require.

After dinner he indemnified himself for the kindergarten lecture by boldly taking possession of Miss Adair for the short walk over to the private car. The entire world of work was still ahead, and a corps of expert stenographers was at the moment awaiting his return to the C.P. & D. offices, where he had established temporary headquarters; but he shut the door upon the exigencies and listened to Miss Alicia.

"I am so sorry we are not going to be here to see your triumph," she was saying; adding: "It is a triumph, isn't it?"'

"Only a beginning," he amended. "And it won't be spectacular, if we can help it. Besides, this east-end affair is only a preliminary. A little later on, if our tackle doesn't break, we shall land the really big fish for which this is only the bait."

"Shall you never be satisfied?" she asked jestingly. And then, more seriously: "What is your ambition? To be able to buy what your neighbor can not afford?"

"Big money, you mean? No, I think not. But I like to win, as well as other men."

"To win what?"

"Whatever seems worth winning—this fight, in the present instance, and the consequent larger field. Later, enough money to enable me to think of money only as a stepping-stone to better things. Later still, perhaps—"

He stopped abruptly, as though willing to leave the third desideratum in the air, but she would not let him.

"Go on," she said. "Last of all?"

"Last of all, the love of a true woman."

"Oh!" she scoffed, with a little uptilt of the admirable chin. "Then love must come trailing along at the very end, after we have skimmed the cream from all the other milk pans in orderly succession."

"No," he rejoined gravely. "I put it clumsily—as I snatch purses. As a matter of sober fact, love sets the mile-stones along any human road that is worth traversing."

She glanced up at him and the blue eyes were dancing. Miss Alicia Adair knew no joy to compare with that of teasing, and it was not often that the fates gave her such a pliable subject.

"Tell me, Mr. Ford; is—is she pretty?"

"She is beautiful; the most beautiful woman in the world, Miss Adair."

"How fine! And, of course, she is a paragon of all the virtues?—an angel without the extremely inconvenient wings?"

"You have said it: and I have never doubted it from the moment I first laid eyes on her."

"Better and better," she murmured. Then: "She has money?"

"I suppose she has; yes, she certainly has money. But that doesn't make any difference—to her or to me."

"It is simply idyllic!" was the ecstatic comment. "After all this there remains but one other possible contingency. Has she a willing mind, Mr. Ford?"

They had reached the steps of the Nadia, and the others had gone within. Ford looked soberly into the depths of the laughing eyes and said: "I would give all my chances of success in this Pacific Southwestern affair to be able to say 'yes' to that."

The station gong was clanging the departure signal for the New York train, and he swung her lightly up to the step of the car.

"Good-by," she said, turning to smile down upon him. And then, "I don't believe you, you know; not the least bit in the world."

"Why don't you?" he demanded.

"Because the woman doesn't live who would be worth such a sacrifice as that would be—to Mr. Stuart Ford."

And this was her leave-taking.

X
THE SINEWS OF WAR

The general offices of the C.P. & D. Railway were crowded into a half-dozen utilitarian rooms on the second floor of the company's freight station building in the Chicago yards. In two of these rooms, with a window outlook upon a tangle of switching tracks with their shifting panorama of cars and locomotives, Ford set up his standard as chief executive of the three "annexed" roads, becoming, in the eyes of three separate republics of minor officials and employees, the arbiter of destiny.

Naturally, the announcement that their railroads had been swallowed whole by the Pacific Southwestern had fallen as a thunderclap upon the rank and file of the three local companies; and since, in railway practice, a change of owners usually carries with it a sweeping change in department heads, the service was instantly demoralized.

During the first few hours of Ford's administration, therefore, the wires were buzzing with hasty resignations; and those whose courage was not whetted to the quitting point took a loose hold upon their duties and waited to see what would happen. Under such chaotic conditions Ford took his seat in the mean little office over the freight station, and flung himself ardently into the task of bringing order out of the sudden confusion. Effectively to support Adair and the reconstructionists on the board it was critically necessary that there be immediate and cheering news from the front.

It was in the preliminary wrestle with disintegration that the young engineer's gift of insight and his faculty of handling men as men stood him in good stead. He was fresh from his trip over the new extension, on which he had met and shrewdly appraised the men who were now his subordinates. With the human field thus mentally mapped and cross-sectioned he was enabled to make swift and sure selections, cutting out the dead timber remorselessly, encouraging the doubtful, reassuring the timid, assorting and combining and ordering until, at the close of the second day of fierce toil, he was ready to make his first report to Adair.

> Track connections at junction points completed to-day. General and division operating and traffic departments in the saddle and effectively organized. With proper coöperation on part of General Manager North, grain should begin to move eastward to-morrow. Can get no satisfactory replies from North. Have him disciplined from your end. Answer.   FORD.

To this telegram there was a prompt and voluminous reply from the seat of war in the East. In a free fight on the Stock Exchange, a battle royal generaled by Brewster and Magnus in which every inch of ground had been sharply contested by brokers buying up P. S-W. in the interest of principals unnamed, a majority of the Southwestern stock—safe but exceedingly narrow—had been secured by the reconstructionists.

In accordance with Ford's suggestion, North had been "called down" by wire, and Ford was instructed to report instantly any failure of effort on the part of the Denver headquarters to set the grain trains in motion.

Otherwise, and from the New York point of view, the situation remained most hopeful. The fight in the Street had unified the factions in the board of directors, and even the timid ones were beginning to clamor for an advance into the territory of the enemy.

Ford read Adair's letter-length and most unbusiness-like telegram with the zest of the fine wine of triumph tingling in his blood. With the Chicago outlet fairly open and in working order, and a huge tributary grain crop to be moved, it should be only a matter of days until the depressed Pacific Southwestern stock would begin to climb toward the bonding figure.

This was the first triumphant conclusion, but afterward came reaction and a depressive doubt. Would the stock go up? Or would the enemy devise some assault that would keep it down in spite of the money-earning, dividend-promising facts? Upon the expected rise hung the fate of Ford's cherished ambition—the building of the western extension. Without a dividend-paying Chicago-Denver main line, there could be no bond issue, no thirty millions for the forging of the third and most important link in the great traffic chain.

Ford walked the floor of his office, called by courtesy, "private," for an anxious hour, balancing the probabilities, and finally determined to take the desperate chance. There was a vast mountain of preliminary work to be leveled, huge purchasing expenses to be incurred, before the first step could be taken in the actual building of the western extension; and the summer was advancing day by day. He did not hope to get the extension completed in a single season. But to get it over into the promising mining field on the lower Pannikin before snow-flying meant work of the keenest, without the loss of a single day. Could he afford to play the safe game and wait until the building capital should be cannily in Mr. Magnus' bank vaults?

He decided that he could not; and when he reached a decision, Ford was not the man to hesitate before taking the plunge. On the morning of the third day he called Truitt, sometime superintendent of the C.P. & D., and now acting manager of the Chicago Extension, and gave him his instructions.

"You say there are three grain trains moving on the line now, Mr. Truitt: there will be three more before night. Keep them coming, and give them the right of way over everything but the United States mails. Can you handle this without help from me?"

"We'll give it a pretty stiff try," was the prompt rejoinder. "But you are not going to leave us, are you, Mr. Ford?"

"No; but for the next forty-eight hours I am going to lock my door, and I don't want to be disturbed for anything less than a disaster or a wire from New York. Please give orders accordingly, will you?"

The orders were given; and, left with his force of stenographers, Ford began to walk the floor, dictating right and left. Letters and telegrams to steel mills, to contractors, to bridge builders, to the owners of grading outfits, and to labor agencies, clicked out of the typewriters in a steady and unbroken stream, and the din was like that of a main-line telegraph office on a hot piece of track.

All day long, and far into the night, the office force wrought unceasingly, digging away at the mountain of preliminary correspondence; and by the next morning the wire replies were beginning to come in.

Then came the crux. To insure prompt delivery of material, definite orders must be placed immediately. A delay of a single day might entail a delay of weeks in the shipments. Yet the risk of plunging the company into debts it might never be able to pay was appalling. What if the stock should not go up as prefigured?—if the bonds could not be floated?

It was with the feeling that he might well be signing his own death-warrant that Ford put his name to the first order for two hundred thousand dollars' worth of steel rails for immediate delivery to the company's line in Chicago. But after the first cold submergence it came more easily, and when he left the office an hour before midnight, a cool million would not have covered the obligations he had assumed during the strenuous day.

Kenneth was sitting up for him when he reached his hotel, and the usually impassive face of the general counsel reflected trouble.

"Out with it," said Ford wearily; and suddenly the new million of indebtedness became a mountain weight to grind him to powder.

"We're blocked," was the brief announcement. "Two of the grain trains are in, and the Transcontinental lawyers have won the toss. We're enjoined by the court from using the service tracks to the elevators. Didn't your local people tell you?"

"No," said Ford. "I had given orders that I was not to be disturbed. But what of it? You expected something of the sort, didn't you?"

"Yes; and I provided for it. The injunction will be dissolved when we have our final hearing; but long before that time the mischief will be irreparable, I'm afraid."

"How?"

"It will be blazoned far and wide that we can't deliver the goods—that the opposition has done us up. I've tried to keep it out of the newspapers, or, rather, to persuade them not to make too much of it. But it wouldn't go. The Transcontinental has all the pull in this town, it appears."

"And you think it will affect the price of the stock?"

"It is bound to, temporarily, at least. And coming upon the heels of to-day's sudden tumble—"

"What's that?" demanded Ford, dry-lipped, adding: "I haven't seen a paper since morning."

Kenneth wagged his head gloomily. "It's pretty bad. P. S-W. closed at thirty-three—five points off yesterday's market."

"Good Lord!" Ford's groan was that of a man smitten down in the heat of the fight. "Say, Kenneth, within a single sweep of the clock-hands I have contracted for more than a million dollars' worth of material for the western extension—more than a million dollars' worth!"

"Well, I'm afraid you have sinned in haste to repent at leisure," said the lawyer, with a weary man's disregard for the amenities. Then he added: "I'm going to bed. I've had about all I can stand for one day."

Ford went to the room clerk for his key; reeled would be the better word, since his brain was whirling. There was a telegram in his box, and he tore it open with fresh and sharper misgivings. It was from Adair.

> The sick man's getting sicker. What is the matter with your prescription? Stock gone off five points, and the bears are squeezing us to beat the band. Stories flying on the Street that we are a kite without an effective tail; that the courts will keep us out of the elevators. What do you say?

Ford consulted his watch. There was barely time to catch the midnight train for New York, and his determination was taken on the spur of the moment. It was all or nothing, now.

Hastily writing a wire to the cashier of the Denver bank where he kept his personal account, and another to Adair, and leaving brief notes for Kenneth and Truitt, he took a cab and had himself driven at a gallop to the Union Station. He was the last man through the platform gates, but he made his train, and was settling himself in the sleeper when another telegram was thrust into his hand. This was from Frisbie, at Saint's Rest; and that it brought more bad news might be argued from the way in which he crushed it slowly in his hand and jammed it into his pocket. On this day, if never before, he was proving the truth of the old adage that misfortunes do not come singly.

Upon arriving in New York late the following evening, he had himself driven to the Waldorf, where he found Adair waiting for him. A few words sufficed to outline the situation, which the lapse of another day had made still more desperate. So far from recovering, the falling stock had dropped to twenty-nine and a half, and there was every indication that the bottom was not yet reached.

"How do you account for it?" asked Ford, when the dismal tale had been told.

"Oh, it's easy enough, when you know how," was the light-hearted rejoinder. "As I wired you, there was something of a scramble on the floor of the Exchange last week when we were fighting to find out whether we should control our own majority or let the Transcontinental have it. Our pool got its fifty-one per cent. all right, but in the nature of things the enemy stood as the next largest stockholder in P. S-W., since they'd been buying right and left against us. Now, since we don't need any more, and nobody else wants it, all the Transcontinental people have to do is to unload on the market, and down she goes."

Ford looked incredulous, and then wrathful.

"Adair, tell me: did I have to stop my work when my time is worth fifty dollars a minute, and come all the way to New York to tell you folks what to do?" he demanded.

Adair's laugh was utterly and absolutely care-free.

"It looks that way, doesn't it? Have you got the compelling club up your sleeve, as usual?"

"A boy might carry it—and swing it, too," was the disgusted answer. "When does the board meet again? Or has it concluded to lie down in the harness?"

"Oh, it gets together every morning—got the meeting habit, you know. Everybody's in a blue funk, but we still have the daily round-up to swap funeral statistics."

"All right. Meet me here in the morning, and we'll go and join the procession. Can you make it nine o'clock?"

"Sure. It's too late to go home, and I'll stay here. Then you'll be measurably certain that I can't escape. May I see the tip end of the club?"

"No," said Ford grumpily. "You don't deserve it. Go to bed and store up a head of steam that will carry you through the hardest day's work you ever hoped to do. Good night."

They met again at the breakfast-table the following morning, and Ford talked pointedly of everything save the P. S-W. predicament. One of Adair's past fads had been the collecting of odd weapons; Ford discovered this and drew the young man skilfully into a discussion of the medieval secrets of sword-tempering.

"I've a bit of the old Damascus, myself," said the engineer. "Tybee— he was on the Joppa-Jerusalem road in the building—picked it up for me. Curious piece of old steel; figured and flowered and etched and inlaid with silver. There were jewels in the pommel once, I take it; the settings are still there to show where some practical-turned vandal dug them out."

Adair was quite at a loss to guess how old swords and their histories could bear upon the financial situation, but he was coming to know Ford better. Some one has said that it is only the small men who are careful and troubled on the eve of a great battle. So the talk was of ancient weapons until the time for action arrived; and a smooth-faced gentleman sitting at a near-by table and marked down by Ford—though not by Ford's companion—listened for some word of enlightenment on the railroad situation, and was cruelly disappointed.

"Why wouldn't you talk?" asked Adair, when they were driving down-town in the young millionaire's auto. "Or rather, why did you persist in keeping me to the old swords?"

Ford laughed.

"For one reason, I enjoy the old swords—as a relaxation. For another, Mr. Jeffers Hawley, who was once one of the Transcontinental lawyers in Denver, was sitting just behind you, with eager ears. You didn't know that. Hold on a minute; tell your man to stop at the Chemical Bank. I want you to introduce me to the cashier."

"Now, what the deuce are you starting a New York bank account for?" queried Adair, as they came out of the bank together and climbed into the tonneau of the waiting touring car. "Couldn't you draw on the treasurer? What's the use of your being the assistant to the president, I'd like to know?"

"Wait," was the answer; and the questioner waited, perforce.

The board was already in session when the two young men were admitted to the private room in the rear of the Broad Street offices, and Ford was welcomed as a man who has recklessly steered the ship upon the rocks. There were even some open recriminations, notably on the part of the president; but Ford sat quietly under them, making no defense, and folding and refolding a slip of paper in his fingers as he listened.

When they gave him leave to speak, he still made no attempt to explain. Instead, he rose, walked to the other end of the table, and tossed the bit of folded paper across to Mackie, the broker.

"I inherited a little money, and I have made and saved enough more to make it an even twenty thousand dollars," he said. "I don't know of any more promising investment just now than Pacific Southwestern at twenty-nine and a half. Will you be good enough to buy for my account, Mr. Mackie?"

The effect was electrical. President Colbrith sat up very straight in his chair; two or three of the anxious ones opened on Ford with a rapid fire of questions; and Brewster, the copper magnate, sat back and chuckled softly in his beard.

"No, gentlemen; there is no change in the situation, so far as I know. Of course, you are not so foolish as to let the newspaper talk of the tie-up at the Chicago elevators influence you," Ford was saying to the anxious inquirers. "And, apart from that, everything is going our way. As I have remarked, our stock at the present figure is good enough for me, and I only wish I had two hundred thousand, instead of twenty thousand, to put into it."

Brewster stopped chuckling long enough to hold up a finger to the broker. "You may buy for my account, too, Mackie, while you are at it—and keep on buying till I tell you to quit."

This broke the deadlock instantly, and for a few minutes the board room was as noisy as the wheat pit with a corner threatening. Brewster, still laughing in his beard, pulled Ford out of the press at the broker's end of the table.

"I'm going to ask only one thing of you, young man," he began, his shrewd little eyes twinkling. "Just let me know when you are going to get out, so I can pull through without having to take the bankruptcy."

"I'll do it, Mr. Brewster," laughed Ford. "Only I'm not going to get out—unless you folks freeze me out."

"Then it isn't a long bluff on your part?"

"It is, and it isn't. We still stand to win if we have the nerve to hold on—in which event P. S-W. at twenty-nine and a fraction is a gold mine. That's one view of it, and the other is this: we've simply *got* to corner our own stock if we expect to sell thirty millions additional bonds."

"Well, I guess you've gone the right way about it. But are you sure about these Chicago terminals? A legal friend of mine here says you'll never get in."

"He was possibly paid to say it," said Ford hotly. "There has never been a shadow of doubt touching our trackage rights on the C.P. & D. contracts, or upon our ability to maintain them. All the Transcontinental people hoped to do was to make a newspaper stir to help keep our stock down. They know what we are going to do to them over in their western territory, and they won't stop at anything to block us."

"Will you be good enough to buy for my account, Mr. Mackie"

"Of course; I think we were all inclined to be a little short-sighted and pessimistic here, Mr. Ford. When do you go back to your fighting ground?"

"To-night."

"You won't wait to see what happens here?"

"I don't need to, I am sure. And the minutes—my minutes—are worth dollars to the company just now."

"Well, go in and win—only don't forget to give me that tip. You wouldn't want to see a man of my age going to the poorhouse."

"One other word, Mr. Brewster," Ford begged, as the copper magnate was pointing for the door of escape. "Please don't let any of these timid gentlemen sell till we get our bonds floated. You mark my word: the temptation to make a big killing is going to be very great, within a week."

The copper king laughed; openly, this time.

"You overrate my influence, Mr. Ford; but I'll do what I can—by word of mouth and by example. You can count on me—as long as you let me stay on your side of the market."

Ford had three several invitations to luncheon after the meeting adjourned, but he accepted none of them. To Adair he made the declination courteous while they were trundling back to the Waldorf in the big touring car.

"I have lost an entire day because I could not take the time to secure a stenographer before leaving Chicago night before last. I must find one now and go to work."

"All right; if you must. But I was hoping I could take you out to Overlook to dinner this evening. Can't you come anyhow, and take a later train west?"

"Don't tempt me," said Ford. And then: "The ladies are quite well, I hope?"

"Oh, yes; they are in town to-day, and we are all going to luncheon together—though I shan't know just where until I go to the club. Failing the dinner, won't you make a knife and fork with us at one o'clock?"

"I should like to—more than anything else in the world," Ford protested, meaning it. "But you'll make my excuses to Mrs. Adair, won't you? We've simply got to get a three-cornered hustle on now, if we want to save the day in the West."

"Why? Is there anything new in that quarter?"

"There is: something that I didn't dare to mention back yonder in the board meeting. You may remember that I told you I had left a man in my place on the Plug Mountain—Frisbie? I had a wire from him, night before last, just as I was leaving Chicago. As you know, the Pacific Southwestern inherits, from the old narrow-gauge purchase, the right-of-way over Plug Pass and down the valley of the Pannikin. Frisbie wires that the Transcontinental people have begun massing building material at the terminus of their Saguache branch, only twenty miles from the Pass."

"And that means?—I'm lame on geography."

"It means that they'll cut in ahead of us, if they can. Plug Pass is the only available unoccupied outlet through the mountains for thirty or forty miles north or south; and if we don't get our building force on the ground mighty suddenly, we'll find it fortified and held by the enemy."

The touring car had turned into Broadway, and the traffic roar precluded further talk. But when Ford was dismounting from the tonneau at the entrance to his hotel, Adair said: "There appears to be no rest for the wicked. You ought to have some of that thirty million dollars to spend right now."

Ford's smile was little more than a sardonic grin.

"Adair," he said, "I'm going to tell you something else that I didn't dare tell those money-tremulous people in McVeigh and Mackie's private office. I have been signing contracts and buying material by the train-load ever since the first grain shipment was started eastward on our main line. Also, I've got my engineering corps mobilized, and it will take the field under Frisbie as its chief not later than to-morrow. Putting one thing with another, I should say that we are something over a fresh million of dollars on the wrong side of solvency for these little antics of mine, and I'm adding to the deficit by the hundred thousand every time I can get a chance to dictate a letter."

Adair lighted a cigarette and made a fair show of taking it easily. But a moment later he was lifting his hat to wipe the perspiration from his forehead.

"Lord! but you have the confidence of your convictions!" he said, breathing hard. "If we shouldn't happen to be able to float the bonds—"

"We are in too deep to admit the 'if.' The bonds must be floated, and at the earliest possible moment that Magnus will move in it. You wanted something big enough to keep you interested. I have been trying my best to accommodate you."

Adair leaned forward and spoke to his chauffeur. The man watched his chances for room to turn in the crowded street.

"Where are you going?" asked Ford.

"Back to McVeigh and Mackie's—where I can watch a ticker and go broke buying more Pacific Southwestern," was the reply, and just then the chauffeur found his opening and the big car whirled and plunged into the down-town stream.

In the financial news the next morning there was a half-column or more devoted to the sudden and unaccountable flurry in Pacific Southwestern. Ford got it in the Pittsburg papers and read it while the picked-up stenographer was wrestling with his notes. After the drop in the stock, caused, in the estimation of the writer, by the company's sudden plunge into railroad buying at wholesale, P. S-W. had recovered with a bound, advancing rapidly in the closing hours of the day from the lower thirties to forty-two, with a strong demand. The utmost secrecy was maintained, but it was shrewdly suspected that one of the great companies, of which the Pacific Southwestern was now a competitor on an equal footing for the grain-carrying trade, had gone in to absorb the new factor in trans-Missouri traffic. Other and more sensational developments might be expected if the battle should be fought to a finish. Then followed a brief history of the Pacific Southwestern, with a somewhat garbled account of the late dash for a Chicago terminal, but lacking—as Ford remarked gratefully—any hint of the company's designs in the farther West.

"If Adair and Brewster and the others only have the nerve to keep it up!" said Ford to himself. Then he tossed the paper aside and dived once more into the deep sea of extension building, working the picked-up stenographer until the young man was ready with his resignation the moment the final letter was filed for mailing in the Chicago station.

Five days the young engineer waited for news from New York—waited and worked like a high-pressure motor while he waited. Each day's financial news showed the continued and growing success of the home-made "corner," and now the reporters were predicting that the stock would go to par before the price should break.

Ford trembled for the good faith of his backers on the board. When one has bought at twenty-nine and a half and can sell within the week for eighty-seven, the temptation is something tremendous. But at the closing hour of the fifth day the demand was still good; and when Ford reached the hotel that night there was a telegram from Adair awaiting him.

He tore it open and read it, with the blood pounding through his veins and a roar which was not of the street traffic drumming in his ears.

P. S-W. closed at ninety-two to-day, and a Dutch syndicate will take the bonds. Success to you in the Western wilderness. Brewster wants to know how soon you'll reach his Utah copper mines.   ADAIR.

XI
HURRY ORDERS

"I'm no cold-water thrower, Ford, as you know. But if I were a contractor, and you were trying to get me to commit myself to any such steeplechase, I should say no, and confirm it with a cuss-word."

It was a week after the successful placing of the Western Extension building-fund bonds with the Dutch syndicate, and Ford, having ordered things to his liking on the newly opened Chicago line, had taken the long step westward to Denver to begin the forging of the third link in the great railway chain.

Frisbie, now first assistant engineer in charge of construction, had come down from Saint's Rest for a conference with his chief, and the place of conferrings was a quiet corner in one of the balconies overlooking the vast rotunda of the Brown Palace Hotel; this because the carpenters were still busy in the suite of rooms set apart for the offices of the assistant to the president in the Pacific Southwestern headquarters down-town.

"You mean that the time is too short?" said Ford, speaking to Frisbie's emphatic objection.

"Too short at both ends," contended the little man with the devilish mustaches and chin beard. "The Copah mining district is one hundred and twenty miles, as the crow flies, from the summit of Plug Pass—say one hundred and forty by the line of our survey down the Pannikin, through the canyon and up to the town. Giving you full credit for more getting-ready than I supposed any man could compass in the three weeks you've been at it, I still think it is impossible for us to reach Copah this season."

"You must change your belief, Dick," was the curt rejoinder. "This is to be a campaign, not only of possibilities, but of things done. We go into Copah with the steel gangs before snow flies."

"I know; that's what you've been saying all along. But you're looking at the thing by and large, and I'm figuring on the flinty details. For example: you'll admit that we can't work to any advantage west of the mountains until we have made a standard gauge out of the Plug Mountain branch. How much time have you been allowing for that?"

"No time at all for the delay: about three weeks, maybe, for the actual changing of the gauge," said Ford coolly.

"All right," laughed Frisbie. "Only you'll show us how. It doesn't lie in the back of my head—or in Crapsey's, unless he's a better man than I hired him for."

"Who is Crapsey?"

"He is a Purdue man that I picked up and started out on the branch to make figures on the change of gauge. The other three parties, under Major Benson, Jack Benson and Roy Brissac, are setting the grade stakes down the Pannikin, and Leckhard is wrestling with the construction material you've been dumping in upon us at Saint's Rest. That left me short, and I hired Crapsey."

"Good. If he is capable, he may do the broadening. Call him in and set him at it."

"But, man! Don't you want the figures first?"

"My dear Dick! I've had those figures for two years, and there's nothing very complicated about that part of our problem. Call your man in and let him attack the thing itself."

"Everything goes: you may consider him recalled. But broadening the Plug Mountain to standard gauge doesn't put us into Copah this summer, does it?"

"No; our necessities will do that for us. See here; let me show you." Ford took out his note-book and on a blank page of it outlined a rough map, talking as he sketched. "Three weeks ago you wired me that the Transcontinental people were massing building material at the terminus of their Saguache branch."

"So I did," said Frisbie.

"And the day before yesterday you wired again to say that it was apparently a false alarm. What made you change your mind?"

"They are hauling the stuff away—over to their Green Butte line, I'm told."

"Why are they hauling it away?"

"The bluff—their bluff—was called. We had got busy on Plug Pass, and they saw there was no hope of cutting in ahead of us at that point."

"Exactly. Now look at this map for a minute. Here is Saint's Rest; here is the Copah district; and here is Green Butte, the junction of their narrow gauge with the standard-gauge Salt Lake and Eastern. If you were on the Transcontinental executive committee and saw an active competing line about to build a standard-gauge railroad through the Copah district and on to a connection with your narrow gauge's outlet at Green Butte, what would you advise?"

Frisbie nodded. "It's easy, when you know how, isn't it They'll standardize their narrow gauge to Green Butte, make an iron-clad traffic contract with the S.L. & E. to exclude us, and build a branch from Jack's Canyon, say, up into the Copah country." And then in loyal admiration: "That's what I call the sure word of prophecy— your specialty, Stuart. How many nights' sleep did you lose figuring that out?"

"Not any, as it happens," laughed Ford. "It was a straight tip out of the East. The plan, just about as you've outlined it, was adopted by the Transcontinental powers that be, sitting in New York last week. By some means unknown to me, Mr. Adair got wind of it, and made a flying trip to Chicago to put me on—wouldn't even trust the wire with it. Now you understand why we've got to wake the Copah echoes with a locomotive whistle this season."

"Copah—yes," said Frisbie doubtfully. "But that is only a way station. What we need is Green Butte and the Pacific coast outlet over the S.L. & E.; and they stand to euchre us out of that, hands down. What's to prevent their making that traffic contract with the Mormon people right now?"

"Nothing; if the S.L. & E. management were willing. But just here the political situation in Mormondom fights for us. Last year the Transcontinental folk turned heaven and earth over to defeat the Mormon candidate for the United States Senate. The quarrel wasn't quite mortal enough to stand in the way of a profitable business deal; but all things being equal, the Salt Lake line will favor us as against its political enemy."

"You're sure of that?" queried Frisbie.

"As sure as one can be of anything that isn't cash down on the nail—with the money locked up in a safety deposit vault. By the sheerest good luck, the Mormon president of the S.L. & E. happened to be in New York at the time when Adair had his ear to the Transcontinental keyhole. Adair hunted him up and made a hypothetical case of a sure thing: if our Western Extension and the Transcontinental, standard-gauged, should be knocking at the Green Butte door at the same time, what would the S.L. & E. do? The Mormon answer was a bid for speed; first come, first served. But Adair was given to understand, indirectly, that on an equal footing, our line would be given the preference as a friendly ally."

"Bully for the Mormon! But you say Copah—this summer. When we reach Copah we are still one hundred and forty miles short of Green Butte. And if you can broaden the Plug Mountain in three weeks—which you'll still allow me to doubt—the Transcontinental ought to be able to broaden its Green Butte narrow gauge in three months."

"If you had cross-sectioned both lines as I have, you wouldn't stumble over that," said Ford, falling back, as he commonly did, upon the things he knew. "We shall broaden the Plug Mountain without straightening a curve or throwing a shovelful of earth on the embankment, from beginning to end. On the other hand, the Green Butte narrow gauge runs for seventy miles through the crookedest canyon a Rocky Mountain river ever got lost in. There is more heavy rock work to be done in that canyon than on our entire Pannikin division from start to finish."

"That's bully for us," quoth the first assistant. "But, all the same, we shouldn't stop at Copah, this fall."

"We shall not stop at Copah," was the decisive rejoinder. "The winters on the western side of the range are much milder than they are here, and not to be spoken of in the same day with your Minnesota and Dakota stamping-ground. If we can get well out of the mountains before the heavy snows come—"

Frisbie wagged his head.

"I guess I've got it all, now—after so long a time. We merely break the record for fast railroad building—all the records—for the next six months or so. Is that about it?"

"You've surrounded it," said Ford tersely.

"Good enough: we're ready to make the break when you give the word. What are we waiting for?"

"Just at this present moment, for the contractors."

"Why, I understood you had closed with the MacMorrogh Brothers," said Frisbie.

"No. At the last moment—to relieve me of a responsibility which might give rise to charges of favoritism, as he put it—Mr. Colbrith took the bids out of my hands and carried the decision up to the executive committee. Hence, we wait; and keep a growing army of laborers here under pay while we wait," said Ford, with disgust thinly masked. Then he added: "With all due respect to Mr. Colbrith, he is simply a senile frost!"

Frisbie chuckled.

"Been cooling your fingers, has he? But I understood from the headquarters people down-town, that the MacMorroghs had a sure thing on the grading and rock work. Their bid was the lowest, wasn't it?"

"Yes; but not the cheapest for the company, Dick. I've been keeping tab on the MacMorroghs for a good while: they are grafters; the kind of men who take it out of the company and out of their labor in a thousand petty little steals—three profits on the commissary, piece-work for subs where they know a man's got to lose out, steals on the working hours, fines and drawbacks and discounts on the pay-rolls, and all that. You know how it's done."

"Sure," agreed Frisbie, with his most diabolical grin. "Also, I know how it keeps the engineering department on the hottest borders of Hades, trying to hold them down. The good Lord deliver us!"

"I wanted to throw their bid out without consideration," Ford went on. "But again Mr. Colbrith said 'No,' adding that the MacMorroghs were old contractors on the line, and that Mr. North had always spoken very highly of them."

"Ah; the fine Italian hand of Mr. North again," said Frisbie. "And that reminds me: are we going to be at war with the main line operating department?"

Ford shook his head. "Not openly, at least. North was down to meet my train when I came in last night, and you would never have suspected that I left Denver six weeks ago without his blessing. And now I'm reminded. I have a luncheon appointment with him at twelve, and a lot of letters to dictate before I can keep it. Go down and do your wiring for Crapsey, and if we lose each other this afternoon, I'll meet you here at dinner this evening."

It was while Ford was working on his mail, with one of the hotel stenographers for a helper, that a thick-set, bull-necked man with Irish-blue eyes and a face two-thirds hidden in a curly tangle of iron-gray beard, stubbed through the corridor on the Pacific Southwestern floor of the Guaranty Building, and let himself cautiously into the general manager's outer office. The private secretary, a faultlessly groomed young fellow with a suggestion of the Latin races in his features, looked up and nodded.

"How are you, Mr. MacMorrogh?" he said; and without waiting for a reply: "Go on in. Mr. North is expecting you."

The burly one returned the nod and passed on to the inner room. The general manager, a sallow, heavy-visaged man who might have passed in a platform gathering for a retired manufacturer or a senator from the Middle West, swung in his pivot-chair to welcome the incomer.

"Glad to see you, MacMorrogh. Sit down. What's the news from New York?"

The contractor found a chair; drew it close to the general manager's desk, and filled it.

"I'm thinking you'll know more about that than I will, Misther North," he replied, in a voice that accorded perfectly with the burly figure and piratical beard. "Ford's fighting us with his fishtes."

"Why?" asked the general manager, holding his chin in his hand—a gesture known the entire length of the Pacific Southwestern as a signal of trouble brewing, for somebody.

"God knows, then; I don't," said the MacMorrogh. "I wint to Chicago to see him when the bid was in, and d'ye think he would lave me talk it over with him? Not him! Wan day he'd be too busy;

and the next, I'd have to call again. 'Twas good for him I was not me brother Dan. Dan would've kicked the dure in and t'rown him out av the windy."

The wan ghost of a smile flitted across the impassive face of the big man at the desk.

"Let me tell you something, MacMorrogh. If you, or your brother Dan, ever find it necessary to go after Ford, don't give him notice by battering down doors. You won't, I know. But about the contract: you haven't heard from the executive committee?"

"Not the half of wan wor-rd."

"Have you any idea of what is causing the delay?"

"'Tis dommed well I know, Misther North. Ford is keeping the wires hot against us. If I could have Misther Colbrith here with you for wan five minutes—"

The general manager broke in, following his own line of thought.

"Ford is in Denver; he came in from Chicago last night. Why don't you go up to the Brown and have it out with him?"

"Fight it out, d'ye mean?"

"Certainly not. Make friends with him."

The contractor sat back in his chair and plunged his stubby hands deep into his pockets.

"Give me the sthraight tip, Misther North."

"It ought to suggest itself to you. This is a big job, with a great deal of money passing. Your profits, over and above what you will make out of the company, will be quite large. Ford is an ambitious young man, and he is not building railroads for his health."

The MacMorrogh was nodding slowly. Nevertheless, he made difficulties.

"Me hand's not light enough for that, Misther North."

Again the general manager smiled.

"You require a deal of prompting, sometimes, Brian. What's the matter with a trusty go-between?"

"H'm, that's it, now. But where to lay me finger on the right man. 'Tis a risk to run—with a yooung fire-brand like Ford holding the other end iv the string."

"Still I think the man can be found. But first we must make sure of your contract, with or without Ford. Your suggestion about taking the matter up with Mr. Colbrith in person strikes me favorably. Can you spare the time to go to New York?"

"Sure I can."

"At once?"

"The wan minute for sthriking is whin the iron's hot, Misther North."

The general manager put aside the thick file of papers he had been examining when MacMorrogh entered, and began to set his desk in order.

"I have been thinking I might make it convenient to go with you. I presume you have no objection to going as my guest in the Naught-Seven?"

"'Tis an honor you're doing me, Misther North, and I'll not be forgetting it."

"Not at all. There are some matters connected with this contract that I'd like to talk over with you privately, and if we can agree upon them, I may be able to help you with Mr. Colbrith and the executive committee."

The general manager pressed one of the electric buttons on the side of the desk, and to the clerk who answered gave a brief order: "Have the Naught-Seven provisioned and made up to go east as a special at twelve-ten to-day. Tell Despatcher Darby to make the schedule fast—nineteen hours or less to the River."

The clerk nodded and disappeared, and North turned again to MacMorrogh.

"Now about that other matter: I'll find you a go-between to approach Ford; but to be quite frank with you, you'll have to be liberal with the young man for his services. When you go into the diplomatic field, you have to spend money." He was pressing another of the electric buttons as he spoke, and to the office boy who put his face in at the door, he said: "Ask Mr. Eckstein to step in here a minute."

It was the private secretary, the well-groomed young man with the alien eyes and nose who answered the summons. North gave him his instructions in a curt sentence.

"Mr. MacMorrogh would like to have a little talk with you, Eckstein: take him into the other room where you can be undisturbed."

It was half an hour later when the door of the library opened to readmit the private secretary and the contractor, and in the interval the division superintendent's clerk had returned to say that the special train schedule was made up, and that the Naught-Seven would be waiting at the Union Station at twelve-ten.

"Well?" said the general manager, lifting a slow eyebrow at MacMorrogh and compressing into the single word his wish to know what had been done in the conference of two.

"'Tis all right, Misther North," said the contractor, rubbing his hands. "'Tis a crown jewel ye have in this yooung—"

North cut the eulogy short in a word to his secretary.

"I go east, special, at twelve-ten, Eckstein, as Mr. MacMorrogh has probably told you. I have a luncheon appointment at twelve with Mr. Ford. Meet him when he comes, and make my excuses—without telling him anything he ought not to know. If you can take my place as his host, do so; but in any event, keep him from finding out where we have gone until we are well on the way. That's all."

This was why Ford, walking the few blocks from his hotel at noon to keep his engagement with North, found the general manager's private office closed, and a suave, soft-spoken young man with a foreign cast of countenance waiting to make his superior's excuses.

"Mr. North was called out of town quite unexpectedly on a wire," was the private secretary's explanation. "He tried to telephone you at the Brown, but the operator couldn't find you. He left me to explain, and I've been wondering if you'd let me take his place as your host, Mr. Ford."

Now Ford's attitude toward his opponents was, by reason of his gifts, openly belligerent; wherefore he fought against it and tried to be as other men are.

"I am sure Mr. North is quite excusable, and it is good-natured in you to stand in the breach, Mr. Eckstein," he said. "Of course, I'll be glad to go with you."

They went to Tortoni's, and to a private room; and the luncheon was an epicurean triumph. Eckstein talked well, and was evidently a young man of parts. Not until the cigars were lighted did he suffer the table-talk to come down to the railroad practicalities; and even then he merely followed Ford's lead.

"Oh, yes; we have made arrangements to give you a clear deck in the Denver yards for your material and supplies," he said, in answer to a question of Ford's about side-track room and yard facilities at the point which would have to serve as his base. "Following your orders, we have been forwarding all that your Plug Mountain rolling stock could handle, but there is considerable more of it side-tracked here. After the MacMorrogh grading outfit has gone to the front, we shall have more room, however."

"The MacMorrogh outfit?" queried Ford. "Do they store it in our yards?"

"Oh, no. They have a pretty complete railroad yard of their own at their headquarters in Pueblo. But they have three train-loads of tools and machinery here now, waiting for your orders to send them to the front."

Ford weighed the possibilities thoughtfully and concluded that nothing could be lost by a frank declaration of principles.

"They have given you folks a wrong impression, Mr. Eckstein," he said mildly. "The contract for the grading on the Western Extension is not yet awarded; and if I can compass it, the MacMorrogh Brothers' bid will be thrown out."

The private secretary tried to look mystified, with just the proper touch of a subordinate's embarrassment.

"I'm only a clerk, Mr. Ford," he said, "and, of course, I'm not supposed to know more than I see and hear in the regular way of business. But I understood that the MacMorroghs were in the saddle; that they were only waiting for you to provide track-room at Saint's Rest for their tool cars and outfit."

"No," said Ford. "It hasn't got that far along yet."

Eckstein looked at his watch.

"Don't let me keep you, if there is anything else you want to do, Mr. Ford; but I'll confess you've aroused my curiosity. What is the matter with the MacMorroghs?"

Ford answered the question by asking another.

"Do you know them, Mr. Eckstein?"

"Why—yes; as Mr. North's chief clerk would be likely to know the firm of contractors which has been given a good share of the Pacific Southwestern work for a number of years."

"Do you know any good of them?"

"Bless me! yes: I don't know anything else of them. Three hearty, bluff, rough-tongued Irishmen; lacking diplomacy and all the finer touches, if you like, but good fellows and hustlers of the keenest."

Ford fastened his companion in a steady eye-grip. "One question, Mr. Eckstein; do they play fair with all concerned?"

"They are more than fair; they are generous—with the company, and with the company's representatives with whom they have to do business. On two contracts with us they have lost money; but I happen to know that in both instances they kept their promises to the engineering department to the letter."

Ford had cast off the eye-grip and he appeared to be studying the fresco design of the ceiling over the private secretary's head.

"And those promises were—?"

Eckstein laughed boyishly. "You needn't make a mystery of it with me, Mr. Ford. I'm one of the family, if I haven't any initials after my name. I know—we all know—that there are certain profits—not made out of the company, of course—that a contractor is always willing to share with his good friends, the engineers."

Ford's attitude instantly became that of a freshman wishing to learn the ropes.

"Consider me, Mr. Eckstein," he said. "I'm new to the construction business—or at least, I've never been at the head of it before. What are these—er—perquisites?"

The private secretary thought he had entered the thin edge of the wedge and he drove it heartily.

"They are perfectly legitimate, of course. The contractors run a commissary to supply the workmen—nobody suspects them of doing it at cost. Then there are the fines imposed to secure faithful work, the *per capita* commission paid on the labor sent in by the engineers, the discounts on time-checks, the weekly hospital and insurance dues collected from the men. All those things amount to a good round profit on a contract like ours."

"To about how much, in figures, should you say?" queried Ford, with an air of the deepest interest.

"To enough to make your share, as head of the construction department, touch ten thousand a year, on a job as big as ours—with a liberal provision for Mr. Frisbie, besides."

Ford blew reflective smoke rings toward the ceiling for a full minute or more before he said quietly: "Do I understand that you are authorized to guarantee me ten thousand a year in commissions from the MacMorrogh Brothers, Mr. Eckstein?"

Eckstein laughed.

"You forget that I'm only a clerk, and an onlooker, as you may say. But if you accept MacMorrogh's bid, and he doesn't do the square thing by you and Mr. Frisbie, you may call me in as a witness, Mr. Ford. Does that clear up the doubt?"

"Perfectly," was the quiet rejoinder. "Under these conditions, I suppose it is up to me to wire the executive committee, withdrawing my objections to the MacMorroghs, isn't it?"

"That is the one thing Mr. MacMorrogh asks." The secretary whipped out a note-book and pencil. "Shall I take your message? I can send it when I go back to the office."

"Thank you," said Ford; then he began to dictate, slowly and methodically: "To S.J. Colbrith, care McVeigh and Mackie, New York. This is to recall my objections to MacMorrogh Brothers, as stated in letter of the twenty-fifth from Chicago. Further investigation develops the fact that they are quite honest and capable, and that they will pay me ten thousand dollars a year for withdrawing my opposition."

Eckstein's pencil had stopped and he was gasping for breath.

"Great Scott!" he ejaculated. "That won't do, Mr. Ford! You can't put a thing like that into a telegram to the president!"

"Why not?" was the cool inquiry. "You said it was perfectly legitimate, didn't you?"

"Yes, but—" the entrance of a waiter to clear the table provided a merciful stop-gap, and Eckstein, hurriedly consulting his watch, switched abruptly. "By Jove! I'm due at the office this minute to meet a lot of cattlemen," he stammered, and escaped like a man hastening for first aid to the mistaken.

Ford laughed long and silently when he found himself alone in the private dining-room; and he was still chuckling by fits and starts when, after an afternoon spent with Auditor Evans, he recounted his adventure to Frisbie over the Brown café dinner table that evening. But Frisbie took all the humor out of the luncheon episode when he said soberly:

Eckstein's pencil had stopped and he was gasping for breath

"He laughs best who laughs last, Stuart. Eckstein took a fall out of you one way, even if he did fail in the other; he kept you safely shut up at Tortoni's while Mr. North and the chief of the MacMorroghs got away on a special train for New York. Beard, the Union Station operator, told me. Which means that they'll have a full day with Mr. Colbrith and the executive committee before you can possibly get there to butt in."

"No, it doesn't; necessarily," Ford contradicted, rising suddenly and signaling a waiter.

"What are you going to do?" queried Frisbie, dropping his knife and fork and preparing to second his chief.

"Come and see. I'm going to get out another special train and give Mr. North a run for his money," was the incisive answer. "Hike down to the despatcher's office with me and help cut out the minutes."

XII
THE ENTERING WEDGE

Has civilized humanity, in the plenitude of twentieth century sophistication, fully determined that there is no such thing as luck?—that all things are ordered, if not by Providence, at least by an unchangeable sequence of cause and effect?

Stuart Ford was a firm believer in the luck of the energetic; which is to say that he regarded obstacles only as things to be beaten down and abolished. But in the dash to overtake and pass the general manager's one-car special, the belief was shaken almost to its reversal.

He knew the Pacific Southwestern locomotives—and something of the men who ran them. The 1016 was one of the fast eight-wheelers; and Olson, the engineer, who had once pulled passenger on the Plug Mountain, was loyal and efficient. Happily, both the man and the machine were available; and while Frisbie was calling up the division superintendent at his house to ask the loan of his private car for the assistant to the president, Ford was figuring the schedule with the despatcher, and insisting upon speed—more speed.

"What's come over you big bosses, all at once?" said Darby, to whom Ford's promotion was no bar to fellowship or free speech. "First Mr. North wants me to schedule a special that will break the record; and now you want to string one that will beat his record."

"Never mind my troubles, Julius," was the evasive reply. "Just you figure to keep things out of my way and give me a clear track. Let's see—where were we? Cheyenne Crossing at 2 a.m., water at Riddle Creek, coal at Brockton—"

The schedule was completed when Frisbie came back to say that the 1016, with the superintendent's car attached, was waiting on track Six. Ford went down, looked the gift horse in the mouth, and had the running gear of the car overhauled under his own supervision before he would give Olson the word to go, pressing the night car inspectors into service and making them repack the truck journals while he waited.

"I'm taking no chances," he said to Frisbie; and truly it seemed that all the hindrances had been carefully forestalled when he finally boarded the "01" and ordered his flagman to give Olson the signal. Yet before the one-car train was well out of the Denver yards there was a jolting stop, and the flagman came in to report that the engine had dropped from the end of an open switch, blocking the main line.

Ford got out and directed the reënrailment of the 1016, carefully refraining from bullying the big Swede, whose carelessness must have been accountable. It was the simplest of accidents, with nothing broken or disabled. Under ordinary conditions, fifteen minutes should have covered the loss of time. But the very haste with which the men wrought was fatal. Enrailing frogs have a way of turning over at the critical instant when the wheels are climbing, and jack-screws bottomed on the tie-ends do not always hold.

Eight several times were the jack-screws adjusted and the frogs clamped into position; but not until the ninth trial could the perverse wheels be induced to roll workmanlike up the inclined planes and into place on the rails. Ford looked at his watch when his special was free of the switches and Olson was speeding up on the first long tangent. With the chase still in its opening mile, Mr. North's lead had been increased from seven hours to eight.

Leaving Denver on the spur of the moment, Ford had necessarily left many things at a standstill; and his first care, after he had assured himself that the race was fairly begun, was to write out a handful of telegrams designed to keep the battle alive during his enforced absence from the firing line. The superintendent's desk was hospitably unlocked, and for a busy half-hour Ford filled blank after blank, steadying himself against the pounding swing of the heavily ballasted car with a left-handed grip on the desk end. When there remained no one else to remind, he wrote out a message to Adair, forecasting the threatened disaster, and urging the necessity of rallying the reconstructionists on the board of directors.

"That ought to stir him up," he said to himself, bunching Adair's telegram with the others to be sent from the first stop where the Western Union wires could be tapped. Then he whirled around in the swing chair and scowled up at the little dial in the end of the car; scowled at the speed-recorder, and went to the door to summon the flagman.

"What's the matter with Olson?" he demanded. "Has he forgotten how to run since he left the Plug Mountain? Climb up over the coal and tell him that forty miles an hour won't do for me to-night."

The flagman picked up his lantern and went forward; and in a minute or two later the index finger of the speed-recorder began to mount slowly toward the fifties. At fifty-two miles to the hour, Ford, sitting in the observation end of the car where he could see the ghostly lines of the rails reeling backward into the night, smelled smoke—the unmistakable odor of burning oil. In three strides he had reached the rear platform, and a fourth to the right-hand railing showed him one of the car-boxes blazing to heaven.

He pulled the cord of the air-whistle, and after the stop stood by in sour silence while the crew repacked the hot box. Since he had made the car inspectors carefully overhaul the truck gear in the Denver station, there was no one to swear at. Olson bossed the job, did it neatly and in silence, and no one said anything when the fireman, in his haste to be useful, upset the dope-kettle and got its contents well sanded before he had overtaken it in its rolling flight down the embankment.

Ford turned away and climbed into his car at the dope-kettle incident. There are times when retreat is the only recipe for self-restraint; and in imagination he could see the general manager's special ticking off the miles to the eastward while his own men were sweating over the thrice-accursed journal-bearing under the "01."

Now, as every one knows, hot boxes, besides being perversely incurable, are the sworn enemies of high speed. At forty miles to the hour the journal was smoking again. At forty-five it burst into flames. Once more it was patiently cooled by bucketings of water drawn from the engine tank; after which necessary preliminary Olson spoke his mind.

"Ay tank ve never get someveres vit dat hal-fer-damn brass, Meester Ford. Ay yust see if Ay can't find 'noder wone." And he rummaged in the car lockers till he did find another.

Unfortunately, however, the spare brass proved to be of the wrong pattern; a Pullman, instead of a P. S-W. standard. Olson was a trained mechanic and a man of resources, and he chipped and filed and scraped at the misfit brass until he made it serve. But when he climbed again to the cab of his engine, and Ford swung up to the steps of the car, the white headlight eye of an east-bound freight, left at a siding a full hour's run to the rear, came in sight from the observation platform of the laboring special.

These were the inauspicious beginnings of the pursuit; and the middle part and the ending varied only in degree. All the way up to midnight, at which hour a station of a bigness to supply a standard brass was reached, the tinkered journal-bearing gave trouble and killed speed. Set once more in running order upon its full quota of sixteen practicable wheels, the special had fallen so far behind its Denver-planned schedule as not only to be in the way of everything else on the division, but to find everything else in its way. Ford held on stubbornly until the lead of the train he was trying to outrun had increased to twelve hours. Then he gave it up, directing his crew to turn the train on the nearest "Y," and to ask for retracing orders to Denver. After which he went to bed in the state-room of the borrowed car, and for the first time in his experience was a man handsomely beaten by the perversity of insensate things.

The request for the retracing orders was sent from Coquina; and when it came clicking into the despatcher's office at Denver, a sleep-sodden young man with an extinct cigar between his teeth rose up out of his chair, stretched, yawned, and pointed for the door.

"Going to leave us, Mr. Eckstein?" said the trick despatcher who was sitting at the train table.

"Yes. If Mr. Ford has changed his mind, I may as well go home and go to bed."

"Reckon he forgot something, and has to come back after it?" laughed the operator.

"Maybe," said the private secretary, and he went out, shutting the door behind him with the bat-like softness and precision that was his distinguishing characteristic.

The sounders were clicking monotonously when the trick man turned to the relief operator who was checking Darby's transfer sheet.

"What do you suppose Eckstein was up to, sitting here all night, Jim?"

"Give it up," said the relief man. "Ask me something easy."

"I'll bet a hen worth fifty dollars I can guess. He didn't want Mr. Ford to make time."

The relief man looked up from his checking.

"Why? He didn't do anything. He was asleep more'n half the time."

"Don't you fool yourself," said the other. "He heard every word that came in about that hot box. And if the hot box hadn't got in the way, I'll bet a cockerel worth seventy-five dollars, to go with that fifty-dollar hen, that he would have tangled me up somehow till I had shuffled a freight train or something in Mr. Ford's way. He's Mr. North's man, body and soul; and Mr. North doesn't love Mr. Ford."

"Oh, rats, Billy!" scoffed the relief man, getting up to fill his corn-cob pipe from the common tobacco bag. "You're always finding a nigger in the wood-pile, when there isn't any. Say; that's 201 asking for orders from Calotte. Why don't you come to life and answer 'em?"

Frisbie, breakfasting early at the Brown Palace on the morning following the night of hinderings, was more than astonished when Ford came in and took the unoccupied seat at the table-for-two.

"Let me eat first," said the beaten one, when Frisbie would have whelmed him with curious questions; and with the passing of the cutlets and the coffee he told the tale of the hindrances.

"I guess it was foreordained not to be," he admitted, in conclusion. "We tried mighty hard to bully it through, but the fates were too many and too busy for us."

"Tricks?" suggested Frisbie, suspecting North of covering his flight with special instructions to delay a possible pursuit.

"Oh, no; nothing of that sort: just the cursed depravity of inanimate things. Every man concerned worked hard and in good faith. It was luck. No one of us happened to have a rabbit's foot in his pocket."

"You don't believe in luck," laughed the assistant.

"Don't I? I know I used to say that I didn't. But after last night I can't be so sure of it."

"Well, what's the cost to us?" inquired Frisbie, coming down out of the high atmosphere of the superstitious to stand upon the solid earth of railway-building fact.

"I don't know: possibly failure. There is no guessing what sort of a scheme North will cook up when he and MacMorrogh get Mr. Colbrith *cornered*."

"Oh, it can't be as bad as that. Take it at the worst—admitting that we may have to struggle along with the MacMorroghs for our general contractors; they can't addle the egg entirely, can they?"

Ford tabulated it by length and breadth.

"With the MacMorroghs in the forefront of things to steal and cheat and make trouble with the labor, and Mr. North in the rear to back them up and to retard matters generally, we are in for a siege to which purgatory, if we ever go there, will seem restful, Richard my son. Our one weapon is my present ranking authority over the general manager. If he ever succeeds in breaking that, you fellows in the field would better hunt you another railroad to build."

"It's a comfort to know that you *are* the big boss, Stuart. North can't knock you out of that when it comes to a show-down."

"I don't know," said Ford, whose night ride had made him pessimistic. "I am Mr. Colbrith's appointee, you know—not an elected officer. And what Mr. Colbrith has done, he may be induced to undo. Adair has been my backer in everything; but while he is the best fellow in the world, he is continually warning me that he may lose interest in the game at any minute and drop it. He doesn't care a rap for the money-making part of it—doesn't have to."

"Wouldn't Adair be a good safety-switch to throw in front of Mr. North and MacMorrogh in New York?"

Ford nodded. "I thought of that last night, and sent a wire. We'll hear from it to-day."

Frisbie ate through the remainder of the breakfast in silence. Afterward, at the pipe-lighting, he asked if Ford's wire instructions of the night before still held good.

"They do," was the emphatic reply. "We go on just as if nothing had happened, or was due to happen. You say your man Crapsey will be in this morning: gather up your laborers and turn the Plug Mountain into a standard-gauge railroad while we wait. That's all, Dick; all but one word—hustle."

"Hustle it is. But say: you were going to give me a pointer on that broad-gauging. I've been stewing over it for a day and a night, and I don't think of any scheme that won't stop the traffic."

"Don't you? That is because you haven't mulled over it as long as I have. In the first place, you have no curves to straighten and no cross-ties to relay—our predecessors having set the good example of using standard length ties for their three-foot road. String your men out in gangs as far as they'll go, and swing the three-foot track, as a whole, ten inches out of center to the left. You can do that without stopping trains, can't you?"

"Sure."

"All right. When you swing, spike the right-hand rail lightly. Then string your gangs again and set a line of spikes for the outside of the standard-gauge right-hand rail straight through to Saint's Rest. Got that?"

"Yes; I guess I've got it all. But go on."

"Now you are ready for the grand-stand play. Call in all your narrow-gauge rolling stock, mass your men at this end of the branch, shove the right-hand rail over to the line of gauge spikes in sections as long as your force will cover, and follow up with a standard-gauge construction train to pick up the men and carry them forward as fast as a section is completed. If you work it systematically, a freight train could leave Denver two hours behind your track-gangs and find a practical standard gauge all the way to Saint's Rest."

"Of course!" said Frisbie, in workmanlike disgust for his own obtuseness. "I'm going back to the Tech when your railroad is finished and learn a few things. I couldn't think of anything but the old Erie Railroad scheme, when it was narrowed down from the six-foot gauge. They did it in one night; but they had a man to every second cross-tie over the whole four hundred miles from New York to Buffalo."

Ford nodded, adding:

"And we're not that rich in labor. By the way, how are the men coming?"

"A car-load or two, every little while. Say, Stuart, you must have had a rabbit's foot with you when you touched up the eastern labor agencies. Every other railroad in this neck of woods is skinned, and M'Grath is having the time of his life trying to hold our levies together. There is a small army of them under canvas at Saint's Rest, waiting for the contractors, and another with between two and three hundred hands camped at the mouth of the canyon."

Ford knocked the ashes from his pipe so hard that the pipestem fell in two.

"Yes! all waiting on Mr. Colbrith's leisurely motions! Well, jump in on the Plug Mountain. That will utilize some of the waste for a few days."

Frisbie went down to the Plug Mountain yard office, and to a wire-end, to begin the marshaling of his forces; and Ford, with three picked-up stenographers to madden him, took up the broken threads of his correspondence with a world which seemed to have become suddenly peopled to suffocation with eager sellers of railroad material and supplies.

Late in the afternoon, when he was tired enough to feel the full force of the blow, a New York telegram came. It was from Miss Alicia Adair, and Ford groaned in spirit when he read it.

Brother left here yesterday in the Vanderdecken yacht for Nova Scotia. Can not reach him by telegraph until next Friday or Saturday. Aunt Hester wants to know if there is anything she can do.

One way to save a man's life at a crisis is to appeal to his sense of humor. Miss Alicia's closing sentence did that for Ford, and he was smiling grimly when he put the telegram away, not in the business file, but in his pocket.

Three days later, however, when Frisbie was half-way to Saint's Rest with his preliminary track-swinging, another New York telegram found Ford in his newly established quarters in the Guaranty Building. This was from some one acting as President Colbrith's secretary, and its wording was concisely mandatory.

Contract has been awarded MacMorrogh Brothers. President directs that you afford contractors every facility, and that you confer with Mr. North in all cases of doubt.

XIII
THE BARBARIANS

It was some little time after the rock had begun to fly from the cuttings on the western slopes of the mountains that Kenneth, summoned by Ford, made the run from Denver to Saint's Rest over the standardized Plug Mountain branch and found the engineer-manager living in a twenty-foot caboose car fitted as a hotel and an office-on-wheels.

The occasion of Kenneth's calling was a right-of-way dispute on the borders of the distant Copah mining district; some half-dozen mining claims having been staked off across the old S.L. & W. survey. The owners, keen to make a killing out of the railroad company, threatened injunctions if the P. S-W. persisted in trespassing upon private property; and Ford, suspecting shrewdly that the mine men were set on by the Transcontinental people to delay the work on the new line, made haste to shift his responsibility to the legal shoulders.

"If I hadn't known you for a pretty good mountaineer, Kenneth, you would have missed this," he said, making his guest free of the limited hospitality of the caboose-hotel. "Are you good for a two-hundred-and-eighty-mile cayuse ride, there and back, on the same trail we tramped over a year ago last spring?"

"I'm good for everything on the bill of fare," was the heartening reply. "How are things going?"

Ford's rejoinder began with a non-committal shrug. "We're building a railroad, after a fashion."

"After a good fashion, I hope?"

Another shrug.

"We're doing as well as we can with the help we have. But about this right-of-way tangle—" and he plunged his guest into a discussion of the Copah situation which ran on unbroken until bedtime.

They took the westward trail together in the morning, mounted upon wiry little mountain-bred ponies furnished by one Pacheco, the half-breed Mexican who had once earned an easy double-eagle by spying upon two men who were out hunting with an engineer's transit. For seven weeks Frisbie had been pushing things, and the grade from Saint's Rest to the summit of the pass was already a practicable wagon road, deserted by the leveling squads and ready for the ties and the steel.

From the summit of the pass westward, down the mountain and through the high-lying upper valley of the Pannikin, the grade work was in full swing. The horse trail, sometimes a rough cart-road, but oftener a mere bridle-path, followed the railroad in its loopings and doublings; and on the mountain sections where the work was heaviest the two riders were never out of sight of the heavily manned grading gangs.

"To a man up a tree you appear to be doing a whole lot, and doing it quickly, Ford," commented the lawyer, when they had passed camp after camp of the workers. Then he added: "You are not having any trouble with the MacMorroghs, are you?"

"Not what the legal department would call trouble," answered Ford evasively; and for ten other miles the narrowness of the bridle-path discouraged conversation.

Farther down in the valley of the Pannikin the activities were less thickly sown. On many sections the work was light; no more than the throwing up of an embankment in the park-like intervales, with now and then a rock-or earth-cutting through some jutting spur of the inclosing mountains. Here the men were bunched on the rock work and the fills, though the camp sites were commonly in the park-like interspaces where wood and water, the two sole commodities for which the contractors could make no deductions on the pay-roll, lay conveniently at the doors of the rude sleeping shacks.

Since he was not required to talk, Kenneth had time to be curiously observant of many things in passing. Each camp was the fellow of its neighbor; a chaotic collection of hastily built bunk shanties, a mess tent for those who, shunning the pay-devouring Scylla of the contractors' "commissary," fell into the Charybdis of the common table, and always, Kenneth remarked, the camp groggery, with its slab-built bar, its array of ready-filled pocket bottles, and its sad-faced, slouch-hatted, pistol-carrying keeper.

"What is that Bible-saying about the shadow of a great rock in a thirsty land?" said Kenneth, as they were passing one of the wilderness bar-rooms buttressing a huge boulder by the trail side. "I should think you'd rule those fellows emphatically and peremptorily out of the game, Ford. They must make a lot of trouble for you, first and last."

"They do," was the sober response. "But how would you go about it to rule them out?"

The lawyer laughed. "My writs don't run this far. But I thought yours did. Why don't you fire 'em bodily; tell 'em their number is 23—skiddoo! Aren't you the Sublime Porte—the court of last resort—the big boss—over here?"

Ford pulled his horse down to a walk.

"Kenneth, let me tell you: behind those barkeepers are the contractors; behind the contractors is Mr. North; behind Mr. North, the president. My little lever isn't long enough to turn the world over."

"Pshaw!" said Kenneth. "Mr. Colbrith wouldn't stand for anything like that! Why, he's a perfect fanatic on the whisky question."

"That's all right," said Ford acidly. "It doesn't go as far as Mr. Colbrith in the matter of the debauching particulars. It stops in Denver; and Mr. Colbrith approves Denver in the lump—signs the vouchers without looking at them, as Evans would say. I tell you what I believe—what I am compelled to believe. These individual saloon-keepers are supposed to be in here on their own hook, on sufferance. They are not; they are merely the employees of a close corporation. Among the profit sharers you'll find the MacMorroghs at the top, and Mr. North's little ring of Denver officials close seconds."

"Do you honestly believe that, Ford?"

"I do. I can't prove it, of course. If I could, I'd go to New York and fight it out. And the whisky isn't all of it, or even the worst: there are women in some of these camps, and there would be more if Leckhard didn't stand guard at Saint's Rest and turn them back."

"Heavens—what a cesspool!" said the attorney. "Does a laboring man ever get out of here with any of his earnings?"

"Not if the MacMorroghs can help it. And you can figure for yourself what the moral atmosphere must be. We are less than two months old on the work, but already the Western Extension is a streak of crime; crime unpunished, and at times tacitly encouraged. You may say that my department isn't responsible—that this is the contractors' day and game. If that is true now—which it isn't—it will no longer be true when we come in with our own employees, the track-layers."

But now Kenneth was shaking his head.

"I can't believe it, Ford. You're blue because Mr. Colbrith has thrown Mr. North into your boat as ballast. I don't blame you: but you mustn't let it make you color-blind."

Ford said nothing. The day was yet young, and the long journey was still younger. It was at the noon halt, made at a subcontractor's camp near a great earth-cutting and a huge fill, that Kenneth had his object lesson.

They were standing at the door of the timekeeper's shanty—they had been the timekeeper's guests for the noon meal—and the big gang of Italians, with its inevitable Irish foreman, was already at work. Out at the head of the great fill a dozen men were dumping the carts as they came in an endless stream from the cutting. Suddenly there was a casting down of shovels, a shrill altercation, a clinch, a flash of steel in the August sunlight, and one of the disputants was down, his heels drumming on the soft earth in the death agony.

"Good God!" said Kenneth. "It's a murder!" and he would have rushed in if Ford and the timekeeper had not held him back.

The object lesson was sufficiently shocking, but its sequel was still more revolting. Without one to kneel beside the dying man; indeed, without waiting until the drumming heels were still; the men callously put their shovels under the body, slid it over the lip of the dump and left it to be covered by the tumbling cataract of earth pouring from the tip-carts whose orderly procession had scarcely been interrupted by the tragedy.

Kenneth was silent for many minutes after they had left the camp of the Italians. He was a Western man only by adoption; of Anglo-Saxon blood, and so unable to condone the Latin's disregard for the sacredness of human life.

"That was simply terrible, Ford," he said finally, and his voice was still in sympathy with the shaking hand that held the bridle-reins. "Will nothing be done?"

"Nothing; unless the murdered man chances to have relatives or clansmen in one of the near-by camps—in which case there'll be another killing."

"But the law," said Kenneth.

"There is no law here higher than the caprice of Brian MacMorrogh. Besides, it's too common—a mere episode; one of those which you said you couldn't believe, a little while back."

"But can't you make the MacMorroghs do a little police work, for common decency's sake?"

Ford shook his head. "They are quite on the other side of the fence, as I told you in the beginning. By winking at lawlessness of all kinds, their own particular brands of lawlessness, by which they and their backers make money, go unquestioned. So far from helping, they'd make it exceedingly difficult for any sheriff who should have the temerity to come in here in the discharge of his duty."

"You foresaw all this before the contract was awarded?"

"Not all—though I had been told that the MacMorroghs ran 'open camps' where the work was far enough from civilization to take the curse off. What you've seen, and what I've been telling you, is bad enough, God knows; but it will be worse before it is better. After we've had a few pay-days, and the men begin to realize that they are here to toil and to be robbed ... Kenneth, it will be hell on earth; and the company will pay for it—the company always pays in the end."

"I've got a notion," said the attorney, after another plodding mile of reflection; but what it was he did not say.

Ford and his companion reached Copah in the afternoon of the third day out from Saint's Rest, and, singularly enough, the mine owners who were disputing the extension right-of-way were found amenable to reason. What Kenneth did to secure the P. S.-W. right-of-way across the mining claims, Ford did not know, or seek to know; though a word or two let fall by the attorney led him to believe that the Transcontinental encouragement was not quite specific enough in dollars and cents to warrant the obstructors in holding out.

Ford was for starting back the next morning: he had missed Brissac and both of the Bensons on the way over. But Kenneth confessed to being saddle-sore, and begged for another day's respite. Ford agreed without giving the matter a second thought. Upon such unconsidered trifles—an indifferent "yes" or "no"—turn the poised scales of life. For one other day the two Southwestern representatives put up at the Grand Union, Copah's tar-paper-covered simulacrum of a hotel; and during that day Ford contrived to sell his birthright for what he, himself, valued at the moment as a mess of pottage.

It was in this wise. At this period of its existence Copah, the future great, was merely a promise; a camp of magnificent prospects. Isolated by one hundred and fifty miles of wagon-road and pack-trail from one railroad base, and by forty miles of mountains from the other, its future turned upon the hope of cheaper transportation. As a gold camp it was an anomaly. With a single exception its ores were low grade, and the wagon-road and pack-trail freightage made them practically profitless to the miners.

The single exception was the "Little Alicia," and it was the coincidence of the name, rather than the eloquence of its impoverished owner, that first attracted Ford. From first to last he did not know the exact location of the mine. It was somewhere in the hills back of Copah, and Grigsby, the prospector who had discovered and opened it, had an office in the camp.

It was in Grigsby's town office that Ford saw the ore specimens and the certified assays, and listened not too credulously to Grigsby's enthusiastic description of the Little Alicia. To be a half-owner in this mine of mines was to be rich beyond the dreams of avarice—when the railroad should come: if one might take Grigsby's word for it.

It is a curious fever, that which seizes upon the new-comer in an unexploited mining field. Ford was far from being money-mad; but there were times when he could not help contrasting a railroad salary with Miss Adair's millions. True, he had once said to her, in the fulness of confident belief, that the money of the woman he loved would make no difference—to her or to him. But the point of view, wise or foolish, is not always the same. There were moments when the Adair millions loomed large, and the salary of an assistant to the president—who was in fact little more than a glorified chief of construction—shrank in proportion. He was free of obligation and foot-loose. His twenty thousand dollars invested in P. S-W. stock at twenty-nine and a half had grown with the rising market to sixty-odd. What did it matter to any one if he chose to put ten thousand of the sixty-odd on a turn of the Little Alicia card?

While it was gambling, pure and simple, he did not bet with his eyes shut. Inquiry at the Bank of Copah established Grigsby's reputation for truth-telling. The specimens and the assay certificates were beyond doubt genuine. More than this, Grigsby had made a number of ore shipments by freighters' wagon and jack train over the range, and the returns had enabled him to keep a small force of men at work in the mine.

Ford made his bet through the bank. The cashier was willing to take a P. S-W. official's note of hand, to be canceled when Ford could deposit to the bank's credit in Denver, and to give Grigsby an open account for his immediate needs. Grigsby accepted joyfully, and the thing was done. Ford's mess of pottage was a deed of half-ownership in the Little Alicia, executed and recorded in the afternoon of the day of stop-overs, and he was far enough from suspecting that he had exchanged for it all that a man of honor holds dearest. But, as a matter of fact, the birthright had not yet been handed over: that came later.

XIV
THE DRAW-BAR PULL

Attorney Kenneth had many more object-lessons in the study of "open camps" on the three-day return ride to Saint's Rest. The day of stop-over in Copah chanced to be the MacMorrogh Brothers' monthly pay-day, and until the men's money was spent pandemonium reigned along the line of the extension.

Some of it they dodged, riding wide to pass the larger camps, and hearing from afar the noise of carousal, the fierce drinking songs of the Magyars, the fusillades of pistol-shots. So far as they could see, all work appeared to be suspended; and Major Benson, whose camp of engineers they picked up in one of the detours around a gulch head, confirmed that conclusion.

"It was the same way last month," raged the major, twisting his fierce white mustaches and looking as if he would like to blot the name of MacMorrogh from the roster of humanity. "It'll take a full week to get them into the swing again, and MacMorrogh will be up with his estimates just the same as if he had been working full time. I'll cut 'em; by the gods, I'll cut 'em! And you must stand by me, Mr. Ford."

There was the same story to be listened to at Brissac's tie camp; and again at young Benson's headquarters, which were on the mountain section. This last was on the third day, however, when the madness was dying down. Some of the rock men were back on the job, but many of the gangs were still grievously short-handed. Ford said little to Kenneth. The pandemonium spoke for itself. But on the third night, when the long ride was ended, and Pietro, Ford's cook and man-of-all-work, was serving supper in the caboose office-on-wheels, some of the bitterness in Ford's heart slipped into speech.

"Can you see now how it takes the very marrow out of a man's bones, Kenneth? You may think of an engineer as a man of purely bull-headed purposes, merely trying, in a crass, materialistic way, to get a material thing done. I want to do a big thing, and I'd like to do it in a big way. It *is* a big thing—the building of this extension. If it doesn't add another star to the flag, it will at least make one state twice as populous, twice as prosperous. It will add its quota to the habitable surfaces; and it's a good quota—a land that some future generation will love, and swear by, and fight for, if need be. And to think that for one man's narrow-mindedness and another's greed we've got to christen it in blood and muck and filth and dishonesty—it makes me sore, Kenneth; sore and disheartened."

"I don't blame you," said the lawyer, reveling, though he would never have admitted it, in the comfort of the caboose headquarters journey's end. "But you'll pull through; you'll build your railroad, and the mistakes that are made won't be your mistakes. It's a horrible state of affairs, that in the MacMorrogh camps; a blot on our boasted civilization. But you can't help it. Or rather you will help it if, and when, you can."

Ford was shaking his head dejectedly.

"I don't know, Kenneth. It's getting next to me, even at this early stage of the game. Have you ever stood on the front car platform of a train nearest to the engine and watched the jiggling draw-bar? It is apparently loose; its hold on the engine seems to be no more than that of the touch of clasped hands in a gipsy dance. Yet it never lets go, and the drag of it is always there. By and by, when the coal is all burned, and the fire is out, and the water is drained from the tank, those gentle little multiplied jerks will pull the big engine down—kill it—make it a mere mass of inert metal blocking the way of progress."

"Well?" said the attorney.

"It's an allegory. I'm beginning to feel the draw-bar pull. Sooner or later, North and his clique will drag me down. I can't fight as the under dog—I never learned how; and they've fixed it so that I can't fight any other way."

Kenneth had lighted his cigar and was lying back against the cushion of the car-seat. After a little, he said: "Just after we saw the Italian killed last week I told you I had a notion, Ford. I've got it yet, and I've been turning it over in my mind and wondering if I'd better explode it on you. On the whole, I think I'd better not. It's a case of surgery. If the patient lives, you'll know about it. If the patient dies, you'll be no worse off than you are now. Shall we let it rest at that?"

Ford acquiesced. He was too utterly disheartened to be curious. But if he could have foreseen the results of Kenneth's notion it is conceivable that he would have been aroused to some effort of protest, as even in deep waters one prays sometimes to be delivered from his friends.

It was a week after this farewell supper in the caboose hotel at Saint's Rest when Ford went down to Denver to borrow, on his P. S-W. stock, the ten thousand dollars to be deposited to the credit of the Bank of Copah. Following him, and only one train behind, came Frisbie, new from a confirmatory survey of the extension beyond the Copah district.

On his return from the Green Butte end of the proposed line, the little man with the diabolical fashion of beard trimming had spent a week in and around Copah, picking up yard rights-of-way, surveying approaches, and setting grade stakes for the outlying MacMorrogh gangs. During that week he had made a discovery, and since he believed it to be all his own, he journeyed eastward to share it quickly with his chief.

Ford was dining alone at the Brown Palace when Frisbie, coming straight from the Plug Mountain train, found him. There was an entire western desert to be talked over during the courses, and Frisbie held his discovery in reserve until they had gone to smoke in a quiet corner of the great rotunda. Even then he approached it indirectly.

"In taking up the line down the Pannikin we have followed the old S.L. & W. survey pretty closely all the way from start to finish. What were your reasons, Stuart?" he asked.

"There didn't seem to be any good reason for not following it. Brandreth made the S.L. & W. preliminary, and there isn't a better locating engineer in this country."

"I know," said Frisbie. "But the best of us make mistakes, now and then. Brandreth made a pretty sizable one, I think."

"How is that?"

"You know where the big rock-cutting is to be made in the lower canyon, about ten miles this side of the point where we begin to swing south for the run to Copah—a mile and a half of heavy work that will cost away up into the pictures?"

"Yes; I've estimated that rock work at not a cent less than two hundred thousand dollars."

"You're shy, rather than over, at that. And two hundred thousand would build a number of miles of ordinary railroad, wouldn't it? But that isn't all. The cliffs along that canyon are shale-topped and shale-undermined, the shale alternating with loose rock about fifty feet above our line of grade in quarter-mile stretches all along. That means incessant track-walking day and night through the mile and a half of cutting, and afterward—for all time afterward—a construction train kept handy under steam to clear away débris that will never quit sliding down on the embankment."

"I'm afraid you are right," said Ford. "It's the worst bit on the entire extension; the most costly to build, as it will be the most expensive to maintain. But I guess Brandreth knew what he was about when he surveyed it."

"Brandreth is a short-line man. He wouldn't lengthen his line ten miles to dodge an earthquake. Ford, we can save a hundred thousand dollars on that piece of track in first cost—to say nothing of the future."

"How? I'm always open to conviction."

"By leaving the S.L. & W. survey at Horse Creek, following up to the low divide at Emory's Mine, and crossing to enter Copah from the southeast instead of from the northeast. I came out that way from Copah five days ago. It's perfectly feasible; straight-away, easy earth work for the greater part, and the only objection is that it adds about twelve running miles to the length of the extension. It's for you to say whether or not the added distance will be warranted by the lessened cost and the assurance of safety in operating. If we cut through that lower canyon cliff it will be only a question of time until we bury somebody, no matter how closely it is watched."

Ford took time to consider the proposal. There were objections, and he named one of them.

"The MacMorroghs have based their bid on the present survey: they will not want to let that piece of rock work drop out of sight."

"They'll have to, if you say so. And you can afford to be pretty liberal with them on the substituted twelve miles."

"I'll have to think about it over night," was Ford's final answer. "Arrange to give me an hour to-morrow morning and we'll go over the maps and your notes together."

Frisbie slept soundly on the gained inch, hoping to make it the coveted ell in the morning. He knew the chief objection, which was that Ford, too, was a "short-line" engineer; a man who would lay down his railroad as the Czar of Russia did the St. Petersburg-Moscow line—by placing a ruler on the map and drawing a straight mark beside it between the two cities—if that were an American possibility. But he knew, too, that the safety clause would weigh heavily with Ford, and there was no minimizing the danger to future traffic if the canyon route should be retained.

It turned out finally as the first assistant had hoped and believed it would. Ford spent a thoughtful hour at his office in the Guaranty Building before Frisbie came down—the little man being trail-weary enough to sleep late in the comfortable room at the Brown Palace. The slight change of route was hardly a matter to be carried up to the executive committee, and Ford's decision turned upon quite another pivot—the addition of twelve miles of distance. As against this, safety and economy won the day; and when Frisbie came in the talk was merely of ways and means.

"Fix up the change with the MacMorroghs the best way you can," was Ford's concluding instruction to his lieutenant. "They will kick, of course; merely to be kicking at anything I suggest. But you can bring them to terms, I guess."

"By my lonesome?" said Frisbie. "Aren't you going over to see the new route with your own eyes?"

"No. I'm perfectly willing to trust your judgment, Dick. Besides, I've got other fish to fry. I'm going east to-night to have one more tussle with the steel mills. We must have quicker deliveries and more of them. When I get back, we'll organize the track-layers and begin to make us a railroad."

"Good," said Frisbie, gathering up his maps and sketches of the detour country; and so, in the wording of a brief sentence or two it came to pass that Ford delivered himself bound and unarmed into the hands of his enemies.

A little light was thrown upon this dark passage that night in the office of the general manager, after Ford's train had gone eastward, and Frisbie was on his way back to the MacMorrogh headquarters on the lower Pannikin. North was waiting when Eckstein came in, flushed as from a rapid walk.

"It's all settled?" asked the general manager, with a slow lift of the eyebrow to betray his anxiety.

"To the queen's taste, I should say," was the secretary's not too deferential reply. "Ford's out of the way, to be gone ten days or a fortnight, and Frisbie has gone back to dicker with MacMorrogh, and to survey the new route up Horse Creek. Ford doesn't know; I doubt if he will ever know until we spring the trap on him. The one thing I was most afraid of was that he would insist upon going over the new line himself. Then, of course, he would have found out—he couldn't help finding out."

The general manager squared his huge shoulders against the back of the chair.

"You think he would call it off if he knew?" he queried. "You give him credit for too much virtue, Eckstein. But I think we have him now. By the time he returns it will be too late for him to hedge. MacMorrogh will see to that."

Eckstein nodded. "I made a point of that with Brian," he said. "The minute the word is given he is to throw a little army of graders upon the new roundabout. But Ford won't find out. He'll be too busy on this end of the line with the track-layers. I'm a little nervous about Merriam, though."

"He's the man who talked Frisbie into championing the new route?"

"Yes. He did it pretty skilfully: made Frisbie think he was finding it out himself, and never let the little man out of his sight while they were in Copah. But I am afraid Merriam himself knows too much."

"Get him out of the country—before Ford gets back," was the crisp order. "If he isn't here when the gun goes off, he can't tell anybody how it was loaded."

"An appointment—" Eckstein began.

"That is what I mean," said the general manager, turning back to his desk. "We need a traffic agency up in the Oregon country. See Merriam—to-night. Find out if he'd like to have the general agency at, say, twenty-five hundred a year; and if he agrees, get out the circular appointing him."

"He'll agree, fast enough," laughed the secretary. "But I'll nail him— to-night."

Ford spent rather more than two weeks in his round-up of the eastern steel mills, and there was a terrific accumulation of correspondence awaiting him when he reached Denver. At the top of the pile was an official circular appointing one George Z. Merriam, a man whom Ford remembered, or seemed vaguely to remember, as one of the MacMorrogh bookkeepers, general agent of the P. S-W., with headquarters at Portland, Oregon. And at the bottom of the accumulation was a second official printing, bearing the approval of the president, this; and Ford's eyes gloomed angrily when he read it.

PACIFIC SOUTHWESTERN RAILWAY CO.

Office of the President.

NEW YORK, August 24.

To All Officials and Employees:

At a called meeting of the stock-holders of this company, held in New York, August 23, Mr. John C. North was elected First Vice-President and General Manager of all lines of this company, operative and under construction. All officers and employees will govern themselves accordingly.

By Order of the Executive Committee.

Approved:

SIDNEY J. COLBRITH, President.

XV
AN UNWILLING HOST

Standing in the Pacific portal of Plug Pass, on the old snow-crust which, even in midsummer, never entirely disappears at altitude ten thousand feet, they could look away westward over a billowing sea of mountain and mesa and valley breaking in far-distant, crystalline space against the mighty rampart of the Wasatch range, two hundred and other miles nearer the sunset.

It was an outlook both inspiring and chastening; with the scenic grandeurs to give the exalted uplift, and the still, gray-green face of the vast mountainous desert to shrink the beholder to microscopic littleness in the face of its stupendous heights and depths, its immeasurable bulks and interspaces. Miss Alicia said something like this to Ford, in broken exclamations, when she had taken her first quailing eye-plunge from the lofty view-point.

"Yes; quite so," Ford acquiesced, in the unresponsive tone of one who says what he must, rather than what he would like to say. "It is all the things you have been saying, and more — when one has the time and the mind to be enthusiastic about it."

Miss Adair stood up very straight, and her chin was a protest in Praxitelean harmonies. She knew very well how reluctantly her companion was doing the honors of the mountain vastnesses; how full of wrath he was because President Colbrith had seen fit to precipitate the Nadia and a private-car party into the midst of the strenuous building battle on the western extension. But she argued that this was no reason why he should be crustily impossible with her. Wherefore she said, merely to see him boil over:

"I should think you would come up here often for this glorious view, Mr. Ford. You do, don't you?"

"Come up here for the view? Oh, yes; I presume I have climbed up here a hundred times, first and last, and always for the sake of the view. I began it the first winter I spent in Saint's Rest, when the snow-shoeing was at its best. Really to appreciate the scenery, you should take three hours for the approach from the basin down yonder, dragging a pair of Canadian raquettes by the toe-straps."

The young woman laughed inwardly at the broadsword slash of his sarcasm. It was so like the man; big and vigorous and energetic, and quite without regard for consequences or for the insignificance of the thing to be obliterated. But she would not spare him.

"How enthusiastic you are!" she commented. "I don't believe I should be equal to 'a hundred times, first and last,' or to the snow-shoes. But I can admire such zeal in other people immensely."

"Do you really think so small of a man's work in the world, Miss Adair?" he demanded, not very coherently. "I'm not saying that the scenery doesn't move me. It does; and the first time I stood here on this summit, I presume I felt just as you do now. But my comings and goings have been chiefly concerned with this" — kicking the rail of the new track which threaded the shallow valley of the pass. "I am trying to build a railroad; to build it quickly, and as well as I can. When I get it finished, I may have time to admire the scenery."

It was a little appeal for sympathy, apparent enough in spite of its indirectness; but Miss Adair was still mindful of Ford's too evident willingness to leave her behind at the deserted grading-camp half-way down to Saint's Rest where the Nadia was temporarily side-tracked.

"Another ideal gone," she lamented, in mock despair. "All those trampings and toilings up this magnificent mountain merely to prepare for the laying of some logs of wood in a row, with two strands of iron to fasten them together!"

He smiled at her definition of his railroad, and the keen edge of his annoyance was a little blunted. He had been telling himself that she might be twenty-four, or possibly twenty-five; but evidently she was only a child, with a child's appreciation of a very considerable industrial triumph. Old engineers, one of them an assistant on his own staff, had shaken their heads and declared that the running of a standard gauge railroad over Plug Pass was a sheer impossibility. Yet he had done it.

"I suspect I owe you an apology," he said, yielding a little to the love which was fighting with discouragement and righteous anger for the first place in his heart. "I'm afraid I have been taking you too seriously, all along."

Her laugh was a delicious little ripple of exultation. She had succeeded in avenging herself.

"I can forgive you now," she said, and the blue eyes were dancing. "But you must admit that you were the aggressor. I have *never* been made so pointedly unwelcome in all my life. I believe you were going to refuse to let me walk up here with you if Uncle Sidney had not commanded you to."

This time his smile was a grin, but it was not ill-natured.

"I should, indeed," he confessed quite frankly. "To be brutally candid, I had a decided attack of the 'unwelcomes' when I received Mr. Colbrith's wire announcing his intention of bringing his picnic party out here into the midst of things. We have little time, and none of the civilized conveniences, for entertaining company."

"I think we all understand that," she made haste to say. "Aunt Hetty tried to dissuade Uncle Sidney, but he was bent on showing us how modern railroad building is rushed at the 'front'—is that the right word?—and so here we are."

A small frown gathered between Ford's eyes. He was far enough from suspecting that this was the outworking of Kenneth's "notion"; that Mr. Colbrith's annual inspection tour over the Pacific Southwestern had been extended to cover the new line at Kenneth's suggestion—a suggestion arising out of purely reformatory motives. Nor would it have helped matters much if he had known Kenneth's genuine distress when it transpired that the suggestion bade fair to result in precipitating a private car-load of pleasurers into the pandemonium of the grading-camps.

But the pleasurers were as yet only upon the borders of the pandemonium, and Ford was torturing his ingenuity to devise some argument strong enough to turn back the threatened invasion. There were reasons enough why a party with women among its members should not be projected into the grading and track-laying field. It was no place for women, Ford was telling himself wrathfully; especially for the women of the president's own household.

In the little interval of silence Miss Adair was focusing her field-glass and trying to trace the line of the descending grade into the headwater valley of the Pannikin. Ford did not mean to be ungracious to her—what lover ever means to be curt to the one woman in all the world? But it is not easy to be angry in nine parts and loving-kind in the tenth—anger being one of the inclusive emotions. Nevertheless, he made the effort, for her sake. However inconsiderate Mr. Colbrith was, she was blameless.

"Let me show you," he said, taking the field-glass and adjusting it for her. "Now hold it steadily and pick up the line in the great loop.... Have you found it?... Now follow it slowly until you come to the point where it turns into the valley, and you can trace it for miles by the cuts and fills."

She followed his directions until the line of the extension became a vanishing thread in the distance, and then was content to let the glass sweep the vastnesses beyond. When she spoke it was of the topographic immensities.

"I heard you telling brother at the dinner-table in Chicago that you were able to see more in this wilderness than you have ever been able to make any one else see. Can I see it with the glass?"

"Hardly," he smiled. "I was trying to tell your brother of the magnificent possibilities of the country lying between this and that

135

farthest mountain range; the country we are going to open up. It was a gospel I had been trying to preach to the directors, but none of them believed — not even your uncle."

"I see nothing but vastness and cold gray grandeurs," she said, adding: "and the very bigness of it makes me feel like a mere atom, or a molecule — whichever is the smaller."

"Yet it is a new empire in the rough," he rejoined, with a touch of the old enthusiasm, "waiting only for the coming of this" — putting his foot again upon the steel of the new railroad line. "What you are looking at has been called a part of the Great American Desert — the most forbidding part, in the stories of the early explorers. Notwithstanding, there will come a time when you can focus your glass here on this mountain and look out over what the promoters will then be advertising as a 'peopled paradise,' and these 'logs of wood in a row, with two strands of iron to fasten them together' will bring it to pass."

There was a flash of the enthusiast's fire in the cool gray eyes to go with the words, and Miss Adair wondered at it. He had stood for her as an embodiment of things practical and prosaic; as one too keenly watchful and alert on the purely industrial side to be in any sense a dreamer of dreams. Some part of her thought slipped into speech.

"No, I am not an enthusiast," he denied, in reply to her charge. "At bottom, I'm only an engineer, with an ambition to build railroads. But I should have learned no more than half of my trade if I couldn't tell where it would be profitable to build them."

"Never mind: you seem to have convinced Uncle Sidney and the directors finally," she commented.

"No; your uncle and the directors are not empire builders — meaning to be," he objected. "They are after the present visible dollar in a western outlet for the Pacific Southwestern. If we reach Green Butte before our competitors can broaden their narrow gauge to that point, we shall have a practicable line from Chicago to the Pacific coast."

"I understand," she said. "But yours is the higher ideal—the true American ideal."

"It's business," he asserted.

"Well, isn't business the very heart and soul of the American ideal?" she laughed.

This time he laughed with her, forgetting his troubles for the moment.

"I guess it is, in the last analysis," he said. And then: "I'm sorry to keep you waiting so long, if you are anxious to get back to the Nadia. But I warned you beforehand. I must keep my appointment with Frisbie. Do you see anything of him?" This because she was again sweeping the western wilderness with the field-glass.

"What am I to look for?"

"The smoke of an engine."

She focused the glass on the gorge at the foot of the pass. "I see it!" she cried. "A little black beetle of a thing just barely crawling. Now it is turning into the first curve of the great loop."

"Then we shan't have very much longer to wait. Do you find the ten-thousand-foot breeze chilly? Turn up the collar of your coat and we'll walk a bit."

It was his first appreciable concern for her comfort, and she gave him full credit. Coquetry was no part of Miss Alicia's equipment, but no woman likes to be utterly neglected on the care-taking side, or to be transformed ruthlessly into a man-companion whose well-being may be brusquely ignored. And this young athlete in brown duck shooting-coat and service leggings, who was patiently doing a sentry-go beside her up and down the newly-laid track at the summit of Plug Pass, was quite a different person from the abashed apologist who had paid for her dinner in the dining-car on the night of purse-snatchings.

XVI
THE TRUTHFUL ALTITUDES

A low, tremulous shudder was beginning to lift itself, like the distant growling of thunder, upon the tinnient air of the high summit. A moment later a heavy construction engine shot around the final curve in the westward climb, with Michael Gallagher hanging out of the cab window on the engineer's side.

The two at the summit faced about to watch the approach. The big engine came lumbering and lurching dangerously over the unsurfaced track in a fierce spurt for the mountain-top, its stack vomiting fire, its cylinder-cocks hissing shrilly, and its exhaust ripping the spheral silences like the barking detonations of a machine-gun.

Ford glanced aside at his companion; her expressive face was a study in delighted animation and he decided that he had again misjudged the president's niece. She was beating time softly with her gloved hands and singing the song of the locomotive:

"'With a michnai—ghignai—shtingal! Yah! Yah! Yah!
Ein—zwei—drei—Mutter! Yah! Yah! Yah!

    She climb upon der shteeple,
    Und she frighten all der people,

Singin' michnai—ghignai—shtingal! Yah! Yah!'"

she quoted; and Ford's heart went out to her in new and comradely outreachings.

"You read *Naught-naught-seven*?" he said: "you are one woman in a thousand."

"Merci!" she countered. "Small favors thankfully received. Brother thinks there is only one person writing, nowadays, and the name of that person is Kipling. I get a little of it by mere attrition."

The brakes of the big engine were still gripping the wheels when a small man with wicked mustaches and goatee dropped from the gangway. His khaki suit was weather-faded to a dirty green, and he was grimy and perspiring and altogether unpresentable; but he pulled himself together and tried to look pleasant when he saw that his chief had a companion, and that the companion was a lady.

"I'm sorry if I have kept you waiting," he began. "Gallagher was shifting steel for the track-layers when your wire found me, and the engine couldn't be spared,"—this, of course, to Ford. Then, with an apologetic side glance for the lady: "Riley's in hot water again—up to his chin."

"What's the matter now?" gritted Ford; and Alicia marked the instant change to masterful command.

"Same old score. The Italians are kicking again at the MacMorrogh Brothers' commissary—because they have to pay two prices and get chuck that a self-respecting dog wouldn't eat; and, besides, they say they are quarrying rock—which is true—and getting paid by the MacMorroghs for moving earth. They struck at noon to-day."

The chief frowned gloomily, and the president's niece felt intuitively that her presence was a bar to free speech.

"It's straight enough about the rotten commissary and the graft on the pay-rolls," said Ford wrathfully. "Is the trouble likely to spread to the camps farther down?"

"I hope not; I don't think it will—without whisky to help it along," said Frisbie, with another apologetic side glance for Miss Adair.

"Yes; but the whisky isn't lacking—there's Pete Garcia and his stock of battle, murder and sudden death at Paint Rock, a short half-mile from Riley's," Ford broke in.

Frisbie's smile, helped out by the grime and the coal dust, was triumphantly demoniacal.

"Not now there isn't," he amended; adding: "Any fire-water at Paint Rock, I mean. When Riley told me what was doing, I made a bee line for Garcia's wickiup and notified him officially that he'd have to go out of business for the present."

"Oh, you did?" said Ford. "Of course he was quite willing to oblige you? How much time did he give you to get out of pistol range?"

Frisbie actually blushed—in deference to the lady.

"Why—er—it was the other way round. He double-quicked a little side-trip down the gulch while I knocked in the heads of his whisky barrels and wrecked his bar with a striking hammer I had brought along."

For the first time in the interview the chief's frown melted and he laughed approvingly.

"Miss Adair, you must let me introduce my friend and first assistant, Mr. Richard Frisbie. He is vastly more picturesque than anything else we have to show you at this end of the Pacific Southwestern. Dick—Miss Alicia Adair, President Colbrith's niece."

Frisbie took off his hat, and Miss Alicia gave him her most gracious smile.

"Please go on," she said. "I'm immensely interested. What became of Mr. Garcia afterward?"

"I don't know that," said Frisbie ingenuously. "Only, I guess I shall find out when I go back. He is likely to be a little irritated, I'm afraid.

141

"Miss Adair, you must let me introduce my friend, Mr. Richard
Frisbie"

But there are compensations, even in Pete: like most Mexicans, he can neither tell the truth nor shoot straight." Then again to Ford: "What is to be done about the Riley mix-up?"

"Oh, the same old thing. Go down and tell the Italians that the company will stand between them and the MacMorroghs, and they shall have justice—provided always that every man of them is back on the job again to-morrow morning. Who is Riley's interpreter now?"

"Lanciotto."

"Well, look out for him: he is getting a side-cut from the MacMorroghs and is likely to translate you crooked, if it suits his purposes. Check him by having our man Luigi present when he does the talking act. Any word from Major Benson?"

"He was at the tie-camp on Ute Creek, yesterday. Jack Benson and Brissac are lining the grade for the steel on M'Grath's section, and the bridge men are well up to the last crossing of Horse Creek."

"That's encouraging. How about the grade work on the detour— your new line into Copah?"

It was the assistant's turn to frown, but the brow-wrinkling was of puzzlement.

"There's something a bit curious about that—you don't mind our talking shop like a pair of floor-walkers, do you, Miss Adair? You know we expected the MacMorroghs would kick on the change of route and the loss of the big rock-cut in the canyon. There wasn't a word of protest. If I hadn't known better, I should have said that old Brian MacMorrogh knew all about it in advance. All he said was: 'Sure, 'tis your railroad, and we'll be buildin' it anywheres you say, Misther Frisbie.' And the very next day he had a little army of men on that detour, throwing dirt to beat the band. It'll be ready for the steel by the time we can get to it with the track-layers."

Ford nodded approvingly. "Speed is what we are paying for, and we're thankful to get it whenever, and wherever, we can. Is the bridge timber coming down all right now?"

"Yes; and we are getting plenty of ties since the major put on his war-paint and went after the MacMorrogh subs in the tie-camps. It is the rock work that is holding us back."

Ford nodded again. Then he tried a little shot in the dark.

"The president's car is just below—at the basin switch. He wants to have it taken to the front, and I have been trying to dissuade him. Is the track safe for it?"

Frisbie guessed what kind of answer was desired, and stretched the truth a little.

"I should say not. It's something fierce, even for the construction trains."

Miss Alicia's smile was seraphic.

"You two gentlemen needn't tell fibs for the possible effect on me," she said, with charming frankness. "Nothing I could say would carry any weight with Uncle Sidney."

"Stung!" said Frisbie, half to himself; and the two men laughed shamefacedly.

"Will it disarrange things so very much if the Nadia is taken to the 'front'?" asked Miss Adair.

"Well, rather," said Frisbie bluntly. Then he tried to excuse himself and made a mess of it.

"Just why?" she persisted. "Forget the conventions, Mr. Frisbie, and talk to me as you have been talking to Mr. Ford. Is there any good reason, apart from the inconvenience, why our little pleasure party

144

shouldn't see your new railroad? I am appealing to you because Mr. Ford won't tell me the truth."

Ford stood aloof and let Frisbie worry with it alone.

"There are a dozen reasons, Miss Adair; the track is fearfully rough—really, you know, it isn't safe for a big car like the Nadia. There are only a few sidings, and what there are, are filled up with construction stuff and camp cars, and—"

She was shaking her head and laughing at his strivings.

"Never mind," she said; "you can't tell the truth, either, with Mr. Ford looking on. But I shall find it out."

Frisbie looked horrified.

"You—you certainly will, Miss Adair; if Mr. Colbrith insists upon having his car dragged over the range." Then, being quite willing to make his escape, he turned to his chief. "Is there anything else? If not, I'll be getting back to the Riley mix-up before the trouble has time to grow any bigger."

Ford shook his head, and Frisbie lifted his hat to Miss Adair and turned to climb to his engine cab. But at the moment of brake-releasings Ford halted him.

"One minute," he said; and turning to his charge: "I'll borrow Dick's engine and take you down to the Nadia's siding, if you'd rather ride than walk."

"Oh, will you? That would be fine! But oughtn't Mr. Frisbie to get back to his work?"

"Y-yes," Ford admitted. "Time is rather important, just now."

"Then we'll walk," she said with great decision.

"That's all, Dick," Ford called. "Keep an eye open for Garcia. He might make a fluke and shoot straight, for once in a way."

They stood in silence on the wind-swept summit until the curving down-rush of the western grade had swallowed the retreating engine. Miss Alicia was the first to speak when the iron clamor was distance-drowned.

"I like your Mr. Frisbie," she said reflectively. "Isn't he the kind of man who would have taken the message to the other Garcia?"

"He is the kind of man who would stop a bullet for his friend, and think nothing of it—if the bullet should happen to leave him anything to think with," he returned warmly. And then he added, half absently: "He saved my life four years ago last summer."

There was genuine human interest in her voice when she said gently:

"Would you mind telling me about it?"

"It was up in the Minnesota pineries, where we were building a branch railroad through the corner of an Indian reservation. A half-breed pot-hunter for the game companies had a right-of-way quarrel with the railroad people, and he pitched upon me as the proper person to kill. It was a knife rush in the moonlight; and Dick might have shot him, only he was too tender-hearted. So he got between us."

"Well?" she prompted, when it became evident that Ford thought he had finished.

"That was all; except that it was touch and go with poor Dick for the next six weeks, with no surgeon worthy of the name nearer than St. Paul."

Miss Alicia was more deeply impressed by the little story than she cared to have her companion suspect. Her world was a world of the commonplace conventions, with New York as its starting point and homing place; and she thought she knew something of humankind. But it came to her suddenly that the men she knew best were not at all like these two.

"Shall we go back now?" she asked; and they were half-way down to the siding and the private car before she spoke again. It took some little time to compass sufficient humility to make amends, and even then the admission came to no more than four words.

"I'm sorry, Mr. Ford."

"What for?" he asked, knowing only that he was coming to love her more blindly with every added minute of their companionship.

"For—for trying to be hateful." It was a humbler thing than any she had ever said to a man, but the raw sincerity of time and place and association was beginning to get into her blood.

"If it comes to that, there were two of us," he rejoined, matching her frankness. "And, as you remarked a while back, I was certainly the aggressor. Shall we call it a truce for the present?"

"If you will be generous enough."

"Oh, I am generosity itself, under ordinary conditions; but just now I'll admit that I am fearfully and wonderfully inhospitable. I can't help wishing most fervently that something had happened to prevent your uncle's coming."

"Is it uncle who is in the way?—or the pleasure party?"

"Both."

"We are negligible," she said, meaning the pleasurers.

"No, you are not; and neither is your Uncle Sidney."

"Is he still formidable to you?" she laughed.

"He is, indeed. But, worse than that, he is likely to prove a very considerable disturbing element if I can't keep him from plunging in upon us."

She let half of the remaining distance to the end of the steep grade go underfoot before she said: "I like to help people, sometimes; but I don't like to do it in the dark."

He would have explained instantly to a man for the sake of gaining an ally. But he could not bring himself to the point of telling her the story of graft and misrule in which the MacMorroghs were the principals, and North—and her uncle, by implication—the backers.

So he said: "It is rather a long story, and you would scarcely understand it. We have been having constant trouble with the MacMorroghs, the contractors, and there is a bad state of affairs in the grading camps. It has come to a point where I shall have to fight the MacMorroghs to some sort of a finish, and—well, to put it very baldly, I don't want to have to fight the MacMorroghs and the president in the same round."

"Why should Uncle Sidney take the part of these men, if they are bad men, Mr. Ford?"

"Because he has always distrusted my judgment, and because he is loyal to Mr. North, whom he has made my superior. Mr. North tells him that I am to blame."

"But it must be a very dreadful condition of things, if what Mr. Frisbie said is all true."

"Frisbie spoke of only one little incident. Trouble like this we're having to-day is constantly arising. No money-making graft is too petty or too immoral for the MacMorroghs to connive at. They rob and starve their laborers, and cheat the company with bad work. I've got to have a free hand in dealing with them, or—"

He stopped abruptly, realizing that he was talking to her as he might have talked to a specialist in his own profession. Hence he was not disappointed when she said:

"You go too fast for me. But I think I understand now why our coming is inopportune. And it's comforting to know that the reason is a business reason."

He put shame to the wall and blurted out suddenly: "It is only one of the reasons, Miss Adair. The—the camps are no fit place for a party with women. You—you'll have to be blind and deaf if your uncle persists in taking you with him."

It was said, and he was glad of it, though he was wiping the perspiration from his face when the thing was done. She was silent until they were standing at the steps of the side-tracked private car.

"Thank you," she said simply. "Of course, I'll do what I can to keep Uncle Sidney from going—and taking us. What shall you say to him?"

"I am going to tell him that our track isn't safe for the Nadia—which is true enough."

"Very well. I'll tell Aunt Hetty and Mrs. Van Bruce—which may be more to the point. But don't be encouraged by that. I have reason to believe that Uncle Sidney will have his way in spite of any or all of us."

XVII
A NIGHT OF ALARMS

Ford put Miss Alicia up the steps of the Nadia and followed her into the vestibule, meaning to fight it out with Mr. Colbrith on the spot, and hoping he might have a private audience with the president for the doing of it.

The hope was not denied. Penfield, who was acting as private secretary to Mr. Colbrith, *en route,* appeared in the passageway to say that Ford was wanted in the president's state-room.

"Well, Mr. Ford, what are we waiting for?" was the querulous demand which served as Mr. Colbrith's greeting when Ford presented himself at the door of the private compartment.

Ford's reply lacked the deferential note. He had reached a point at which his job was not worth as much as it had been.

"I have just brought Miss Adair back from the top of the pass, where we met Mr. Frisbie, my chief of construction. I wished to ask him if he thought the track was safe for your car, and he says, most emphatically, that it is not. I can not take the responsibility of sending the Nadia to the end-of-track."

The president's thin face was working irritably. "I haven't asked you to assume any responsibility, Mr. Ford. If the track is safe for your material trains, it is safe enough for my car. But I didn't send for you to argue the point. I desire to have the Nadia taken to the front. Be good enough to give the necessary orders."

Ford tried again. In addition to the precarious track there were few or no unoccupied sidings, especially near the front. Moreover, there was no telegraph service which might suffice for the safe despatching of the special train. There might be entire sections over which the Nadia would have to be flagged by a man on foot, and —

The president cut him off with almost childish impatience.

"I don't know what your object is in putting so many stumbling-blocks in the way, Mr. Ford," he rasped. "A suspicious person might say that you have been doing something which you do not wish to have found out."

Ford was a fair-skinned man, and the blood burned hotly in his face. But, as once before under the president's nagging, he found his self-control rising with the provocation.

"My work is open to inspection or investigation, now or at any time, and I think we need not discuss that point," he said, when he could force himself to say it calmly. "We were speaking of the advisability of taking the Nadia and a pleasure party over a piece of raw construction line, and into an environment which, to put it mildly, could hardly be congenial to—to the ladies of the party. You know, or ought to know, the MacMorroghs: their camps are not exactly models of propriety, Mr. Colbrith."

This was merely waving a red flag at an already exasperated bull. The president got upon his feet, and his shrill falsetto cut the air like a knife.

"Mr. Ford, when I wish to be told what is or is not proper for me to do, I'll ask you for an opinion, sir. But this is quite beside the mark. Will you order this car out, or shall I?"

Ford looked at his watch imperturbably. Now that the president was thoroughly angry, he could afford to be cool.

"It is now five o'clock; and our end-of-track is fully one hundred and ten miles beyond the summit of the pass. Do I understand that you wish to take the added risk of a night run, Mr. Colbrith? If so, I'll give the order and we'll pull out."

"I desire to go *now!*" was the irascible reply. "Is that sufficiently explicit?"

"It is," said Ford; and he left the presence to go forward to the cab of the waiting engine.

"You are to take the car over the mountain, Hector," he said briefly, to the beetle-browed giant in blue denim, when he had climbed to the foot-plate. "I'll pilot for you."

"How far?" inquired the engineer.

"Something like a hundred and ten miles."

"Holy smoke! Over a construction track — in the night?"

"It's the president's order — none of mine. Let's get a move."

The big man got down from his box and made room for Ford. "I'll be pilin' 'em in the ditch somewhere, as sure as my name's Bill Hector," he said. "But we'll go, all the same, if he says so. I've pulled Mr. Colbrith before. Down with you, Jimmy Shovel, and set the switch for us."

The fireman swung off and stood by the switch, and Hector backed his one-car train from the siding. When he had picked up the fireman and was ready to assault the mountain, Ford thrust a query in between.

"Hold on a minute; how is the water?" he asked.

Jimmy Shovel climbed over the coal to see, and reported less than half a tankful.

"That settles it," said the chief to Hector. "You'll have to back down to Saint's Rest and fill up. You'll get no more this side of Pannikin Upper Canyon. We haven't had time to build tanks yet."

Hector put his valve-motion in the reverse gear and began to drop the train down the grade on the air. A dozen wheel-turns brought a shrill shriek from the air-signal whistle. Mr. Colbrith evidently wished to know why his train was going in the wrong direction. Hector applied the brakes and stopped in obedience to the signal.

"Do we send back?" he asked.

"No," said Ford sourly. "Let him send forward."

Penfield was the bearer of the president's question. Would it be necessary to discharge somebody in order to have his commands obeyed?

Ford answered the petulant demand as one bears with a spoiled child. They were returning to Saint's Rest for water. Let the president be assured that his orders would be obeyed in due course.

"He's a piker, the old man is," said the big engineer, once more giving the 1012 the needful inch of release to send it grinding down the hill. "I'd ruther pull freight thirty-six hours on end than run his car for a hundred miles."

There was trouble getting at the water-tank in the Saint's Rest yard. Leckhard, acting as division engineer, telegraph superintendent, material forwarder and yardmaster, found it difficult at limes to bring order out of chaos in the forwarding yard. It was a full hour before the jumble of material trains could be shunted and switched and juggled to permit the 1012 to drop down to the water tank; and four times during the hour Penfield climbed dutifully over the coal to tell Ford and the engineer what the president thought of them.

"Durn me! but you can take punishment like a man, Mr. Ford!" said Hector, on the heels of the fourth sending, sinking rank distinctions in his admiration for a cool fighter. "These here polite cussin's-out are what I can't stand. Reckon we'll get away from here before the old man throws a sure-enough fit?"

"That's entirely with the yard crew," said Ford, calmly making himself comfortable on the fireman's box. "We'll go when we can get water; and we'll get water when the tank track is cleared. That's all there is to it." Whereupon he found his cigar case, passed it to Hector, lighted up, and waited patiently for another second-hand wigging from the Nadia.

As it chanced the tank track was cleared a few minutes later; the 1012 was backed down and supplied, and Ford instructed Leckhard to do what he could with the single, poorly manned construction wire toward giving the president's special a clear track.

"That won't be much," said the hard-worked base-of-supplies man. "We've got our own operator at Ten Mile, and Brissac and Frisbie have each a set of instruments which they cut in on the line with wherever they happen to be. I don't know where Brissac is, but Frisbie is down about Riley's to-night, I think. After you pass him you'll have no help from the wires."

"I'll have what I can get," asserted Ford. "Now tell me what we're likely to meet."

Leckhard laughed. "Anything on top of earth, from Brissac or Jack Benson or Frisbie chasing somewhere on a light engine, to Gallagher or Folsom coming out with a string of empties. Oh, you're not likely to find much dead track anywhere after you get over the mountain."

Ford swung up beside Hector, who had been listening. "You see what we're in for, Hector. Start your headlight dynamo and let's go," he said; and five minutes farther on, just as Penfield was about to make his fifth scramble over the coal in the tender, the 1012 took the upward road with a deafening whistle shriek as its farewell to Saint's Rest.

It was pocket-dark by the time the switch-stand at the basin siding swung into the broad beam of the electric headlight. Ford got down from the fireman's box and crossed over to the engineer's side to pilot Hector.

"How's your track from this on?" inquired the big engineman gruffly.

"It is about as rough as it can be, and not ditch the steel trains. You'll have to hold her down or we'll have results."

"What in the name o' thunder is the old man's notion of goin' to the front with a picnic party and makin' a night run of it, at that, d'ye reckon?"

"The Lord only knows. Easy around this curve you're coming to; it isn't set up yet." The 1012 was a fast eight-wheeler from the main line, and though the grade was a rising four per cent, the big flyer was making light work of her one-car train.

Ford sat gloomily watching the track ahead as the great engine stormed around the curves and up the grades. The struggle against odds was beginning to tell on him. The building of this new line, the opening of the new country, was the real end for which all the planning and scheming in the financial field had been only the necessary preliminaries. For himself he had craved nothing but the privilege of building the extension; of rejoicing in his own handiwork and in the new triumph of progress and civilization which it would bring to pass. But little by little the fine fire of workmanlike enthusiasm was burning itself out against the iron barriers of petty spite and malice thrown up at every turn by North and the Denver junta of obstructionists.

He was at no loss to account for North's motive. It was no longer the contemptuous disregard of a general manager for one of his subordinates who had shown signs of outgrowing his job. It was a fight between rivals—equals—and Ford knew that it must go on until one or the other should be driven to the wall. Thus far, his antagonist had scored every point. The MacMorroghs had been helped into the saddle and held there. Mr. Colbrith had been won over; the authority given Ford by his appointment as assistant to the president had been annulled by making North the first vice-president with still higher authority. With a firm ally in the president, and a legion of others in the MacMorroghs' camps, North could discredit the best engineering corps that ever took the field; and he was doing it—successfully, as Ford had reason to know.

More than once Ford had been on the point of leaving his plow in the furrow while he should go to New York for one more battle with the directory—a battle which should definitely abolish North and Mr. Colbrith—or himself. Again and again he had weighed the chances of winning such a battle. With Brewster for a leader it might be done. The time for the annual stock-holders' meeting was approaching, and an election which should put the burly copper magnate into the presidency would be an unmixed blessing, not only for a struggling young chief of construction, but for the Pacific Southwestern stock-holders, who were sure to pay in the end for the present policy of rule or ruin.

Part of the time it seemed to Ford that it was clearly his duty to make this fight against the grafters in the Denver management. North deserved no consideration, and while Mr. Colbrith was honest enough, his blind prejudice and narrow mentality made him North's unwitting accessory. Three months earlier Ford would not have hesitated; but in the interval a woman had come between to obscure all the points of view. A fight to the death against the Colbrith administration meant the antagonizing of the Adairs—of Alicia, at least. True, she had spoken lightly of her uncle's peculiarities; but Ford made sure she would stand by him in the conflict, if only for kinship's sake.

All this he was turning over in his mind for the hundredth time while the big 1012 hammered up the Plug Mountain grade under the guiding hand of the giant in blue denim. Ford, glooming out upon the lighted stretch ahead, was once more finding the crucial question answerless. Should he draw out of the losing battle with North and his fellow grafters, and thereby save his chance of winning Alicia Adair? Or should he sacrifice his love upon the altar of ambition, abolish Mr. Colbrith and the crew of buccaneers his mistaken policy was sheltering, and win the industrial success and a quieted conscience?

His decision was reached by the time Hector was easing the throttle lever at the summit of Plug Pass. What must be done should be done quickly.

"Right here is where you begin to run on your nerves," he said to the big engineer, as the heavy engine and car lunged over the summit of the pass and began to gather gravity momentum on the downward rush.

Hector nodded, and twitched the handle of the air-brake cock at shorter intervals. Ford glanced back at the following car framed in the red glow from the opened fire-box door. It was surging and bounding alarmingly over the uneven track, not without threatenings of derailment. Ford was willing to give the president the full benefit of his unreasonable pertinacity; but there were others to be considered — and one above all the others.

"Easy, man; easy!" he cautioned. "If you leave the steel on this goat-track there won't be anybody left to tell the story. It's a thousand feet sheer in some places along here. Suppose you let me take her to the bottom of the hill."

The engineer stood aside with a good-tempered grin. He had seen the chief of construction walking the one young lady of the party to the top of Plug Pass and back, and it was not difficult to account for his anxiety.

Throughout the ten long miles of the mountain descent Ford crouched on the driver's seat and put his mind into the business of getting down the slides and around the sagging curves without having a wreck. The 1012's brake equipment was modern, and the Nadia's gear was in perfect order. Now and then on a tangent the big engine would straighten herself for a race or a runaway, but always the steady hand on the air-cock brought her down just before the critical moment beyond which neither brakes nor the steadiest nerve could avail. Thrice in the long downward rush Ford checked the speed to a foot-pace. This was in the rock cuttings where the jagged faces of the cliffs thrust themselves out into the white cone of the headlight, scanting the narrow shelf of the right-of-way to a mere groove in the rock. He was afraid of the cuttings. One of the many tricks of the MacMorroghs was to keep barely within the contract limits on clearance widths, and once the Nadia, sagging mountainward on the roughly leveled track at the wrong moment, touched one of the out-hanging rocks in passing. Hector heard the touch, and so did Ford; but it was the engineman who made a grim jest upon it, saying: "If she does that more'n once or twice, there'll be a job for the car painters, don't you reckon, Mr. Ford? And for the carpenters."

Just below the doubling bend in the great loop they came in sight of the first of the MacMorrogh camps. Since the night was frosty a huge bonfire was burning beside the track; and when Hector blew his whistle, some one flagged the train with a brand snatched from the fire. Ford stopped because he dared not do otherwise.

"Well, what's wanted?" he snapped, when the train came to a stand, and the brand-swinger, backed by a dozen others, made as if he would climb to the cab of the 1012.

"Some of us fellies want to go down to Ten Mile—the liquor's out," said the man, trying to get a fair sight of the strange engineman.

"Get off!" said Ford; and Hector made the order effective by shoving the intruder from the step. That was easy; but before the train had measured twice its length, a pistol barked thrice and the glass in the cab window on Ford's side fell in splinters.

"Holy smoke!" said Hector. "Is them the kind of plug-uglies you've got over here, Mr. Ford?"

Ford nodded. His eyes were on the track again, and he was hoping fervently that the three shots had all been aimed at the engine. A mile farther on, Penfield came sliding over the coal to say that the president wanted to know what the shooting was about.

Ford turned the 1012 over to Hector. The track hazards of the mountain grade were safely passed.

"Did any of the shots hit the car?" he asked of Penfield.

"No."

"Well, if you have to say anything before the ladies it might be advisable to make a joke of it. Signal torpedoes sound very much like pistol-shots, you know."

Penfield nodded. "But to Mr. Colbrith?"

"To Mr. Colbrith you may say that a gang of drunken MacMorrogh surfacers flagged us down, and when we wouldn't let them have the train, made a little gun play."

"Heavens!" said the clerk, whose curiosity stopped short at the farthest confines of any battle-field. "Is that sort of thing likely to happen again, Mr. Ford?"

"Your guess is as good as anybody's," said Ford curtly. "Better get back to the car as quickly as you can, before Mr. Colbrith whistles us down to find out what has become of you."

Below the camp of the surfacers there were a few miles of better track, and Hector made fair time until the train circled the mountain shoulder at the lower end of the great loop. Beyond this the roughnesses began again, and there were more of the skimped rock cuttings. At Ten Mile, which was a relay station in the upper canyon for the halting of supplies and material for which there was no room at the ever-advancing "front," they stopped to try for track-clearings.

As Leckhard had foretold, the operator could give them little help. Two hours earlier, a train of empties in two sections had left the end-of-track, coming eastward. Whether it was hung up at one of the intervening side-tracks, or was still coming, the operator could not say; and there were no means of finding out. Also, Mr. Frisbie, who had reached Riley's camp late in the afternoon, had left there after supper and was somewhere on the line with his light engine— probably on his way to the front, the operator thought.

Hector removed his great weight from the telegraph counter and the woodwork creaked its relief. What he said was indicative of his frame of mind.

"Humph!" he growled. "If we don't get tangled up with Mr. Frisbie's light engine, it's us for a head-ender with the string of empties. Isn't that about it, Mr. Ford?"

"That's it, precisely."

"Which means that Jimmy Shovel trots ahead of us for a hundred mile 'r so, carryin' a lantern like a blame' Dio-geenes huntin' for an honest man."

"That is the size of it," said Ford; but just then the sounder on the table began to click and the operator held up his hand for silence.

"Hold on a minute," he interrupted, "here's a piece of luck—it's Mr. Frisbie, cutting in with his field set from Camp Frierson. He is asking Saint's Rest about you."

"Break in and tell him we're here," said Ford; and when it was done: "Ask him about that string of empties."

The reply was apparently another piece of luck. Frisbie, going westward, had passed the first section of the freight train at Siding Number Twelve. It was hung up with a broken draw-head on the engine, and was safe to stay there, Frisbie thought, until somebody came along with a repair kit, which, it might be assumed, would not be before morning.

At this point Ford went around the counter and took the wire for a little personal talk with the first assistant. It ignored the stalled freight train, and Ford's rapid clickings spelled out an order. Frisbie was to drop everything else, and constitute himself the president's *avant-courrier* to the end-of-track camp, which, at the moment, happened to be the MacMorroghs' headquarters at the mouth of Horse Creek. All liquor-selling was to be stopped, the saloons closed, and the strictest order maintained during the president's stay—this if it should take the entire field force of the engineering department to bring it to pass.

"Don't," clicked Frisbie, from the other end of the long wire. And then at the risk of giving it away to every operator on the line: "You're doing yourself up. Let the president see for himself what he has let us in for."

Ford's reply was short and to the point. "The order stands. There are others besides the president to be considered. Good night."

"Well, we go to this here Siding Number Twelve, do we?" said Hector, when they were clambering once more to the foot-plate of the 1012.

"Safely, I think," said the chief, adding: "You can't run fast enough over this track to get into trouble anyway."

That was the way it appealed to Hector for the succeeding twenty miles. When the track was not too rough to forbid speed, the cuts were too numerous, and the big flyer had to be bitted and held down until some of Hector's impatience began to get into the machinery. This shall account as it may for what happened. A mile or two below Riley's, where the lights were all out and the turmoil of the day of strikes had apparently subsided, the canyon opened out into a winding valley, and when Ford called across to Hector: "There are no rock cuts on this section, and we are partly surfaced. You can let her out a little for a few miles," the engineer took the permission for all it was worth and sent the eight-wheeler flying down the newly-ballasted stretch.

Two long curves were rounded in safety, and the special was approaching a third, when to Ford, track-watching even more anxiously than Hector, a dull red spot appeared in the exact center of the white field of the electric. For a moment it puzzled him, but the explanation came with a vigorous shock an instant later. It was the oil-lamp headlight of the freight!

Hector was huge enough to be slow, if bigness were a bar to celerity. But no drill-master of the foot-plates could have brought the flying train to a stand with the loss of fewer seconds. Happily, too, the 1012's electric headlight served as a danger signal seen from afar by the engineer of the freight. So it chanced that the two great engines merely put their noses together; and by the time Penfield came scrambling over the coal with the inevitable query from the president, the jolting stop was a thing of the past, and the train was in motion again, following the freight, which was backing, at Ford's order, to the nearest siding.

"No more hurry for us to-night, Hector," was the boss's dictum, when the obstructing string of empties was safely passed. "We take it slow and sure from this on, with your fireman to flag us around the curves and through the cuts. This was only the first section of the train that left Horse Creek at eight o'clock—the section that was broken down at Siding Twelve. We're due to pick up the second section anywhere between here and the end-of-track."

"Slow it is," said Hector. "I'm no hog, if I do take a little swill now and then: I know when I've got enough."

This was at ten-forty, while the night was still young. And for seven other hours the one-car special inched its way cautiously toward the goal, with Ford scanning every mile of the hazardous way as it swung into the beam of the headlight arc, with Hector's left hand stiffening on the brake-cock, and with a weary fireman dropping from his gangway at every curve approach to flag for safety.

It was not until three o'clock in the morning that they met and passed the second section of empties, and the dawn of a new day was fully come when the shacks and storehouses of the MacMorroghs' headquarters at the mouth of Horse Creek came in sight. Ford got down from his seat on the fireman's side and stretched himself as one relaxing after a mighty strain.

"That's the end of it for a little while, Billy," he said, addressing the big engineer as a man and a brother. "Crawl in on the first siding you come to, and go hunt you a bed. I don't think the president will be perniciously active to-day—after such a night as we've had."

But in this, as in other instances when Mr. Colbrith's activities had figured as a factor, he reckoned without his host.

XVIII
THE MORNING AFTER

Ford was awake for all day, and was colloguing with Frisbie about the carrying out of the sumptuary order for the forcible camp-cleaning, when Penfield came with the request that the chief report at once to the president in the Nadia.

"Tell him I'll be there presently," was the answer; and when Penfield went to do it, the interrupted colloquy was resumed.

"You say the camp has already gone dry?" said Ford incredulously.

Frisbie nodded. "Everybody's on the water-wagon; here and at all the camps above and below—bars not only closed, but apparently wiped out of existence. I went for old Brian last night as soon as I reached here. He looked at me reproachfully, and said: 'It's you to be always naggin' me about thim whisky dives that I'm forever thryin' to run out, and can't. Go and thry it yourself, Misther Frisbie, an' I'll stand at your back till you're black in the face.' But when I went through the camp, everything was quiet and orderly, and Jack Batters' bar was not only closed—it was gone; vanished without leaving so much as a bad smell behind it."

"And then?" said Ford.

"Then I got out my horse and rode up the creek and through some of the camps on the Copah detour. The star-eyed goddess of reform had evidently landed on that coast, too. Donahue's Hungarians were singing war-songs around their camp-fire, as usual, and Contadini's Tuscans were out in full force, guying the night-shift track-layers. But there was no bad blood, and no whisky to breed it. You're done up again, Stuart."

"I don't see that," said Ford, who, besides being short on sleep, was rejoicing in the thought that Alicia and the other women of the private-car party would not have to be blind and deaf.

164

"Don't you? You've been protesting to beat the band about the lawlessness and dissipation of the MacMorrogh camps. Accordingly, Mr. Colbrith comes over here to see for himself: and what will he see? Decency on a monument smiling reproachfully at her unprincipled traducer. MacMorrogh will rub it into you good and hard. Can't you feel the Sunday-school atmosphere right here in the headquarters this morning? Look down yonder at the Nadia— wouldn't that soothe you, now?"

Ford looked and the scowl which was coming to be a habit transformed itself into a cynical smile. A hundred or more of the MacMorrogh laborers, hats off and standing at respectful attention, were clustered about the rear platform of the private car, and Mr. Colbrith was addressing them; giving them the presidential benediction, as Frisbie put it irreverently.

"Don't you see how you are going to be hoisted with your own ammunition?" the little man went on spitefully. "What becomes of all your complaints of drunkenness and crime, when Mr. Colbrith can see with his own eyes what truly good people the MacMorroghs are? And what conclusion will he arrive at? There's only one, and it's a long-armed one so far as your reputation is concerned: you are so desperately bent on having your own way that you haven't scrupled to tell lies about these angelic contractors."

"Let up, Dick," said Ford gruffly. "I've got about all I can carry till I catch up on sleep a little. But you're right: this is the place where the fireworks come in. I think I'll go and light the fuses while I'm keyed up to it."

The crowd of laborers had dispersed by the time Ford reached the Nadia, and the president, benign from the reactionary effect of his own early-morning eloquence, was waiting for him.

"Ah; we did reach the front safely, after all, didn't we, Mr. Ford?" was Mr. Colbrith's mildly sarcastic greeting. And then: "Come aboard, sir; we are waiting breakfast for you."

Ford would have declined promptly, if the invitation had been anything less than a command. He had met none of the members of the private-car party save Miss Alicia, and he did not want to meet them, having the true captain-of-industry's horror of mixing business with the social diversions. But with one example of the president's obstinacy fresh in mind, he yielded and climbed obediently to the railed platform. Whatever happened, he should see Alicia again, a privilege never to be too lightly esteemed, whatever it cost.

The social ordeal was not so formidable. The private-car party was made up of the president and his sister-in-law, the president's family physician, Doctor Van Bruce, the doctor's wife, his sister, a maiden lady of no uncertain age, and Alicia. These, with Penfield and Ford, made the eight at table in the open compartment in the Nadia; and Ford, in the seating, was lucky enough to find his place between Miss Van Bruce, who was hard of hearing, and Miss Alicia, who was not. Luckily again, Mr. Colbrith omitted all talk of business, drawing his end of the table into a discussion of the effects of the dry altitudes in advanced stages of tuberculosis.

"What a dreadful night you must have had, Mr. Ford," said Alicia, when the tuberculotic subject was well launched at the other end of the table. "Were you on the engine all the time?"

"Most of the time," he confessed. "But that was nothing. It wasn't my first night in the cab, as it won't be the last, by many, I hope."

"Why? Do you like it?"

"Not particularly. But I hope to live a while longer; and while I live I shall doubtless have to ride with the enginemen now and then."

"Was it very bad—last night?" she asked.

"I am afraid you know it was. Could you sleep at all?"

"Oh, yes; I slept very well—after that terrible shaking up we had just before bedtime. What was happening then?"

"Nothing much. We were about to try the old experiment of passing two trains on a single track."

"Mercy!" she exclaimed.

It was safely retrospective now, and Ford could smile at her belated shock.

"Were the others alarmed?" he asked.

"Mrs. Van Bruce and Aunt Hetty were. But Uncle Sidney fairly coruscated. He said that an engineer who would make such a stop as that ought to be discharged."

"Hector was willing to quit," laughed Ford. "He grumbled for a full hour afterward about the wrenching he had given the 1012. You see he might have taken about six feet more for the stop, if he'd only known it."

Miss Alicia said "Mercy!" again. "Were we as near as that to a collision?" she asked, in a hushed whisper.

"We were, indeed. The freight was supposed to be on a siding— broken down. The crew tinkered things up some way, and the train proceeded. Luckily, the freight engineer saw our electric headlight farther than we could see his oil lamp, and the track happened to be measurably straight."

Miss Adair was silent for a little time, waiting for the lapsed tuberculotic discussion to revive. When it was once more in full swing, she asked quickly:

"What is the programme for to-day? Must we all stay in the car as you intimated yesterday?"

Ford glanced across the table to make sure that Penfield was not eavesdropping.

"It will not be necessary. Your coming—or the president's—has reformed things wonderfully. Frisbie says—but never mind what he says: the miracle has been wrought."

He said it with such an evident air of dejection that she wondered. And with Miss Alicia Adair the step from wonderment to investigation was always short.

"You say it as if you were sorry," she said. "Are you?"

"Oh, no; I'm glad—for your sake. But I wonder if you could understand if I say that it will make it a thousand times harder for me?"

"I can understand when I'm told," she retorted.

The table-for-eight was no place for confidences; and Ford knew Penfield's weakness for soaking up information. Yet he took the risk.

"You remember what I hinted at, yesterday," he said in low tones; "about the rough-house we have been having in the camps. It hasn't stopped short of murder. I objected to the MacMorroghs before the contract was given to them; and since, I have fought the lawlessness as I could. Now your uncle comes over here and doesn't find any lawlessness. What is the inference?"

"That you have been—" she took him up quickly, and there was swift indignation in the blue eyes.

"—lying to gain a personal end," he finished for her.

Penfield had been apparently listening avidly to the president's praise of the dry altitudes as a sure cure for consumption, but now he had his face in his plate. Ford devoted himself for the moment to the deaf Miss Van Bruce, and when he turned back to Alicia he was telegraphing with his eyes for discretion. She understood, and the low-toned tête-à-tête was not resumed. Later, when they had a moment together in the dispersion from the breakfast-table, he tried to apologize for what he was pleased to call his "playing of the baby act." But she reassured him in a low-spoken word.

"Brother told me—I know more than you give me credit for, Mr. Ford. Mr. North doesn't like you—he would be glad if you would resign. *You must not resign!*"

The others, personally-conducted by Mr. Colbrith, were crowding to the rear platform for an after-breakfast view of the headquarters camp. Ford and Alicia followed, but without haste.

"You have chanced upon the word, Miss Adair," Ford was saying. "I decided last night that I should resign."

"No," she objected.

"Yes; I must. Sometime I may tell you why."

"I say you must not. That was the last word in brother's letter; and he wished me to repeat it to you," she insisted.

"Where is your brother?" he asked.

"He was in London when he wrote."

"He has thrown up his hand." Ford was pessimistic again.

Miss Adair looked about her despairingly for some means of prolonging the whispered confidence. Penfield, deferentially in the rear of the platform group, was never safely out of earshot.

"I want to see the engine that so nearly plunged us into a collision last night," she said aloud; and Penfield's visible ear betrayed the listening mind.

Ford took his cue promptly. "We can go out the other way," he said; and the secretary *pro tempore* had no excuse for following.

They found the cab of the 1012 deserted, with the steam in the huge boiler singing softly at the behest of the banked fire. Miss Adair lost her curiosity as soon as Ford had lifted her to the foot-plate.

"Now you are to tell me all about it—quickly," she commanded. "Uncle Sidney will be calling for you as soon as he misses you. Why are you so foolish as to talk about resigning? Don't you see what they will say then?—that you were afraid?"

Ford was leaning against the centered reversing-lever, and his face was gloomy again.

"Possibly I am afraid," he suggested.

"You should be more afraid of dishonor than of—of the other things. Do you suppose Mr. North will be content with your resignation now?"

Ford looked up quickly. Here was a new revelation—an unsuspected facet of the precious gem. He could hardly believe that this steady-voiced, far-seeing young woman was the insouciant, school-girlish—though none the less lovable—young person with whom he had tramped to the wind-swept summit of Plug Pass in the golden heart of the yesterday.

"You mean—?" he began.

"I mean that you will be discredited; disgraced if possible. Are you sure you haven't been doing anything over here that you wouldn't want Uncle Sidney to find out?"

"Not consciously, you may be sure," he asserted unhesitatingly.

"Think; think hard," she urged. "Is there nothing at all?"

He could not help smiling lovingly at her scarce-concealed anxiety—though it was merely the anxiety of a noble soul unwilling to stand by and see injustice done.

"My methods never get very far underground," he averred. "Not far enough for my own safety, Frisbie says. If I had been keeping a diary, I think I should be quite willing to let Mr. Colbrith read it—or print it, if he cared to."

"And yet there *is* something," she asserted, and the straight brows went together in a little frown of perplexity. "You don't ask me how I know: I'm going to tell you, Mr. Ford—though it's rather shameful. Three days ago, while we were in Denver, Mr. North came down to the car to see Uncle Sidney."

"Yes?" he encouraged.

"They were closeted in Uncle Sidney's state-room for a long time," she went on. "I—I was walking with Miss Van Bruce, up and down on the station platform beside the Nadia, Uncle Sidney had told me not to go very far away because we were likely to start at any moment. The—the car windows were open—"

Her embarrassment was growing painfully apparent, and Ford came to the rescue.

"You were not even constructively to blame," he hastened to say. "They must surely have seen you passing and repassing, and if they wished for privacy they might have closed the windows."

"I didn't hear much: only a word or two, now and then. They were talking about you and brother; and—" She stopped short and laid her hand on the throttle-lever of the big engine: "What did you say this was for?" she asked ingenuously.

Ford's up-glance of surprise was answered by a glimpse of Penfield sauntering past on the other side of the track. She could not have seen, but she had doubtless heard his footsteps on the gravel.

"It's the throttle," said Ford, answering her question. And then: "Please go on: he is out of hearing."

"They were speaking of you and brother; and—and of *me*. I can't repeat a single sentence entire, but I know Mr. North was accusing you in some way, and apparently implicating me. Perhaps I listened in self-defense. Do you think I did, Mr. Ford?"

"You certainly had a good right to," said Ford, who would have sworn in her behalf that the morally black was spotlessly white. "But how could you be implicated?"

"That was what puzzled me then—and it is puzzling me still. They said—or rather Mr. North said—that you—that you had *bought* me!"

Ford did not say that he would like to buy, beg, borrow or steal any kind of right to call her his own, but if his lips did not form the words they were lying at the bottom of the steady gray eyes for her to take or leave as she chose.

"I am sure you couldn't have heard that part of it quite straight," he said, almost regretfully.

"But I did, because it was repeated. Mr. North insisted that you had bought me; and I didn't like the way in which he said it, either. He called me 'the little Alicia'."

"What!" said Ford; and then a flood of light burst in upon at least one of the dark places. "It's only a mine," he said sheepishly. "And I did buy it, or half of it."

She was regarding him accusingly now.

"Did you—did you name it?" she asked, and there was the merest breath of frost in the air.

He was glad to be able to tell the truth without flinching.

"No; it is one of the earliest of the Copah prospects, and I suppose the discoverer named it. I am willing to defend his choice, though. He couldn't have found a prettier name."

She went back to the matter in hand with womanly swiftness. "But the mine: you had a right to buy it, didn't you?"

"I should suppose so. I paid for it with my own money, anyway."

"Then why should Mr. North use it as an argument against you in speaking to Uncle Sidney? He did that—I am sure he did that."

"Now the water has grown too deep for me," said Ford. "Why, North, himself, is interested in Copah, openly. He owns half a dozen claims."

"Near yours?" she queried.

Ford stopped to consider. "To tell the truth, I don't know where mine is," he confessed. "I bought it as the school-boys trade pocket-knives—sight unseen. You wouldn't believe it of a grown man, would you?"

"What made you buy it at all?"

Again he told the simple truth—and tried not to flinch.

"You won't mind if I say that the name attracted me? I thought a mine, or anything, that bore your name, ought to be good and—and desirable. And it is a good mine; or it will be, by and by. Some morning I shall wake up and find myself rich. At least that is what my partner, Grigsby, assures me; and I believe him when I happen to remember it."

She neither approved nor disapproved. When she spoke, it was of the present necessity. "We must go back to the others now," she said. "Or at least I must. Do you know what is to be done to-day?"

Ford spread his hands.

"Your uncle will set the pace. I wouldn't venture a guess, after last night."

He was handing her down from the engine step and she went back in a word to the former contention.

"You haven't promised me yet that you will not resign under fire — you are under fire, you know."

"Am I?"

"Brother thinks you are."

Once more he took the pessimistic view.

"Your brother isn't losing any sleep over the Pacific Southwestern situation. You said he was in England, didn't you?"

"I said he was in London when he wrote."

"London is a long way off: and what I do must be done to-day or to-morrow. Mr. North will force the fighting, now that your uncle is on the ground, and your brother safely on the opposite side of the earth. And I can't afford to fight this time, Miss Alicia."

"Why can't you?"

They were walking slowly back toward the Nadia when he said: "Because a victory would cost me more than I am willing to pay. There is no longer room in this service for Mr. North and me. If we come to blows one of us will have to go."

"I can understand that," she said quietly.

"And to obliterate Mr. North, I shall be obliged to efface — your uncle."

She caught her breath.

"Mr. Ford, you have intimated that Mr. North isn't an honest man. Do you ask me to believe that Uncle Sidney is his accomplice?"

"He is not, knowingly. But he will stand or fall with the man he has made. I should have to ride him down before I could get at North."

Her lip curled and the straight-browed little frown came again. "There is no such thing as mercy in business, is there, Mr. Ford? My uncle is an old man and his presidency means more to him—"

"I understand that perfectly," said Ford soberly. "That is why I prefer to step down and out and let some other man have the glory of finishing the extension."

She looked up quickly.

"Would you do that for Uncle Sidney? He hasn't been very lenient with you, has he?"

Ford ignored the query.

"He is your uncle, Miss Alicia; and I'd do it for your sake or not at all."

They had reached the steps of the private car, and Frisbie was waiting with evident impatience for a word with Ford. Miss Adair's eyes signaled emotion, and Ford thought it was resentment. But her parting word was not resentful; it was merely a repetition.

"Go to Mr. Frisbie," she said from the car step; "he is waiting for you." And then: "Remember; whatever happens, *you must not resign*—not even if Uncle Sidney asks you to."

Frisbie's information, given after Miss Adair had gone in, was rather mystifying. Young Benson, who was just in from the grade work beyond Copah, brought word of a party of strange engineers

175

running lines on the opposite side of the river from the rejected S.L. & W. short-cut through the canyon of shale slides. Questioned by Benson, they had told what Frisbie believed to be a fairy tale. The chief of the party claimed to be the newly-elected county surveyor from Copah, running the lines for some mining property recently filed for entry. Benson had not been over curious; but he was observant enough to note that the tale was a misfit in three important particulars. He saw no locating stakes, such as a prospector always sets up conspicuously to mark his claim; and there were no signs of the precious metal, and no holes to indicate an attempt to find it.

"What's your guess, Dick?" said Ford tersely.

The assistant shook his head.

"I haven't any coming to me. But I don't like mysteries."

"Where was this party?"

"About a mile and a half below here. It was going out toward Copah when Jack met it—its work, whatever it was, all done, apparently."

It was one of Frisbie's gifts to be suspicious; but Ford was lacking on that side.

"It's barely possible that the man was telling the truth, in spite of Benson's failure to find any prospect holes," he remarked. "We'll let it go at that until we know something different. It couldn't be a Transcontinental party, this far from home, and we haven't anybody else to fear."

Frisbie dropped the subject as one of the abstractions and took up the concrete.

"What are the orders for to-day?" he asked.

"I don't know. I'm waiting for Mr. Colbrith to say."

"There are two buckboard teams here, in the MacMorrogh stables — came over from Copah last night. What are they for?"

"I don't know. Another of the president's little surprises, I suppose. We'll know when he sends for me."

The expected summons came at that precise moment, transmitted by Penfield. Mr. Colbrith would like to see Mr. Ford in his private state-room in the Nadia. The secretary had a sheaf of telegrams in his hand, and wished to be directed to the wire office. Frisbie took him in charge, and Ford went to obey the summons.

The president was sitting very erect in his swing chair when the young engineer let himself into the box-like compartment, and his voice was at its thinnest when he said: "Be seated, Mr. Ford."

Ford sat down on the divan-couch, and the president plunged at once into business.

"Some time ago, you advised me, as chairman of the executive committee, that you had decided upon a change of route, Mr. Ford," he began raspingly. "What were your reasons for making the change?"

"I stated them in my letter of advice," said Ford; "economy in construction and greater safety in operating, as against a slight increase in the length of the line."

"Twelve miles, I believe you said: that is a very considerable increase, I should say. The great eastern companies are spending millions of dollars, Mr. Ford, to shorten their lines by half-mile cut-offs."

Ford had his reply ready.

"The conditions are entirely different. It will be many years before a fast through service is either practicable or profitable over the extension; and when it comes to that, we shall still have the short line from Denver to Green Butte by forty-two miles. But I explained all this at the time, Mr. Colbrith, and I understood that I had the executive committee's approval of the changed route."

"Qualifiedly, Mr. Ford; only qualifiedly. Yet you have gone ahead in your usual impetuous way, abandoning the short line through the canyon and building the detour. Your motive for haste must have been a very strong one—very strong."

"It was. I am not here to kill time."

"So it appears. But I am here, Mr. Ford, to consider carefully, and to investigate. We shall go first over this route you have abandoned. I wish to see for myself the difficulties you have so painstakingly described."

Ford shrugged.

"I'm quite at your service, of course. But you will find it a hard trip. Indeed, if we drive, we shall have to cross the river and take the other side. The canyon on this side is impassable in places for a man on foot."

"I provided for that," said the president, letting his ferrety eyes rest for a moment upon the reluctant one. "You will find two buckboards with their drivers at the MacMorrogh headquarters. Be good enough to order them around, and we'll start at once. No; no protests, Mr. Ford. My responsibilities are not to be shirked. Penfield will drive with me, and you may take Mr. Frisbie with you, if you see fit. I understand he is implicated with you in this matter."

Ford bridled angrily at the word.

"There is no implication about it, Mr. Colbrith. You continually refer to it as if it were a crime."

"Ah! the word is yours, Mr. Ford. We shall see—we shall see. That is all, for the present."

Ford was raging when he found Frisbie and gave the order for the vehicles.

"He turned me out of his office state-room as if I had been a messenger boy or tramp! Get those teams out, Dick, and give me a chance to cool down. If my job is to last through this day—"

Frisbie laughed. "Go and dip your head in the Pannikin while you wait. Or, better still, chew on this. It's a cipher message that Durgin has just been sending for Penfield to Vice-President North. Wouldn't that make you weep and howl?"

Ford was still puzzling over the meaningless code words when he took his seat in the second of the two buckboards with Frisbie. The first assistant waited until the horses had splashed through the shallows of the river crossing; waited further until the president's vehicle had gained a little start. Then he said: "Is it possible that you had Penfield for a spy on you as long as you did without working out his cipher code? Good Lord! I got that down before I did anything else—last spring when you left me to run the Plug Mountain. Here's what he says to North"—taking the code message and translating: "Ford suspects something. Don't know how much. He and Miss Adair are putting their heads together. She has authority of some kind from her brother. President goes with Ford to examine abandoned route, as arranged. Will wire result later.'"

"'As arranged,'" was Ford's wrathful comment.

"Apparently, everything is arranged for us. Some day, Dick, I'll lose my temper, tie Penfield in a hard knot and throw him into the river! It's like a chapter out of Lucretia Borgia!"

XIX
THE RELUCTANT WHEELS

It was possibly an hour after Penfield's cipher message reached the Southwestern Pacific headquarters in the Colorado capital, when a fair-haired young man in London-cut clothes, and with a tourist's quota of hand-luggage, crossed the Denver Union Station platform from the Pullman of a belated Chicago train.

Ascertaining from a gateman that the Plug Mountain day train had long since gone on its way up the canyon, the young man left his many belongings at the check-stand and had himself driven up-town to the Guaranty Building. It was Eckstein who took his card in Mr. North's outer office. The private secretary was dictating to a stenographer, and was impatient of the interruption. But the name on the card wrought a miracle.

"Mr. North? Why, surely, Mr. Adair. He is always at liberty for you. Right through this way"—holding the gate in the counter railing at its widest—"we're mighty glad to see you in Denver, always."

Adair had acquired the monocle habit on his latest run across the Atlantic, and to keep in practice he gave the secretary the coldest of stares through the disconcerting glass. "Really! I'm quite delighted. Who is the other member of the 'we,' Mr.—er—er—"

"Eckstein," prompted the secretary; but he said no more, being prudently anxious to be quit of the transfixing stare before a worse thing should befall.

In the inner room the vice-president was less effusive, but no less cordial. It was a rare thing to see one of the company's directors in the Denver business offices. Mr. North was of the opinion that it would be a good investment of time and effort for all concerned if the members of the board used their privilege oftener. So on through half a dozen polite time-killers to the reluctant query: What could the general manager do for Mr. Adair?

Given leave to speak, Adair stated his needs succinctly. He wanted a special train to Saint's Rest; he wanted it suddenly, and he asked that it be given the right of the road.

"My dear sir!" protested the vice-president, "you mustn't ask impossibilities! You shall have the train at once, of course: you shall have my private car. But when it comes to the right of way, you'll have to appeal to Mr. Ford. Why, he doesn't scruple to lay out the United States mails for his material trains!"

"Um," said Adair. "Where can I reach Ford?"

Mr. North did not equivocate; he never lied when the truth would answer the purpose equally well.

"He is out on the extension; or more correctly speaking, somewhere beyond the present end of the construction telegraph line. I'm afraid you couldn't reach him by wire."

"And the president?" queried the visitor.

"Mr. Colbrith's car is at the end-of-track. You wished to join the party in the Nadia?"

"That is what I had in mind," said Adair, not too anxiously.

Mr. North shook his head.

"I don't think you'd enjoy the run over the construction track. Mr. Colbrith went over it last night because—well, because he believes it to be a presidential duty to inspect everything. If you leave to-day, you will probably meet the Nadia coming out—possibly at Saint's Rest."

Adair suddenly became wary.

"Perhaps that would be the easy thing to do," he said. "I suppose the engineers at Saint's Rest could put me up if I have to stay over night?"

"You needn't ask them. You will have my car—with the best cook this side of Louisiana. Keep it, live in it, till Mr. Colbrith picks you up on his return."

"All right. But you'll give me the special. And let it make as good time as it can, Mr. North; I'm fierce when I have to ride a slow train."

The vice-president's promise was freely given; and to expedite matters, the division superintendent's chief clerk went down to the station with Adair to see the special train properly equipped and started on the mountain-climbing run. Adair left the details to this orderly from the general offices; not knowing how to compass them himself, he had to. If he could have seen the broad grins on the faces of his train crew when Dobson, the clerk, gave them the despatcher's order—but at that moment he was lounging in Mr. North's easiest chair in the central compartment of the "01," reading for the twentieth time a crease-worn telegram.

The telegram was from Alicia, and it was dated at Denver, three days gone. It was not very explicit; on the contrary, it was rather incoherent.

"You would better come on as fast as you can if you want to save your friend's life. He has been tried and found guilty — of just what, I don't know—and will be hanged pretty soon—within a few days, I think."

"Now that's a nice way to stir a fellow up, isn't it?" soliloquized the pleasure-lover. "Just as I was getting ready to go up to Mount Ptarmigan for the shooting. She knew that, too. I'll bet a picayune it's just a girl's scare. Ford's plenty good and able to take care of himself."

That was Mr. Charles Edward Adair's care-free phrasing of it; but three hours later, when the cook of the "01" served him the most appetizing of luncheons in the big open compartment, and the steeply pitched walls of the lower Blue Canyon were still stinting the outlook from the car windows, he began to grow impatient.

"Whereabouts are we now, Johnson?" he asked of the cook's second man.

"Between Cutcliff and No-Horse; yes, sah. 'Bout forty mile from Denver."

"Great Scott! Fifteen miles an hour? Say, Johnson, what do you do when you want 'em to run faster—pull this string?"

"Yes, sah; dat's it," grinned the negro.

Adair pulled the air-cord, and it brought results—of a kind. Only the train came to a sudden stop, instead of going ahead faster; and Conductor Barclay, who had been riding on the engine, came back to see what had happened.

"Did you stop us, Mr. Adair?" he asked pleasantly.

"Not meaning to, you may be sure," said Adair. "But now you're here, I'll ask if there is any objection to my getting off and walking. I could stop and rest and let you overtake me now and then, you know."

The conductor tweaked the air-cord and the train moved on again.

"I've been expecting you'd shout at us," he said good-naturedly. "But we're doing the best we can. There's a freight wreck on ahead, and we've been dallying along, hoping they'd get it picked up by the time we reach it. I thought you'd rather keep moving than to be hung up for three or four hours at the wreck."

Adair saw his helplessness and made the best of it. He was in Mr. North's hands, and if Mr. North was playing for delay, the delay would be forthcoming. None the less, he contrived to make Barclay uncomfortable.

"I'm only a director in the Pacific Southwestern, and I suppose directors don't count," he said nonchalantly. "Yet, I presume, if I should ask it as a personal favor, I might get a conductor's or an engineer's head to take home with me for a souvenir. How would that be? Do you think I could make it win?"

"You could do it, hands down, Mr. Adair. But I hope you won't feel as if you'd got to go into the head-hunting business. It's like the boy throwing stones into the pond; it's fun for the kid, but sort o' hard on the toad-frogs."

Adair laughed. He was not one of those who find it easy to bear malice.

"You don't talk half as bad as you act," he said genially. "Down at bottom I dare say you're a pretty good kind of a fellow. Had anything to eat?"

Barclay shook his head. "No; we was laying off to get coffee and sinkers at Clapp's Mine, if we ever get there."

"'Coffee and sinkers'," said Adair. "That doesn't sound very uplifting. Sit down here and help me out with my contract."

Barclay did it, rather unwillingly. He was not accustomed to eating at the vice-president's table, but there was no resisting the curly-headed young man when he chose to make himself companionable. Barclay sat on the edge of his chair, ate with his knife or fork indifferently, and had small use for the extra spoons and cutlery. But he made a meal to be remembered. Afterward, the young man found a cigar-case, and his own box of Turkish cigarettes; and still the special was going at the same slow cow-gallop up the canyon.

"How many are there of you up ahead?" asked Adair, when Barclay's cigar was going like a factory chimney.

"Only Williams and his fireman."

"Dinner-buckets?"

"No; neither one of 'em, as it happens. Hurry call to go out with you, and both of 'em live too far to go home after the grub-cans."

"Johnson," said the dispenser of hospitality, calling the second man. "Think you could climb over the coal with some dinner for the enginemen? No? Let me make it possible"—flipping a dollar into the ready palm. "Tell the cook it's an order, and if he stints it there'll be consequences."

Barclay grinned his appreciation. The curly-headed young man was far enough removed from any species of railway official hitherto known to the conductor. But Adair was only paving the way.

"Do you know," he said, after a little interval of tobacco-charmed silence, "one of the things I am most anxious to see is a real railroad wreck. Suppose you quicken up a little and let us have our dead time at the scene of this disaster you speak of."

Barclay was tilting uneasily in his chair.

"I reckon they've about got it picked up and cleaned out o' the way by this time, Mr. Adair. I shouldn't be surprised if we could hardly find the place when we get there."

"Nor I," said Adair; and he sat back and chuckled. "It's considerably difficult to sit up and pull your imagination on a man who has been decently good to you, isn't it, Barclay? Let me ask you: are you Mr. North's man?"

"Mr. North is the big boss."

"But this Plug Mountain division is a part of Mr. Ford's line, isn't it?"

"It used to be all his. There's a white man for you, Mr. Adair."

Adair saw his opportunity and used it.

"Now see here, Barclay; I'm only a director, and I don't cut much ice out this way. But back in New York I'm one of three or four people who can tell Mr. North what he can do, and what he can't. You wouldn't want to see Mr. Ford getting it in the neck, would you?"

"By Jacks! There ain't a man in the service that wouldn't fight for him. I tell you, he's *white*."

"Well, Mr. Ford is in trouble: I don't know but he is likely to lose his job, if I don't see the president before the big ax comes down. That is between us two."

The conductor sprang out of his chair.

"By gravy! Why didn't you say that at first? Say, Mr. Adair, you stand between us and Mr. North—tell him you gave the orders yourself—and you'll have the ride of your life from here to Saint's Rest!"

"Go it," said Adair; and two minutes after Barclay had let himself out of the forward door of the "01," the train took a sudden start and darted ahead at full speed.

This bit of diplomacy on the part of Adair saved two full hours in the run to Saint's Rest. Nevertheless, it was after dark when the "01" pulled into the crowded material yard in the high mountain basin and Leckhard came aboard to find out what had brought this second private-car visitation. He was relieved not to meet North—to be confronted only by a pleasant-faced young man who seemed to have the car all to himself.

"My name is Leckhard," announced the man-of-all-work, "and I represent the engineering department. I saw it was Mr. North's car, and—"

"And you came to see what you could do for the vice-president and general manager," Adair finished for him. "Mighty sorry to disappoint you, Mr. Leckhard, but my name isn't North; it's Adair, and I'm only a director. How much authority is a director allowed— at this altitude and distance from New York?"

Leckhard laughed.

"I reckon you might call yourself the ranking officer in the field, Mr. Adair. What you say, goes."

"Then I say 'go'; which means that I'd like to go—on to the end of the extension."

But now the engineer was shaking his head.

"Ask me anything but that, Mr. Adair. None of our enginemen is at this end of the line, and your man Williams, who brought you up from Denver, doesn't know the way. More than that, if we had a man and an engine, I'd be afraid to send you out for a night run. Mr. Ford made it last night with Mr. Colbrith's car, and they used up ten hours in covering less than a hundred and twenty miles, and came within six feet of killing everybody."

Adair had lighted a cigarette, and he did not reply until the match flare had gone out. Then he said, in a way that made Leckhard his friend for life:

"I'm entirely in your hands, Mr. Leckhard; can't turn a wheel unless you say so. And I believe you're telling me the truth, as man to man. Can you reach Ford or Mr. Colbrith by wire?"

"I'm sorry to say I can't. We have only the one wire, and it's on temporary poles most of the way. It broke down on us this morning, and I can't raise the end-of-track."

"Block number two," said Adair cheerfully. "We seem to be out of luck this evening." Then, with searching abruptness: "Do you call yourself Ford's friend, Mr. Leckhard?"

"Rather," said the Saint's Rest Pooh Bah. "He hired me; and when he goes, I go."

"Ah! now we are warming ourselves at the same fire. Let me invite your confidence in one word, Mr. Leckhard. I dislike Mr. North."

The burly engineer laughed again.

"You have a geniusful way of putting your finger on the sore spot without fumbling. We all dislike Mr. North at this end of things— with reason."

"And that reason is?"

"That he'd fire the entire engineering department if he could find half an excuse. I'm afraid he's going to do it, too, in the most effectual way—by forcing Mr. Ford out. If Ford goes, every man in the department will quit with him. I'm afraid it's coming to that."

Johnson, the porter, had lighted the Pintsch globes and was laying the covers for dinner.

"Make it two, Johnson," said Adair; and, then to Leckhard: "You dine with me—don't say no; I couldn't stand it alone." And when that point was settled: "Now, sit down till we thresh, this out a bit finer. How far has this forcing business gone? You're talking to the man who has backed Ford from the first."

"It has gone pretty far. North has obstructed, quietly but persistently, ever since the first blow was struck on the extension. He has delayed material, when he could do it unofficially, he scants us for rolling stock and motive power, he stands in with the MacMorroghs and backs them against Ford every time there is a dispute. Ford is a patient man, Mr. Adair, but I think he has about reached the limit."

"H'm. Do you attach any particular importance to the president's trip over the extension?"

Leckhard shook his head. "I'm only a passenger—I see what goes by the car-windows. Mr. Colbrith was dead set on pushing over to the end-of-track—wouldn't even wait for daylight. You probably know him better than I do—"

"He is my uncle," Adair cut in.

"Oh; then I can't tell you anything about him. He was hot at Ford last night; what for I don't know, unless it was because Ford opposed a night run over a raw construction track with the Nadia. He was right about that, though. If I had been in his place I would have thrown up my job before I would have taken the risk."

Adair appeared to be considering something, and when he had thought it out, the porter had announced dinner and they had taken their places at the table.

"I have told you I am Ford's friend, Mr. Leckhard; I have ridden a couple of thousand miles out of my way to give him a lift. Tell me frankly; have you any reason to believe it will come to blows between him and the president while they are together at the front?—Try this celery; it's as good as you'd get at Sherry's."

Leckhard helped himself to the relish, and waited until the negro, Johnson, had gone back to the cook's galley.

"The little I know comes in a roundabout way," he replied slowly. "Penfield, who is known all over the Southwestern as Mr. North's private detective and spy, is with Mr. Colbrith acting as the president's secretary. Yesterday, while the Nadia was side-tracked here, Penfield had a lot of telegraphing to do for Mr. Colbrith. He did it himself—he's a lightning operator, among other things—and I happened into the office just as he was finishing. His final message was a cipher, to Mr. North, and he signed it with his own name."

"Well?" said Adair.

Again the engineer waited until the negro was out of hearing.

"A little later, just as the Nadia was about to pull out, there came a rush call from Denver for Penfield. I answered and said the car was on the point of leaving, but that I'd take the message and try to catch Penfield if I could. It came, on the run, and it was signed by Eckstein, North's chief clerk. It wasn't ciphered—lack of time, I reckon—and Eckstein took the chance that I wouldn't catch on."

"You kept a copy?" suggested Adair.

"I did. I wasn't able to deliver the original until the Nadia came back from the foot of the pass in the evening to fill the engine tank. But I couldn't make anything out of it. It was an order to Penfield not to let anything interfere with the president's buckboard trip—whatever that might be—with authority to incur any expense that might be necessary, using the telegram as his credential with the MacMorrogh Brothers if more money were needed."

"To pay for the buckboards?" asked Adair.

"You may search me," said Leckhard. "Only it could hardly be that—we have an open account at the Bank of Copah for legitimate expenses. No; there's a nigger in the woodpile, somewhere. Penfield is only a clerk; but for some purpose he is given *carte blanche* to spend money."

Adair was absently stirring his black coffee.

"All of which points to one conclusion, Mr. Leckhard. They are plotting against Ford—without the president's connivance. But the president is going to be made to swing the club. I know rather more than you do about it—which isn't saying very much. My—a relative of mine who is with the party in the Nadia wired me three days ago from Denver that Ford had been tried and condemned, and was only waiting to be hanged. That's why I am here to-night. You've got to get me to the end-of-track before it comes to blows between Mr. Colbrith and Stuart Ford. I know both men, Mr. Leckhard. If the iron comes to a certain heat, the past master of all the peacemakers won't be able to patch things together."

"Ford will resign," said the engineer.

"That is what I'm afraid of; and we can't let him resign. That would mean Mr. North for everything in sight, and the ultimate ruin of the Pacific Southwestern. On the other hand, I can't have Ford fighting the family—or my uncle—which is just what he will do if he gets his blood up—and doesn't quit in a huff. It's up to you to trundle this car over to the seat of war, Mr. Leckhard."

The division engineer was thinking hard.

"I can't see how it's to be done, right now, Mr. Adair. But I'll tell you what I will do. Our empty material trains come back from the front in the night, as a rule. When they get in, and I can be sure that the track's clear, I'll double one of the construction engines out with you. It will be along toward morning, I'm afraid; but, with nothing in the way, you ought to make the run in four or five hours—say by late breakfast time."

That was the way it was left when Leckhard went back to his telegraph den at ten o'clock; and some six hours later, Adair, sleepily conscious of disturbances, wakened sufficiently to hear the wheels once more trundling monotonously under the "01."

191

XX
THE CONSPIRATORS

"How far do we go, and what do we do when we get there?" asked Frisbie of his chief, when the two buckboards, heaving and lurching over the rock-strewn talus at the foot of the canyon cliff, had passed beyond sight and sound of the headquarters camp at the mouth of Horse Creek.

"I'm not guessing any more," said Ford crustily. He was finding that his temper deteriorated as the square of his distance from Alicia Adair increased. "The president said he wanted to drive over this short-cut, and he's doing it."

"Humph!" growled Frisbie. "If he wanted to rub salt into your bruises, why didn't he take you in the cart with him? And where do *I* come in?"

"You are 'implicated' with me; that was his word."

Another mile passed in discomforting plungings. The trail had become all but impassable for the staggering horses; yet the leading buckboard held on doggedly. There were places where both drivers had to get out and lead; bad bits where all save the president descended to walk. But through the worst as well as the best, Mr. Colbrith clung to his seat like a man determined to ride. It was well past noon when the two vehicles reached the western portal of the canyon, and the dottings of the Copah mine workings came in sight on the hillsides to the southward. Ford's driver had fallen a little behind in the final half-mile, and when the gap was closed up, the president was waiting.

"Well, Mr. Ford," he began, somewhat breathless but triumphant, "are you fully satisfied?"

"I have learned nothing that I did not know before we began to build the extension," was the non-committal rejoinder.

"Oh, you haven't? You reported that canyon impracticable for a railroad, and yet I have just driven through it without once dismounting from this buckboard. Moreover, we shall find in Copah to-morrow a re-survey of the line showing its entire practicability, Mr. Ford—a report not made by your engineers."

Ford and Frisbie exchanged swift glances of intelligence. The presence of the strange engineering party in the canyon was sufficiently explained. At first sight the president's expedient seemed childishly puerile to Ford. Then suddenly in a flash of revealment he saw beyond the puerilities—beyond the stubborn old man who, with all his narrow self-will and obstinacy was merely playing the game for others.

"We can discuss these matters later, if you wish," he said placably. "I think you will find our ground well taken. Do you want to drive back as we came? Or will you let me find you an easier road to the mouth of Horse Creek?"

But Mr. Colbrith was not to be balked or turned aside.

"Mr. Ford, I wish to be fair and impartial. I desired to satisfy myself, personally, that this route we have driven over is practicable, and it was also my desire that the investigation should be conducted in your presence. You will admit now that you made a mistake—a very costly mistake for the company—in abandoning this short cut."

"I admit nothing of the kind. The difficulties remain as they were, quite unchanged by our pleasure trip from the end-of-track, Mr. Colbrith. Assuming that the re-survey will report that the north bank of the river is practicable, while the south bank is not, I have only to say that the cost of the two bridges would offset the easier grading conditions, while the danger to future traffic would remain the same. But that is neither here nor there. You must either give us credit for knowing our business, or you must discredit us entirely."

Frisbie was grinding his heel into the hard soil of the mesa. The argument was growing rather acrid; and Penfield and the two drivers were interested listeners. It was high time for a diversion to be made, and the assistant made it.

"We have used five hours getting down here, and we'll need as many going back," he put in. "Unless there is something more to be done on the spot, I think we'd better take the road over the hills. It's with you, Mr. Colbrith."

The president signified his assent by climbing into his buckboard, and the return journey was begun with the two engineers in the lead for pathfinding purposes. Once safely out of earshot, Frisbie voiced his disgust.

"A wild goose-chase, pure and simple! Stuart, that old man is in his second childhood."

"Not at all," said Ford. "He is merely following out North's suggestions. Dick, my name is Dennis."

"Nonsense! Things are no worse than they have been all along."

"My time with the Pacific Southwestern is shorter by just the number of hours it has taken us to drive down here. Mr. Colbrith has convinced himself that I was wrong in abandoning the canyon. To-morrow he will convince himself that I was doubly wrong in approving the detour. I shall hand in my resignation to-night."

"So be it," said Frisbie shortly. "That means good-by to the extension. I'm predicting that it will never get to Green Butte—never get beyond Copah. And your name will go out to the railroad world as that of a man who bit off a number of large things that he couldn't chew."

"Confound you!" said Ford; and after that, Frisbie could get no more than single-syllabled replies to his monologue of Job's comfortings.

The returning route was a detour, winding, through the greater part of it, among and over the swelling heights north of the Pannikin. On each hilltop the vast sweep of the inter-mountain wilderness came into view, and from the highest point in the trail, reached when the sun was dipping toward the western horizon, the eye-sweep took in the broken country lying between the Pannikin and the path of the Transcontinental narrow gauge forty miles away.

Jack's Canyon, the Transcontinental station nearest Copah, was the beginning of a combined pack trail and stage road connecting the Copah district with what had been, before the advent of the Southwestern Extension, its nearest railroad outlet. Along this trail, visible to the buckboarders as a black speck tittuping against the reddening background of the west, galloped a solitary horseman, urging his mount in a way to make Frisbie, getting his glimpse from the hilltop of extended views, call Ford's attention.

"Look at that brute, pushing his horse like that at the end of the day! He ought to be—"

But the hastening rider was getting his deserts, whatever they should be, as he went along. For three hours, with three relays of fresh horses picked up at the stage stations in passing, he had been galloping southward, and to whatever other urging he might confess was added the new one of fear, the fear that in the approaching day's-end he would lose his way.

Seen from the nearer point of view, the tittuping horseman seemed curiously out of harmony with his environment. Instead of the cow-boy "shaps," or overalls, he wore the trousers of civilization, which the rapid night had hitched half-way to his knees. In place of the open-breasted shirt with the rolled-up sleeves there were tailor-made upper clothes, with the collar and cravat also of civilization, and the hat—it was perhaps fortunate for the rider that he had not met any true denizens of the unfettered highlands on the lonely trail from Jack's Canyon. His hat was a Derby of the newest shape; and the cow-men beyond the range are impatient of such head-gear.

Recognition, after one has ridden hard for three hours over a dusty road, is not easy; but there are faces one never forgets, and the features, dust-grimed and sweat-streaked though they were, had still the South-of-Europe outline, the slightly aquiline nose, and the piercing black eyes of Mr. Julius Eckstein, whom we saw, on the morning of this same road-wearying day, welcoming Adair over the counter railing in the Denver office. How does it come that a few short hours later we find him galloping tantivy over the dusty hills, no less than two hundred miles, as the birds fly, from the counter railing of welcomings?

That is the story of another, and a more successful special train than Adair's. No sooner was the care-free young director safely on his way to meet the delays so painstakingly prearranged for him than the wires began to buzz with a cipher message of warning to Penfield. A precious half-hour was lost in ascertaining that the wire connection to the end-of-track was temporarily out of commission; but during that half-hour Mr. North had held his chin in his hand to some good purpose.

With the fresh complications promised by Adair's projection into the field, a stronger man than Penfield should be in command on the firing line. The vice-president decided swiftly that Eckstein was the man; but how to get him to the MacMorrogh headquarters before Adair should arrive?

It proved to be simpler in the outcarrying than in the planning. A special light engine over the Transcontinental to Jack's Canyon—an exchange of courtesies which even fighting railroads make in war as well as in peace—a wire request on the stage company for relays of saddle horses, and the thing was done. And Eckstein, pushing his jaded beast down the final hill in the dusk of the evening, and welcoming, as only the saddle-tormented can welcome, the lights of the headquarters camp, confessed in cursings quite barbaric in their phrasings that he, too, was done.

The conference held that night behind locked doors in the MacMorroghs' commissary office was a council of five, with Eckstein, as the mouthpiece of the vice-president, in the chair. Penfield was present, with no vote, and the three MacMorroghs voted as one; but as to that, there were no divisions. A crisis was imminent, and it must be met.

"As I have said, I am here with power to act," said Eckstein, gripping the chair with wincings after the day of torment. "The plan outlined at first by Mr. North must go through as it was outlined. Part of it has already been carried out, you say: Ford and the president have been over the short-cut together. To-morrow the entire private-car party goes to Copah over the detour. Are the buckboards here for that?"

"They're here wid the drivers. I saw to that part of it myself." It was the youngest of the three MacMorroghs who gave the assurance.

"So far so good," commented the chairman. "The other thing we have to provide for, or rather, to prevent, is the possibility of Mr. Adair's reaching here in time to join the party. The last definite information we had of Mr. Adair he was crawling up Blue Canyon, with a train crew which was under orders to give him ample time to study the scenery. He has probably reached Saint's Rest before this, however, and once there, Leckhard will give him anything in sight. The question is, will he attempt to run the extension to-night?"

The middle MacMorrogh thought not, and his younger brother agreed with him. But the senior partner voted aye, and stuck to it. Thereupon ensued a conflict of opinion. Dan MacMorrogh pointed out that the construction motive power was all at the west end, or in transit eastward; it would be daylight of another day before an engineer familiar with the hazards could be obtained for Adair's special over the construction line. But Brian MacMorrogh argued with equal emphasis that this was a mere begging of chances. Without a telegraph wire to verify the guess, no man could say at what hour one of the trains of empties would pull through to Saint's Rest; and whatever the hour, Leckhard would doubtless turn the engine and crew to double back with Adair's car.

Eckstein was gripping the arms of his chair and setting his teeth deep into his cigar while the probabilities were getting themselves threshed out. At the end of the dispute he said quietly: "It's a hell of a pity we can't have the use of the wire for this one night. But, gentlemen, we can't stop for trifles. There are five of us here in this room who know how much is at stake. One of two things is due to happen. If we can keep Adair out of it for another twelve hours, Ford will be disgraced and asked to resign. If he gets to that point, we're safe. I know Ford's temper. If Mr. Colbrith puts it as he is likely to put it, Ford will say and do things that will make it impossible for Adair or any one else to get him back into the service."

"Thrue for you, Misther Eckstein; ye have 'im down to the crossin' of a 't'," agreed the eldest of the brothers MacMorrogh.

"That is one of the due things," Eckstein went on smoothly. "The other isn't pretty to look at. If Adair gets here in time, it will be another story. He can handle Ford; and he has proved once or twice that he can handle Mr. Colbrith. If he hadn't been out of the way when you went to New York with Mr. North, you'd never have seen the thin edge of this contract, Brian. Well, then what happens? With Adair on the ground to back him, Ford wins out. Do you know what that means? Investigations, muck-rakings, and worse. There are two or three of us here, and some more on the other side of the range, who won't get off with less than ten years apiece. I'm willing to take the chance of a few more years for another play on the red. How is it with the rest of you?"

The elder MacMorrogh spread his hands.

"It's all in the same boat we are. You've a notion in the back par-rt of your head, Misther Eckstein; lave us have it."

"As I've said, we can't stick at trifles. If Adair's train is on the extension, it mustn't get here. Somebody goes up the line on a hand-car to-night and stops it."

"Is it to ditch it, ye mane?" asked the youngest of the brothers in a hoarse whisper.

Eckstein laughed cynically. "What a lot of crude cutthroats you are!" he jeered. "Now if it were Ford, instead of Adair—but pshaw! a rail or two taken up and flung into the river well beyond walking distance from this camp does the business. Only the man who does it wants to make sure he has gone far enough back to cover all the possible chances."

"That's me," said Dan MacMorrogh; and he rose and let himself out, with the younger brother to lock the door behind him.

The door-keeping attended to, the younger brother drew closer into the circle.

"There's wan thing," he said, looking furtively at Eckstein. "I was in Copah this day: I got the buckboards for Misther Colbrith. Goin' past the bank, who would I see but our old bookkeeper, Merriam, chinnin' wid the bank president. I thought he was out o' the way entirely."

Stiff and saddle-sore as he was, Eckstein leaped out of his chair with an oath.

"Merriam? What the devil is he back here for? It's a put-up job!"

It was the chief of the MacMorroghs who flung in the calming word.

"'Tis only a happen-so, Misther Eckstein. Merriam owns a mine or two in the Copah, and ye know the fever: a man can't keep away from thim."

"That may be; but it's a cursed unlucky combination, just the same. I tell you, Brian, he knows too much—this fellow Merriam. He knew what was up when he was steering Frisbie. You told him too much. And afterward, when we gave him the Oregon job, he knew why he was being bribed to go away. You let us in for this: you've got to muzzle him, some way."

The MacMorrogh looked at his remaining brother meaningly. "'Tis up to you, this time, Mickey, b'y. Find your way over to the minin' camp this night, and make a clane job av it.'"

Penfield was moving uneasily in his chair. The plotting waters were deepening swiftly, much too swiftly for him. Loyalty to his superior officer, the unquestioning loyalty that disregards motives entirely and does not look too closely at methods, was his fetish. But these men were not merely loyal to Mr. North. They were criminals—he stuck at the word, but there was no other—fighting for their own hand.

"I guess—I guess I'd better go back to the Nadia," he stammered, trying to keep his voice steady. "Mr. Colbrith may need me."

Eckstein turned on him like a snarling animal.

"No you don't, Arthur, my boy. I know you like a book. You stay here till you're in as deep as the rest of us. Like Merriam, you know too damned much."

Penfield sat still, with the cold chills running up and down his spine, while Eckstein went on talking to the two MacMorroghs.

"This Merriam business complicates things like hell"—he was growing coarsely profane in the grinding mill of events. "But it shows us where we stand. This thing has got to go through, and if it doesn't work out the way we've planned it, it's for us to find another way."

"There's always the wan other way," said the elder MacMorrogh slowly. "'Tis but a drunken fight in wan o' the camps, and Ford tryin' to stop it, as he always does: a bit of a shindy among the b'ys, and this—" crooking his forefinger suggestively.

"Bah!" said Eckstein. "You fellows ought to have lived in the stone age, when a man pulled his enemy to pieces with his bare hands. If it comes to that, there are easier ways—and safer. A premature blast in a rock cut; a weak coupling-pin when he happens to be standing in the way of a pulling engine: they tell me he is always indifferent to his personal safety. But never mind the fashion of it; the point I'm making is that if everything else fails, Ford mustn't live to be the head-foreman of the outfit."

Penfield's face was ashen, and he was cravenly thankful that the lamplight was dim, and that his chair was in the shadow. This was more than he had bargained for; more by the price of a man's life.

Eckstein was lifting himself by painful inches from his chair. A silence as of the grave had fallen upon the two MacMorroghs. It was the senior partner who broke it.

"'Tis as ye say, Misther Eckstein. A man—a safe man, that'll do what he's told to do—will be at Ford's heels till this thing do be settled. And now for yourself: 'tis betther that ye kape dark. Four of us know that you're in the camp—no wan else need know. I've a room and a bed, and ye'll be nadin' the lasht, I'm thinking."

The two MacMorroghs were bestirring themselves, and Penfield was slipping through the door into the commissary when Eckstein's fingers closed upon his arm.

"Your part is to keep tab on the programme," he whispered "Get word instantly to Brian if there is any change. And if you weaken, Arthur, I'll promise you just one thing: I'll pull you in with the rest of us if I have to swear to a string of lies a mile long. Remember that."

Penfield escaped at length, and stumbled through the littered end-of-track yard to where the lighted windows of the Nadia marked the berth of the president's car. Out of the shadow of the car a man rose up and confronted him. It was Frisbie, and he asked a single question:

"Say, Penfield, who was that fellow who rode around to the MacMorroghs' back door just after dark?"

"It was Eckstein." The secretary let slip the name before he could lay hold of his discretion.

"Oh: all right That's all," said the engineer; and he vanished.

Climbing to the observation platform, Penfield let himself into the cheerful central compartment of the Nadia quietly enough to surprise two people who were sitting together on one of the broad divans. The two were Ford and Miss Alicia Adair, with Aunt Hester Adair, reading under the drop-light at the table, for the only other occupant of the compartment. It was Miss Alicia who told the secretary that he was not needed.

"Mr. Colbrith was very tired, and he has gone to bed," she said; and Penfield, still pallid and curiously unready of speech, said he believed he'd go, too.

Ford got up when Penfield had disappeared in the curtained vestibule leading to the state-rooms.

"I shall wait one more day, because you want me to," he said, resuming the conversation which had been broken off by Penfield's incoming. "But I'll tell the truth: I came here to-night to have it over with. We were as near quarreling to-day as I want to come, and if Frisbie hadn't got between—"

"Good Mr. Frisbie!" she said. "Some day I hope to get a chance to be very nice to him."

Ford laughed. The evening had healed many of the woundings of the day.

"If you don't get the chance it won't be Dick's fault—or mine. Meantime, I'll be delighted to pose as his substitute."

She had gone with him to the door, and his last word was a reminder. "Don't forget," he said. "I'm to drive your buckboard to-morrow, whatever happens."

"You are the one who will forget," she retorted. "When Uncle Sidney crooks his finger at you, you'll climb up obediently beside him and let him scold you all the way over to Copah."

"Wait and see," said Ford; and then he said good night, not as he wanted to, but as he must, with Aunt Hester sitting within arm's reach.

Frisbie was sitting up for him when he reached the white tents of the engineers' camp pitched a little apart from the MacMorrogh conglomeration of shacks and storehouses.

"Just one question," said the first assistant, "and I've been staying awake to ask it. Are you still my boss?"

"For one more day," said Ford shortly.

"Well, we can't live more than a day at a time, if we try. That will do to sleep on."

"All right; sleep on it, then."

"In a minute; after I've freed my mind of one little news item. Do you remember that fellow we saw riding in on the Jack's Canyon trail as we were coming back this afternoon?"

"Yes."

"Have you any notion who it was?"

"No."

"It was Mr. Julius Eckstein; and he is at present lying doggo in the MacMorrogh quarters. That's all. Now you can turn in and sleep a few lines on *that*."

XXI
THE MILLS OF THE GODS

It was merely by chance that Adair had Michael Gallagher for his engineer when the "01" was made up for the after-midnight run from Saint's Rest to the MacMorrogh headquarters. But it was a chance which was duly gratifying to Leckhard. The little Irishman was Ford's most loyal liegeman, and a word was all that was needed to put him on his mettle. The word was spoken while he was oiling around for the man-killing extra service.

"Pretty well knocked out, Michael?" asked Leckhard, by way of preface.

"I am thot, Misther Leckhard. 'Tis the good half of lasht night, all day yestherday, and thin some."

"It's tough. But if any of the other men were in, I should still ask you to go. Mr. Ford is in a pinch, and Mr. Adair, your passenger, is going to help him out. He can do it if you get him to Horse Creek in time; and I know you'll get him there if the 956 and the '01' will stay on the steel."

"To help Misther Foord out? Thot's me," said Gallagher simply.

"Not having a wire, I can't boost you any from this end. You'll meet Folsom and Graham with the other two sections of empties where you can: you'll run as fast as the Lord'll let you on such a track as you have: but above all, you'll stay on the rails. If you ditch yourself, it'll go hard with Mr. Ford."

"I'll do all thim things and wan more—and thot wan is the shtiffest av thim all: the saints aidin' me, Misther Leckhard, I'll shtay awake."

There was a short siding at the summit of the pass, and by good hap, Gallagher met Folsom with the first string of empties at that point: or rather, giving the bit of good luck full credit, he heard the roaring of

Folsom's exhaust as the first of the opposing trains pounded up the dangerous western grade, and hastily backed up and took the summit siding.

Pitching over the hill with the "01" the moment Folsom's tail-lights had passed the outlet switch, Gallagher had a sharp attack of memory. The day before, in the Horse Creek yard, he had seen and remarked a jagged scratch on the side of the Nadia. Hence, he was watching for the narrow rock cuttings, and the three passages perilous on the cliff face were made in safety.

Once off the mountain, however, the greater peril began to assert itself. For a time the Irishman kept himself fully awake and alert by pushing the 956 to the ragged edge of hazard, scurrying over the short tangents and lifting her around the curves in breath-taking spurts. Later this expedient began to lose its fillip. Since the train was running wholly on the air-brakes there was nothing for the fireman to do, and Jackson, the loyalest understudy Gallagher had ever known, tumbled from his box in a doze, staggered across the gang-way into the half-filled tender, and fell like a man anæsthetized full length on the coal. Gallagher did not try to arouse him.

"'Tis hell for wan, an' twice hell for two," he muttered; and then he shifted his right hand to the brake-cock and grasped the hot throttle lever with the ungloved left. And for a time the pain of the burn sufficed.

It was another piece of luck, good or bad, that made Ten Mile station the special train's meeting point with the second train of empties. This time it was Graham, the other engineer, who heard. He had stopped at Ten Mile on the bare chance that the wire between that point and Saint's Rest had been repaired; public opinion to the contrary notwithstanding, an engineer does not run "wild" when he can help it.

The engineer of the third section had come out of the night operator's office disappointed, and was climbing to his engine to pull out, when he heard, or thought he heard, the dull rumble of a train racing down the canyon. It came in sight while he listened, and the yellow flare told him that it was either Gallagher or Folsom doubling back on one of the construction engines. What startled him was the fact that the coming train appeared to be running itself; there was no warning whistle shriek and no slackening of speed.

Graham was a Scotchman, slow of speech, slow to anger, methodical to the thirty-third degree. But in an emergency his brain leveled itself like a ship's compass gimballed to hang plumb in the suddenest typhoon. Three shrill whistle calls sent a sleepy flagman racing to set the switch of the siding. With a clang the reversing lever came over and the steam roared into the cylinders.

The Scotchman had the grade to help him, which was fortunate. When he had the string of empties fairly in retreat, the beam of Gallagher's headlight was shining full in his face and blinding him. For a heart-breaking second he feared that the opposing train would follow him in on the siding; there was but an instant for the flicking of the switch. But by this time the sleepy flagman was wide awake, and he jerked the switch lever for his life the moment Graham's engine had cleared the points. It was the closest possible shave. Gallagher's cab ticked the forward end of the other engine's running board in passing, and if Graham had not been still shoving backward with the throttle wide open, the "01," being wider than its piloting engine, would have had its side ripped out.

Graham had a glimpse into the cab of the 956 as it passed and saw Gallagher, sitting erect on his box with wide-staring eyes. He knew the symptoms, and feared that he had only postponed the catastrophe. The siding was a short one, and he knew that in backing down he must inevitably have shoved the rear end of his train out upon the main line at the lower switch. Once again the level brain righted itself to the emergency. Four sharp shrieks of the whistle for switches, a jamming of the whistle lever to set the canyon echoes yelling in the hope of arousing Gallagher, and Graham slammed his engine into the forward motion without pausing to close the throttle. There was a grinding of fire from the wheels, a running jangle of slack-taking down the long line of empties, and the freight train shot ahead, snatching its rear end out of harm's way just as Gallagher, dreaming that his boiler had burst and that all the fiends of the pit were screeching the news of it, came to life and snapped on the air.

When the stop was made, the little Irishman roused his fireman, got off and footed it up the line to see what he had done. Graham had stopped his engine when he was sure his train was clearing the lower switch, and was on his way back to find out what had happened to Gallagher. The two men met in the shadow of the halted material empties, and it was the Irishman who began it.

"Paste me wan, Scotchie," he said. "'Tis owin' to me."

Without a word the Scotchman gave the blow, catching the little man full in the chest and knocking him half a car-length. That was enough. Gallagher picked himself up out of the gravel, the lust of battle hot upon him.

"Wan more like thot, ye divvle, and I cajo lick ye if ye wor Fin-mac-Coul himself," he panted; and Graham gave it judiciously, this time on the point of the jaw. For five bloody minutes it went on, give and take, down and up; methodically on Graham's part, fiery hot on Gallagher's. And in the end the Irishman had the heavier man backed against the string of empties and yelling for quarter.

"Are you full awake now, ye red-hot blastoderm?" gasped Graham, struggling to free himself when Gallagher gave him leave.

"I am thot, thanks to you, Sandy, lad. 'Twas a foine bit av a scrimmage, an' I'm owin' ye wan. Good night to ye."

"Ye've got a clear track from this," called Graham, swabbing his battered face with a piece of cotton waste drawn from one of the pockets of method. "But ye'd better not take any more cat-naps. Go on with ye, ye wild Irishman; ye're obstructin' the traffic."

For twenty miles below Ten Mile Gallagher sat on his box like a man refreshed. Then the devil of sleep postponed beset him again. Once more the fireman was asleep on the coal, and to the little Irishman's bombardment of wrenches and other missiles he returned only sodden groans. Gallagher nerved himself to fight it through alone. Mile after mile of the time-killing track swung slowly to the rear, and there was not even the flick of speed to help in the grim battle.

Dawn came when the end-of-track camp was still forty miles away, but the breaking day brought no surcease of strugglings. When it came to the bitter end, when his eyelids would close involuntarily and he would wake with a start to wonder dumbly how far the 956 had come masterless, Gallagher took a chew of tobacco and began to rub the spittle into his eyes—the last resort of the sleep-tormented engineman. Like all the other expedients it sufficed for the time; but before long he was nodding again, and dreaming that a thousand devils were burning his eyes out with the points of their red-hot pitchforks.

Out of one of these nightmares he came with a yell of pain to see what figured for the moment as another nightmare. Three hundred feet ahead the track seemed to vanish for three or four rail-lengths. It was second nature to jam on the brakes and to make the sudden stop. Then he sat still and rubbed his smarting eyes and stared again. The curious hallucination persisted strangely. Fifty feet ahead of the stopped engine the glistening lines of the steel ended abruptly, beginning again a car-length or two beyond. Without disturbing the sleeping Jackson, Gallagher got down and crept cautiously out to the break. It was a break. He stooped and felt the rail ends with his hands.

When he straightened up his passenger was standing beside him.

"What is it?" asked Adair. "Have we lost something?"

Gallagher waved a grimy hand at the gap.

"The thrack," he said. "'Twas there whin I pulled me sthring av empties out over ut lasht night. 'Tis gone now, else I'm thot near dead for sleep I can nayther see nor feel sthraight."

Adair was calmly lighting a cigarette.

"Your senses are still in commission," he said; "there is a good-sized piece of track missing. Who sniped it, do you suppose?"

The engineer was shaking his fiery head.

"'Tis beyond me, Misther Adair."

"That's the deuce of it," smiled the young man. "It's beyond the train. How is your engine—pretty good on the broad jump?"

Gallagher was not past laughing.

"She'll not lep thot, this day. But who'd be doin' this job betune dark an' mornin', d'ye think?"

"You will have to ask me something easy, I'm not up in all the little practical jokes of the country. But if I should venture a guess, I should say it was some one who didn't want me to answer the first call for breakfast at your end-of-track camp this morning. What do we do?"

Gallagher was thinking.

"We passed a camp av surfacers tin mile back, and there'd be rails at Arroyo Siding, tin mile back o' thot," he said reflectively.

Adair had passed over to the river side of the line and was looking at a fresh plowing of the embankment.

"The rails have been dragged down here and they are probably in the river," he announced. "If we had men and tools we might fish them out and repair damages."

"Come on, thin," cried the little Irishman, and when he ran back to climb to the footboard of the 956, Adair climbed with him.

Jackson, refreshed by his cat-naps on the coal, was sent to the rear end of the "01" to flag back, and in due time the special picked up the gang of surfacers just turning out to the day's work. An Irish foreman was in command, and to him Gallagher appealed, lucidly but not too gently. The reply was a volley of abuse and a caustic refusal to lend his men to the track-laying department.

Gallagher turned to Adair with his red-apple face wrinkling dismayfully.

"'Tis up to me to push thot felly's face in, Misther Adair; and what wid two nights and a day, shtandin', and wan fight wid a bully twice me size, I'm not man enough."

Adair tossed away the stump of his cigarette.

"You're quite sure that is what is needed?" he queried.

"To knock a grain av sinse into thot Wicklow man?" queried Gallagher. "Sure, it is." And then whispering: "But not for you, Misther Adair; he'd ate you in two bites. L'ave me have a thry wid him."

But Adair was off and fronting the surly MacMorrogh foreman.

"We need a dozen of your men and some tools," he said quietly. "Do we get them?"

"Not by a fistful!" retorted the surly one. "Maybe you think you're enough of a — — — — — — to take 'em."

"I am a better man than you are," was the even-toned rejoinder.

"Prove it, then."

Gallagher, leaning from his cab window, fully awake now, and chuckling and rubbing his hands together softly, saw the blow. It was clean-cut, swift as the lightning's flash, true to a finger's breadth, and the sound of it was as bone upon bone. At its impact the Wicklow man bounded into the air, arched his back like a bow, and pitched on his head in the ditch. When he rose up, roaring blasphemies and doubling his huge fists for the fray, the quiet voice was assailing him again. "Do we get the men and tools?"

"Not—"

Again the lightning-like passes of the hands, and the Wicklow man sat down forcibly and gasped. The Italian surfacers threw aside their picks and shovels and made a ring, dancing excitedly and jeering. The big foreman, whose scepter of authority was commonly a pick-handle for the belaboring of offenders, was not loved.

"Kick-a da shin—kick-a da shin—he like-a da nigger-mans," suggested one of the Italians, but there was no need. Being safely out of range of the catapult fists, the foreman stayed there.

"Take your track gang and be damned to you!" he snarled.

Adair made a forward step and stood over him.

"Are you quite convinced that I am the better man?" he asked very gently.

"It's a trick!" growled the Wicklow man savagely. "I could get onto it in another whirl or two."

"Get up," said the gentle voice. "You'll never have a better chance to learn the trick." But the foreman had the saving grace to shun anti-climaxes.

"G'wan! Take the men, I say; all of 'em, if you like."

"Thanks," said Adair pleasantly. "We'll do it, and we'll take you, as well—to answer for their good behavior. Let me help you up," and he stooped and snapped the big one to his feet as a man would collar a reluctant boy.

"Great judgment!" gasped the foreman. "Say, Mister Cock-o'-the-walk—where do you hide all that muscle?" And without waiting for an answer he piled a dozen of his men upon the engine and followed them, still muttering.

It was a partly surfaced ten miles over which the special train thundered for the third time since dawn-breaking, and Gallagher took the last wheel-turn out of the 956. None the less, the sun was reddening the western mountains when the Italians took ground at the mysterious gap. The rails were found in the stream, as Adair had predicted, and it was a work of minutes only to snake them up the embankment and to spike them lightly into place. But when Adair, for the healing of wounds, had thrust a bank-note into the hand of the Wicklow man, and the special was once more on its unhindered way westward, the sun had fairly topped the eastern range, and Johnson, the porter of the "01," was shouting across the rocketing tender that breakfast was served.

The young man in the London-cut clothes might have climbed back to the car over the coal; or Gallagher would have stopped for him. But he elected to stay in the cab, and he was still there, hanging from the open window on Jackson's side, when the one-car special woke the echoes with its whistle, clattered in over the switches at Horse Creek, and came to a stand opposite the MacMorroghs' commissary.

It was Brian MacMorrogh who came across the tracks to greet Adair, and, since this was their first meeting, he made the mistake of his life in calling the young director by name.

"The top of the morning to you, Misther Adair. Is it Misther Colbrith you'd be looking for?"

"It is," said Adair shortly, not failing to remark that the barrel-bodied, black-bearded man seemed to recognize and to be expecting him.

"'Tis two hours gone they all are," was the oily-voiced explanation. "Up the grade and over to Copah. But they'll be back to-morrow,

Heaven savin' thim, and we'll make you comfortable here—as comfortable as we can."

"That will be quickly done," said Adair, swinging down from the engine step. "Just give me a horse and tell me which way they have gone, and I'll overtake them."

But here the barrel-bodied one spread his hands helplessly.

"'Tis just our luck!" he protested, in the keenest self-reproach. "There isn't a horse or a mule in camp that you could get a mile an hour out of. In fact, I'm thinking there isn't anny horses at all!"

XXII
THE MAN ON HORSEBACK

Since the weather was rather threatening, and the promise of October in the inter-mountain region is not to be lightly trifled with, Mr. Colbrith pressed for an early start on the seventeen-mile buckboard jaunt to Copah over the detour survey.

It was by his express command that the private-car party was called at daybreak, and that breakfast was served in the Nadia at six o'clock. And at seven sharp, which chanced to be the precise time of day when Adair's commandeered Italians were spiking the last of the displaced rails into position at the gap in the track thirty-three miles away, the buckboards were drawn up at the steps of the president's car.

For reasons charitable, as well as practical, Ford had planned to leave Frisbie out of this second dance of attendance upon the president. The track-layers were well up toward the head of Horse Creek gulch, with Brissac to drive; but during the night the Louisianian had reported in with a touch of mountain fever, and Ford had asked Frisbie to go up and take his place.

This was one of Ford's peg-drivings for the day; and another was timed for the moment of outsetting. For conveyances for the party there were the two double-seated buckboards used on the canyon trip the previous day, and one other with a single seat; but there were only two drivers, the third man, who had brought the single-seated rig from Copah, having been prevailed upon by Ford to disappear.

Ford directed the distribution of the trippers arbitrarily, and was amazed when the president acquiesced without protest. Mr. Colbrith, the doctor's wife, and Penfield, were to go in the leading vehicle; Aunt Hester Adair, Miss Van Bruce, and the doctor, in the second; and Ford drove the single-seated third, with Miss Alicia for his companion.

"I think you must have taken Uncle Sidney unawares," said Alicia, when the caravan was toiling at a slow footpace along the rough wagon road paralleling the Horse Creek grade.

"You mean that he might have objected to your driver? You are a whole lot safer with me than you would be with one of those livery-stable helpers up ahead."

"Oh, no; I didn't mean just that. But you know he usually plans all the little details himself, and—"

"And the fact that somebody else plans them is sufficient excuse for a rearrangement. That is one of the penalties he pays for being the big boss," laughed Ford. Since the yesterday was now safely yesterday, and to-day was his own, there was no room for anything but pure joy.

"You are a 'big boss,' too, aren't you?" she said, matching his light-hearted mood.

"I was, in a way, until your uncle came over and eclipsed me."

"And you will be again when Uncle Sidney moves a little farther along in his orbit."

"That remains to be seen. There is yet plenty of time for him to abolish me, permanently, before he goes on his way rejoicing."

"But you are not going to resign, you know," she reminded him.

"Am I not?" Then he took his courage by the proper grip and went on with sudden gravity: "That rests entirely with you."

"Mr. Ford! Aren't you a little unfair?" She did not pretend to misunderstand him.

"I am open to convincement," he affirmed.

"It is making me Uncle Sidney's executioner, on one hand; or yours, on the other."

He pressed the point relentlessly.

"There are only two horns to the dilemma: either Mr. Colbrith, or a man named Stuart Ford, will have to walk the official plank. Because Mr. Colbrith is your relative, I'm willing to be the victim. But you must say that it is what you wish. That is my price."

"I say it is unfair," she repeated. "Why should you put the burden of the decision upon poor me?"

"Because, if you were not concerned, there would be, to put it in good Hibernian, only one horn to the dilemma—and your uncle would be impaled upon that one."

"Mercy!" she shuddered, in mock dismay. "That sounds almost vindictive. Are you vindictive, Mr. Ford?"

"Terribly," he laughed. "The black-hearted villain of melodrama isn't a patch on me when I'm stirred." And then, more seriously: "But it isn't altogether a joke. There is another side to the thing—what you might call the ethical, I suppose. There are a score or so of men in the company's service—Frisbie and his subordinates—whose jobs hang upon mine. A worse man than I ever aspired to be might be loyal to his friends."

"I wouldn't think of questioning your loyalty to your friends," she admitted.

"Also," he went on determinately, "there is the larger question of right and wrong involved. Is it right for me to step aside and let an organized system of graft and thievery go on unchecked? I know it exists; I have evidence enough to go before a grand jury. I'm not posing as a saint, or even as a muck-raker; but isn't something due to the people who are paying the bills?"

"Now you are involving Uncle Sidney again; and I can't listen to that."

"He is innocent; as innocent as some hundreds of other narrow-minded, short-sighted old men whom chance, or the duplicity of the real rascals, puts at the head of corporations."

"Yet you would make him suffer with the guilty."

"Not willingly, you may be sure. Not at all, if he would listen to reason. But he won't. He'll stand by North till the last gun is fired; and while North stays, there'll be graft, big or little, as the opportunities warrant."

Alicia held her peace while the caravan was measuring another half-mile of the boulder-strewn road. Then she said: "I feel so wretchedly inadequate to help you, Mr. Ford. I wish you could wait until you have talked it over with brother."

"So do I. But I am afraid postponement doesn't lie with me, now. From your uncle's manner and from what he said to me yesterday, I can't help feeling that the crisis is right here. For two days Mr. Colbrith has been very plainly leading up to some sort of dramatic climax. I can't remotely guess what it is going to be; though I can guess that the plot isn't his."

Again she took time to consider, and when she spoke they were nearing the scene of strenuous activities at the moving track-end.

"You don't think you could postpone it?" she asked, almost wistfully, he thought. "I think—I hope—my brother will become interested again. It is your fault that he lost interest, Mr. Ford."

"My fault?" reproachfully.

"Certainly. You didn't give him enough to do. He was happy and contented while you kept him hard at work. But after the bonds were placed and the money raised—"

"I'm a miserable sinner!" Ford confessed. "And I had promised you, too! But the battle has been so fierce at this end of the line; and I couldn't be in two places at one time. Your brother should have been made first vice-president, instead of North. Perhaps we can bring it about yet—if you don't call it all off."

"There it is again," she retorted. "You are dragging me in—and trying to bribe me, too!"

"God forbid!" he said, so earnestly that she forgave him. And then: "I wish your brother were here—now."

"So do I," she admitted. Then she told him of the wire summons sent from Denver, and of the shadowy hope she had based upon it.

"Where was your brother then?" he asked.

"I don't know, positively. I hope he was in New York. He was to come over in the *Campania*, in time for the shooting at Mount Ptarmigan."

"You've had no word from him?"

"None."

They were up with the track-layers, now, in a country of huge bare hills and high-lying, waterless valleys; and the president had halted the caravan to give his guests a chance to see a modern railroad in the actual throes of evolution.

In a specialist in the trade, Ford's genius might have invoked enthusiasm. Speed was the end to which all of the young engineer's inventive powers had been directed; and the pace was furious. On the leveled grade ahead of the track-laying train an army of sweating laborers marched and counter-marched like trained soldiers, placing the cross-ties in position. On a train of specially constructed flat-cars another army was bolting together a long section of track, clamping the double line of rails at intervals to hold them to gauge. At the word, "Ready!" a hauling chain, passing through an anchored pulley-block far up the grade and back to the freed engine of the construction train, was made fast to the forward end of the bolted section; a second word of command, and the engine backed swiftly, dragging the prepared section off over the rollers of the flat-cars and into place on the ties. With the clanging fall of the final pair of rails, a third army, spike-drivers these, fell upon the newly placed steel, shouting their chantey as they swung the great pointed hammers; and in the midst of this fresh turmoil the train, with its brigade of bolters deftly preparing another section, was slowly pushed to the new front for another advance.

"It is like clockwork," was Miss Alicia's enthusiastic comment. "Did you invent it, Mr. Ford?"

Now the combination of flat-car bolting-table, and the shifting and laying by sections, was Ford's invention, but he modestly stood from under.

"Frisbie gets the medal," he said. "It's all in the drill—every man knowing what he has to do, and doing it at the proper moment. I'd give something if I had Dick's knack in detail organizing."

She looked up, laughing. "You have the funniest way of ducking to cover if you think a bit of honest appreciation is coming your way, Mr. Ford. You know you told Mr. Frisbie how to do it."

"Did I? I suppose it wouldn't be polite to contradict you."

"Or any use. Is Mr. Frisbie here now?—Oh, yes; there he is." And then, in a half-awed whisper: "Who is that dreadful, Grand-Opera-villain looking man he is talking to?"

Ford's eyes sought and found Frisbie. He was standing a little apart from the turmoil, talking to a man on horseback; a man with half-closed, beady, black eyes, drooping mustaches, and a face reptilian in its repulsiveness.

"That is 'Mexican George'; the MacMorrogh Brothers' 'killer'," said Ford evenly. "Have you ever heard of a professional man-killer, Miss Adair; a man whose calling is that of a hired assassin?"

She shuddered. "You are jesting, I know. But the word fits his face so accurately. I saw him lounging about the store at the camp yesterday, and it gave me the creeping shivers every time I looked at him. Do you ever have such instantaneous and unreasoning hatreds at first sight?"

"Now and then; yes. But I was not jesting about Mexican George. He is precisely what the word implies; is hired for it and paid for it. Nominally, he guards the commissary and stores, and is the paymaster's armed escort. Really, it is his duty to shoot down any desperate laborer who, in the MacMorroghs' judgment, needs to be killed out of the way."

"Mercy!" Miss Alicia was shuddering again. "What hideously primitive conditions! What is this terrible man doing out here?"

"Oh, he is a free lance; comes and goes as he pleases. No, he's not quarreling with Dick"—answering her look of anxiety.

"How do you know he isn't?"

Ford laughed. "Because Dick wouldn't let him get that near. He knows—Hello; I wonder what your good uncle wants of us."

Mr. Colbrith was standing up in his place in the leading buckboard and making signals to the rear guard of two. Ford shook the reins over his broncos and drove around.

The president was fingering his thin beard and waving an arm toward the track-layers.

"Mr.—ah—Ford," he began critically, "is it necessary to have such a vast army of men as that to lay the track?"

"I don't think we are over-manned," said Ford good-naturedly. It was comparatively easy to be patient with Alicia looking on and listening.

But it was against Mr. Colbrith's principles to let a man off with a single rebuttal.

"I am not at all convinced of the worth of these new-fangled ideas, Mr. Ford; not at all. We built the Pacific Southwestern main line in the old, approved way—a rail at a time—with less than one-quarter of the men you have over there."

"I don't question it: and you were three years building some six hundred miles in a prairie country. We are to-day just six weeks out of Saint's Rest with the track gang, and in six more, if the weather holds, we shall be laying the switches in the Green Butte yards. That is the difference between the old way and the new."

The president was turned aside but not stopped.

"I understand," he objected raucously. "But your expense bills are something tremendous; tre-*men*dous, Mr. Ford! You have spent more money in three months than we spent in a full year on the main line."

"Quite likely," agreed Ford, losing interest in the pointless discussion. "But with us, time is an object; and we have the results to show for the expenditure."

At this, Mr. Colbrith took refuge in innuendo, as seemed to be his lately acquired habit.

"You are very ready with your answers, Mr. Ford; very ready, indeed. Let us see if you can continue as you have begun."

It was Miss Alicia who resented this final speech of the president's when the buckboards were once more in motion, following the unrailed grade around the swelling shoulders of the huge hills.

"I think that last remark of Uncle Sidney's was rather uncalled for," she said, after Ford had driven in grim silence at the tail of the procession for a full mile.

"It is one of a good many uncalled for things he has been saying to me since the day before yesterday," was Ford's rejoinder.

"Yet you can still assure me that you are not vindictive."

"I am not—at the mere actors in the play. But I confess to an unholy desire to get back at the prompter—the stage manager of the little comedy. I am only waiting for your decision."

"Please!" she said; and he saw that the blue eyes were growing wistful again.

"I'm done," he said quickly. "I shan't put it up to you any more. I'll do what I think I ought to do, on my own responsibility."

But now, woman-like, she crossed quickly to the other side.

"No; you mustn't deprive me of my chance," she protested soberly. "After a little while I shall tell you what I think—what I think you ought to do. Only you must give me time."

His smile came from the depths of a lover's heart.

"You shall have all the time there is—and then some, if I can compass it. Now let's talk about something else. I've been boring you with this despicable business affair ever since you gave me leave on that foot-race down Plug Mountain Tuesday afternoon."

"What shall it be?" she inquired gaily. And then: "Oh, I know. One day last summer—just as we were leaving Chicago in the Nadia— you had begun to tell me about a certain young woman who had money, and who was—who was—"

"—who was without her peer in all this world," he finished for her. "Yes; I remember."

"Do you still remember her, as you do the conversation?" she went on teasingly.

"I have never lost a day since I first met her."

"Good Sir Galahad!" she mocked. "And is she still worth all those sacrifices you said you would be willing to make for her?"

"All, and several more."

Silence for a little time, while the hoof-beats of a horse fox-trotting behind them drew nearer. It was the sinister-faced Mexican who ambled into view, and when he overtook the rearmost of the buckboards he was a long time in passing.

"That dreadful man!" murmured Alicia; and she did not go back to the suspended subject until he had trotted on past the caravan. Then she said slowly, taking her companion's complete understanding for granted: "It must be delicious to be away out over one's depth, like that!"

"It is," said Ford solemnly. "It's like—well, I've never been sick a day in my life since I can remember, but I should think it might be like a—a sort of beneficent fever, you know. Haven't you ever had a touch of it?"

"Possibly—without recognizing it. Can you describe the symptoms?"

"Accurately. One day I awoke suddenly to the realization that there was one woman, in the world: before that, you know, there had always been a good many, but never just one. Then I began to discover that this one woman was the embodiment of an ideal—my ideal. She said and did and looked all the things I'd been missing in the others. I wanted to drop everything and run after her."

"How absolutely idyllic!" she murmured. "And then?"

"Then I had to come down to earth with a dull, stunning swat, of course. There were a lot of commonplace, material things waiting to be done, and it was up to me to do them. Before I saw her, I used to think that nothing could divide time with a man's work: that there wouldn't be any time to divide. Afterward, I found out my mistake. Sleeping or waking, every day and all day, she was there: and the work went on just the same, or rather a whole lot better."

The long drive was in its final third, and the wagon track, which had transferred itself to the top of the level railroad grade, admitted speed. By degrees the caravan became elongated, with the president still in the lead, the man on horseback indifferently ahead or behind, and the other two vehicles wide apart and well to the rear. Their isolation was complete when she said:

"Do you want me to say that I don't recognize any of the symptoms, Mr. Ford?"

"Do I—No! Yes!—that is, I—Heavens! that is a terrible way to put it! Of course I hope—I hope you are in love—with the right person. If you're not, I—"

She was weeping silently; weeping because it would have been a sin to laugh.

"You—called it a comedy a little while—ago," she faltered. "In another minute it will be a tragedy. Don't you think we are getting too far behind the others?"

He whipped up obediently, but the horses were in no hurry. At the rounding of the next shouldering hill the railroad grade entered a high, broad valley, the swelling hills on either side dotted with the dumps and tunnel-openings of the Copah gold-diggers. Ford had not been through the upper part of the district since the previous summer of pathfindings, and at that time it was like a dozen other outlying and hardly accessible fields, scantily manned and languishing under the dry rot of isolation. But now—

He was looking curiously across at the opposing hillsides. Black dots, dozens of them, were moving from ledge to ledge, pausing here and there to ply pick and shovel. Now and then from some one of the dry arroyos came the echoes of a surface shot; dynamite cartridges thrust into the earth to clear away the drift to bed-rock. Ford called his companion's attention to the activities.

"See what it does to a mining country when a railroad comes within shouting distance," he said. "The last time I was over here, this valley was like a graveyard. Now you'd think the entire population of Copah was up here prospecting for gold."

"Is that what they are doing?" she asked. Then suddenly: "Where is your mine?—the mine with my name?"

He laughed.

"I told you the simple truth. I don't know where it is; though I suppose it is up this way somewhere. Yes, I remember, Grigsby said it was on Cow Mountain."

The hill on their side of the valley threw out a long, low spur and the railroad-grade driving track swept in a long curve around the spur and crossed over to the foot of a slope dotted with the digging manikins.

"By Jove!" said Ford, still wondering. "There are twice as many prospectors out here as there were inhabitants in Copah the last time I was over. The camp ought to vote bonds and give the railroad company a bonus."

Farther along, the grade hugged the hillside, skirting the acclivity where the shaft-houses of some of the older mines of the district were perched on little hillocks formed by their own dumps, within easy tramming distance of the railroad. Opposite and directly below the nearest of these shaft-houses the two leading buckboards had stopped; and the president was once more standing up and beckoning vigorously to the laggards in the single-seated vehicle.

Ford spoke to his horses and grimaced as one who swallows bitter herbs.

"I wonder what I've been doing now—or leaving undone?" he queried.

He was not kept long in suspense. When they drove up, the president was still standing, balancing himself with a hand on the driver's seat in front. His thin face was working nervously and the aggressive chin whiskers moved up and down like an accusing finger.

"Dear me!" said Alicia, under her breath; "Uncle Sidney is really angry, this time! What could have hap—" She glanced up at the mine buildings perched above the roadway and smothered a little cry. Ford's eyes followed hers. All across the slab-built shaft-house and the lean-to ore sheds was stretched a huge canvas sign. And in letters of bright blue, freshly painted and two feet high, ran the boastful legend:

THE LITTLE ALICIA MINE

THE ONLY PAYING PRODUCER IN THE DISTRICT

Stuart Ford & John Grigsby, Props.

The white-haired old man standing in the leading buckboard was trembling with righteous indignation. Pointing a shaking finger at the incriminating sign, he broke out in a storm of accusation.

"So, Mr. Ford! This is why you changed the route of the extension and added twelve miles to its length!" he raved. "This explains why you suddenly found the shorter route impracticable! Answer me sir: when did you become interested in this mine?"

There was a little stir of consternation among the listeners; and it did not help matters that the man on horseback ambled up at the moment and drew rein behind the doctor's vehicle. Ford's hands were gripping the reins until the stiff leathers were crumpled into strings; but it was Alicia's touch on his arm that enabled him to reply coldly:

"It was something over two months ago, I believe. I can give you the exact date when we reach Copah, though you will permit me to say that it is none of your business."

Mr. Colbrith exploded like a hastily fired bomb.

"I propose to make it some of my business! Was it before or after your purchase here that you decided upon the change of route? Answer me that, Mr. Ford!"

Ford wheeled his bronchos and closed the shouting gap.

"Sit down, Mr. Colbrith," he said half-menacingly. "If it is your purpose to humiliate me before your guests, I shall drive on and leave you."

"You don't answer my question; you can not answer it! You instructed your assistant to change the line of this railroad *after* you had bought this mine!"

"And if I did?"

"You did. And by so doing, Mr. Ford, you diverted the company's money to your own personal ends as wrongfully as if you had put your hands into the treasurer's strong-box. In other words, you became what you have accused others of being — a common grafter!"

Ford's face was very white, and his lips were drawn into thin lines when he opened them to reply. But the restraining hand was on his arm again, and he obeyed it.

"Answer me, sir! When did you become interested in this mine?"

"I don't care to talk with you, about this matter or any other, here and now. Later on, perhaps, when you can speak without being abusive, I shall take the liberty of telling you what I think of you." And at that, he gave his horses the rein and drove on, swiftly, abruptly, leaving the president and his guests to follow as they would.

For some minutes neither of the two in the flying buckboard could find words wherewith to bridge the miserable chasm so suddenly opened between them. Miss Alicia's eyes were tear-brightened and unfathomable; Ford's were hard, and there was a steely light in them. It was Alicia who spoke first.

"I know it is not true, of course—what Uncle Sidney accused you of," she offered. "But tell me how it happened?"

"I don't know—unless the devil planned it," said Ford bitterly. "I bought the mine one day last summer when I was in Copah, without premeditation, without seeing it—without knowing where it was situated, just as I have told you. Some little time afterward, Frisbie came to me with the plan for the change of route. I had considered it before, but had made no estimates. Frisbie had made the estimates, and we decided upon it at once. I haven't been over here since: it wasn't necessary, and I had other things to do."

"Did Mr. Frisbie know about your purchase of the mine?"

"No. I don't think he knows of it yet. To tell the truth, I was a little ashamed: it was a touch of the mining fever that everybody gets now and then in a mining country. Dick would have guyed me."

"But Mr. Frisbie must have been over the line a great many times: how could he miss seeing that enormous sign?" she persisted.

Ford shook his head.

"I venture to say that the paint isn't yet dry on that sign. It was put there for a purpose, and your uncle was told to look for it. Grigsby is just the sort of fool to jump at the chance to advertise the mine, and somebody suggested it and gave him the tip that the president of the railroad was coming in this way. Mr. North is a very careful man. He doesn't neglect any of the little details."

The high valley was falling away into a broken gulch, and the railway-grade driving-path clung closer to the hillsides. At the next turn the town of Copah came into view, and the road became a shelf on the slope two hundred feet above the main street and paralleling it. Alicia was looking down upon the town when she said:

"What shall you do?"

Ford's laugh was not mirthful.

"I have already done it. I shall perhaps be permitted to see you all safely back to the Nadia, and over the rough track to Saint's Rest. More than that I fancy Mr. Colbrith will not allow—and possibly not that much."

Miss Adair was still looking down upon the town; and now Ford looked. Instantly he saw that something unusual was going on. Notwithstanding the number of men afield on the hills, the main street of the camp was restlessly alive. Horsemen were galloping back and forth; in front of the outfitting stores freighters were hastily loading their pack animals; at every gathering place there were knots of excited men talking and gesticulating.

Ford was puzzled. At another time he would quickly have put the obvious two and two together to make the equally obvious four. But now he merely said: "That's curious; mighty curious. Where do you suppose all those people came from?"

Alicia's rejoinder was not an answer to the half-mechanical query.

"Mr. Ford, a little while ago I told you I must have time to consider: I—I have considered. You must fight for your life and your good name. You must make Uncle Sidney see things as they are—that they are not as he thinks they are."

"I can't," he said stubbornly. "Your condition reverses your decision. If I am to fight with any hope of winning, after what has transpired to-day, Mr. Colbrith will have to be eliminated."

He had pulled the broncos down to a walk. There was a soft thudding of hoofs on the yielding earth of the grade behind, but neither of them heard.

"You are disappointing me," she protested, and now the hesitation was all gone. "A few minutes ago, before this miserable thing happened, you were telling me of your ideal ... a woman may have an ideal, too, Mr. Ford."

"Yes?" he said eagerly.

"My ideal is the knight without fear and without reproach—and also without limitations. He will never say, 'I can not.' He will say, 'I will,' and not for my sake, but because his own sense of justice and mercy and loving-kindness will go hand in hand with his ambition."

"One word," he broke in passionately; and now the soft thudding of hoofs had drawn so near that the presence of the overtaking horseman might have been felt. "My little allegory didn't deceive you; you are the one woman, Alicia, dear. I didn't mean to tell you yet, though I think you have known it all along: I had an idea that I wanted to do something worthy—something big enough to be worth while—before I spoke. But you have given me leave; don't say you haven't given me leave!"

"You have taken it," she said softly, adding: "And that is what a woman likes, I think. But you mustn't spoil my ideal, Stuart—indeed, you mustn't. You are young, strong, invincible, as my knight should be. But when you strike you must also spare. You say there is no way save the one you have indicated; you must find a way."

He smiled ruefully.

"You give the cup of water only to take it away again. I'd rather build ten railroads than to attempt to smash North and his confederates through your uncle. You see, I'm frightfully handicapped right at the start—with this mine business hanging over me. But if you say it has to be done, it shall be. I'll win Mr. Colbrith over, in spite of all that has happened; and he shall fire North and the MacMorroghs first and prosecute them afterward. I've said it."

It was just here that the broncos shied—inward, toward the hill. Ford gathered the slack reins, and Miss Adair looked up and gave a little shriek. Noiselessly, and so close upon the buckboard that he might have touched either of its occupants with his rawhide quirt, rode the Mexican. When they discovered him he was leaning forward, his half-closed eyes mere slits with pin-points of black fire to mark them, and his repulsive face a stolid mask. Ford's hand went instinctively to the whip: it was the only available weapon. But the Mexican merely touched his flapping sombrero and rode on at the shuffling fox-trot.

"That man, again!" shivered Alicia, when the portent of evil had passed out of sight around the next curve in the grade.

But Ford's concern was deeper than her passing thrill of repulsion.

"Did you notice his horse's hoofs as he went by?" he asked soberly.

"No," she said.

"I did. He dismounted somewhere behind us and covered them with sacking."

"What for?" she asked, shivering again with the nameless dread.

"You recall what I was saying when the broncos shied: his object was to creep up behind us and listen. He has done it more than once since we left the end-of-track, and this time—"

"Yes?"

"This time he heard what he wanted to hear."

Beyond the curve which had hidden the Mexican, the wagon-road left the grade, descending abruptly upon the town. Ford looked back from the turn and saw that the other two vehicles were not yet in sight.

"Shall we wait for your aunt and the others?" he asked.

Her smile was a sufficient reward for the bit of tactful forethought.

"I'm sure we have left the conventions far enough behind not to be unduly terrified by them. I am not afraid to go in unchaperoned. Besides, I heard Uncle Sidney telling Doctor Van Bruce that our rooms at the hotel had been engaged for us."

Ford drove carefully down the steep side street which was the approach to the hotel. An excited throng blocked the sidewalk, and the lobby seemed to be a miniature stock exchange. Single-eyed, Ford fought a passage through the crowd with Alicia on his arm, heeding nothing until he had seen her safely above stairs and in the sitting-room of the president's reservation, with a cheerful fire in the big sheet-iron stove for her comforting. Then he went down and elbowed his way through the clamorous lobby to the clerk's desk.

"Suppose you take a minute or two off and tell me what this town has gone crazy about, Hildreth," he said, with a backward nod toward the lobby pandemonium.

"Why, Great Scott! Mr. Ford—have you got this far into it without finding out?" was the astounded rejoinder. "It's a gold strike on Cow Mountain—the biggest since Cripple Creek! We've doubled our population since seven o'clock this morning; and by this time to-morrow.... Say, Mr. Ford; for heaven's sake, get your railroad in here! We'll all go hungry within another twenty-four hours—can't get supplies for love or money!"

Ford turned away and looked out upon the stock-selling pandemonium with unseeing eyes. The chance—the heaven-sent hour that strikes only once in a life-time for the builders of empire—had come: and he was only waiting for the arrival of the president to find himself rudely thrust aside from the helm of events.

XXIII
THE DEADLOCK

"No, Mr. Ford; there is no explanation that will explain away the incriminating fact. This is a matter which involves the good name of the Pacific Southwestern company, through its officials, and I must insist upon your resignation."

The battle was on, with the two combatants facing each other in the privacy of the president's room in the Copah hotel. Since Alicia had made him exchange the sword of extermination for the olive branch, Ford was fighting on the defensive, striving good-naturedly and persistently to keep his official head on his shoulders.

"I've admitted that it looks pretty bad, Mr. Colbrith; but you will concede the one chance in a hundred that no wrong was intended. I merely did, on the ground, what thousands of investors in mining chances do the world over—bought an interest in a mine without knowing or caring greatly into what particular mountain the mine tunnel was driven."

Mr. Colbrith frowned. He was of that elder generation of masters which looked with cold disapproval upon any side ventures on the part of the subordinate.

"The company has paid you liberally for your time and your undivided attention, Mr. Ford. No man can serve two masters. Your appointment as assistant to the president did not contemplate your engaging in other business."

Ford carefully suppressed the smile which the bit of industrial martinetry provoked.

"As to that," he said placably, "I can assure you that the gold-digging has been purely an investment on my part."

"But an investment which you should not have made," insisted the president judicially. "If it had not tempted you to the breach of trust, it was still inexpedient—most undeniably inexpedient. An official high in the counsels of a great corporation should be like Cæsar's wife—above suspicion."

This time Ford's smile could not be wholly repressed. "I grant you it was foolhardy, in the economic point of view," he confessed. "I took a long chance of going ten thousand dollars to the bad. But mine-buying is a disease—as contagious as the measles. Everybody in a mining country takes a flyer, at least once. The experienced ones will tell you that nobody is immune. Take your own case, now: if you don't keep a pretty tight hold on your check-book, Mr. Colbrith, Cow Mountain will—"

The president frowned again; more portentously, this time.

"This levity is most reprehensible, Mr. Ford," he said stiffly. "I trust I know my duty as the head of a great railway company too well to be carried away on every baseless wave of excitement that fires the imagination of the mining-camp I chance to be visiting." Mr. Colbrith was not above mixing metaphor when the provocation was sufficiently great.

"Baseless?" echoed Ford. "Surely you don't doubt ... Why, Mr. Colbrith, this strike is the biggest thing that has happened in the mining world since the discovery of the wedge-veins in Cripple Creek!"

The president shrugged his thin shoulders as one whose mission in life is to be sturdily conservative after all the remainder of mankind has struck hands with frenzied optimism.

"Nonsense!" he rasped contemptuously. "What happens? Two men come to town with certain rich specimens which they claim to have taken out of their prospect hole on Cow Mountain. That was at seven o'clock last night, less than twenty-four hours ago, and some two or three thousand lunatics have already rushed here in the belief—

founded upon a mere boast, it may be—that a great gold reef underlies Cow Mountain. By this time to-morrow—"

Ford took him up promptly. "Yes; and by this time to-morrow the Denver Mining Exchange will be howling itself hoarse over Copah mining shares, like those curb-stone fellows down-stairs; the hunt will be up, and every feeder the Pacific Southwestern system has will be sending its quota of gold-seekers to the new field. That isn't what you were going to say, I know; but it is what is going to happen. Mr. Colbrith, it's the chance of a century for the Pacific Southwestern company, and you are deliberately trying to fire the one man who can make the most of it."

The president's lack of sense of humor made it hard for him at times. He was sitting very erect in the straight-backed hotel chair when he said: "Mr. Ford, there are occasions when your conceit is insufferable. Do you imagine for a moment that you are the only engineer in the United States who can build railroads, Sir?"

"Oh, no."

"Then perhaps you will be good enough to explain your meaning?"

"It was a poor attempt at a jest," said the young man, rather lamely. "Yet it had the truth behind it, in a way. I predict that this is the beginning of one of the biggest mining rushes the world ever saw. We are within one hundred and forty miles of Copah with a practicable railroad; we are within twelve miles with a track which must be made practicable while the band plays. If you discharge your entire engineering corps at this crisis—"

"I beg your pardon," interrupted the president crustily. "I have not asked your force to resign."

"Not meaning to, perhaps," countered the young man, maliciously rejoicing in the hope that he had found one vulnerable link in the president's coat of mail. "But if I go, the entire department will go. Every man in it is my friend, as well as my subordinate; and they know very well that if they shouldn't go, your new chief would fire them and put in his own men."

"Ha!" said the president, straightening up again. "Am I to understand that you are threatening me, Mr. Ford."

"No, indeed; I am only stating a fact. But it is a pretty serious fact. Let us suppose, for the sake of the argument, that my prediction comes true; that within thirty-six or forty-eight hours Saint's Rest is packed with people trying to get to Copah. Your new chief, if you shall have found him, will hardly be in the saddle. When he comes he will have to reorganize the department, break in new men, learn by hard knocks what I have been learning in detail—"

Mr. Colbrith thrust out a thin lip of obstinate determination.

"And if he does, your hypothetical rush will simply have to wait, Mr. Ford. We have the key to the Copah door."

"Don't you fool yourself!" snapped Ford, forgetting his rôle of the humble one for the moment. "The Transcontinental is only forty miles away at Jack's Canyon, with a pretty decent stage road. Long before you can get the extension in shape to carry passengers, or even freight, the other line will be known from Maine to California as the keyholder to this district!"

That shot told. The president was not yet convinced that the Copah boom was real; but there was the chance that it might be—always the chance. And to the over-cautious the taking of chances, however remote, is like the handling of a snake: a thing to inspire creeping horrors.

"If you could convince me, Mr. Ford, that your interest in that mine did not influence you in changing the route of the extension," he began; but Ford took him up sharply. "I can't; and I can say no more than I have said."

Mr. Colbrith got up and went to the window to look down upon the excited throng in the street. It did look real.

"Perhaps we might leave matters as they are, pending a future investigation, Mr. Ford," he said, turning back to his victim, who was methodically clipping the end from a cigar.

"No," was the brittle rejoinder.

Again the president took time to look down into the crowded street. His next attack was from the rear.

"But I have understood that you do not wish to resign. Let us be magnanimous, Mr. Ford, and agree to hang this matter up until this supposed crisis is past."

"No," was the curt reply. "I have changed my mind. I don't think I want to work for you any longer, Mr. Colbrith."

"Not if I withdrew my—ah—objections?"

"No."

Silence again. The packed lobby of the hotel had overflowed upon the plank sidewalk, and the din of the buyers and sellers rose like the noise of a frantic street fight. Ford's half jesting remark about the possibility of the microbe finding its way into the blood of the president was not so pointless as the old man's retort sought to make it appear. It was the wheat pit which had given Mr. Colbrith his first half-million; and as he listened to the hoarse cries, the thing which he hoped was safely caution-killed began to stir within him. Suddenly he picked a word of two out of the sidewalk clamor that made him turn swiftly upon the silent young man.

"They are selling 'Little Alicia'—your stock—down there!" he gasped. "Have you—have you—"

"No; I haven't put mine on the market. It's some of my partner's, Grigsby's, stock. I suppose he couldn't stand the push."

Once more the president listened. Only an ex-wrestler in the wheat pit could have picked intelligence out of the Babel of puts and calls.

"It's up to a hundred and fifty!" he exploded. "What did you pay for your shares, Mr. Ford?"

"Twenty," said Ford coolly.

"Good Heavens! I—I hope you hold a safe majority?"

"No; we broke even, Grigsby and I. I have fifty per cent."

The president groaned.

"I—I'll excuse you, Mr. Ford. Get down there at once and buy that other necessary share!"

Ford shook his head with predetermined gloom. "No, Mr. Colbrith, I'm not buying any more mining stock. What I did buy seems to have cost me my job."

"But, my dear young man! This is a crisis. You are likely to lose control of your property! Or, at least, it is soaring to a point at which you will never be able to secure the control."

Ford came up smiling. "You forget that this is mere mad excitement, Mr. Colbrith," he said, handing back the President's own phrase. "To-morrow, I dare say, I shall be able to buy at twenty again."

The president came away from the window and sat down. His face was twitching and the thin white hands were tremulous.

"There may be more in this gold discovery than I have been willing to admit," he said abstractedly, "and in that case ... Mr. Ford, upon what terms will you consent to go on and whip this line of ours into shape?"

Ford came out of the fog of discouragement with a bound.

"A complete change in the management of the Pacific Southwestern, Mr. Colbrith. North and his grafters must go."

The President did not fly into wrathful shards, as Ford fully expected. On the contrary, he was fingering the white goat's-beard with one nervous hand, and apparently listening half-absently to the clamor in the street.

"Don't be unreasonable, Mr. Ford," he said quite mildly. "You know we can't consider anything like that at the present moment."

"It must be considered," Ford persisted. "Ever since I quit being a division superintendent, North has obstructed, lied about me, fought me. The time has come when, if I stay, I must have a free hand. I can't have it while he is out of jail."

"That is strong language to apply to our first vice-president, Mr. Ford. And I can only believe that you are prejudiced — unduly prejudiced. But all this may be taken up later. As you suggest, we may be losing very precious time."

Ford got to his feet.

"Promise me that you will give the Denver management as thorough an investigation as you have given me, Mr. Colbrith; do that, and give me absolute authority over the MacMorroghs and their men for one week; and before the week's end we'll be hauling passengers and freight into Copah over our own rails."

For a moment the president seemed to be on the point of yielding. Then his habitual caution thrust out its foot and tripped him.

"I can't be pushed, Mr. Ford," he complained, with a return of the irritated tone. "Let the matter rest for the present. And—and you may consider yourself relieved from duty until I have gone a little deeper into these charges against you. Mr. North accuses you, and you accuse Mr. North. I must have time to approach those matters deliberately. I don't know which of you to trust."

It was a deadlock. Ford bowed and laid his hand on the door.

"You are still the president of the Pacific Southwestern, Mr. Colbrith, and while you remain president—"

The old man's pride of office took fire like tow in a furnace.

"What do you mean by that, Mr. Ford? Make yourself clear, sir!" he quavered.

"I mean just this: if your niece, Miss Alicia Adair, hadn't been good enough to say that she will be my wife, I'd carry this thing up to the board of directors and do my level best to have you put where you could do the least harm."

"You? Alicia?" the old man shrilled. And then, in an access of senile rage that shook him like a leaf in the wind: "I said you were suspended—you are discharged, sir—here and now! If you give another order as an official of the Pacific Southwestern company, I'll—I'll put you through the courts for it!"

Ford opened the door and went out, leaving the president clutching his chair with one hand and balling the other into a shaking fist. The die was cast, and he had thrown a blank at the very moment when the game seemed to be turning his way. What would Alicia say?

As if the unspoken query had evoked her, the door of her room opened silently and she stood before him in the corridor.

"Tell me," she commanded.

"We have fought it out, and I've had my beating," he said soberly. "When I thought I had him fairly down,—he was actually begging me to stay on with the company,—we got tangled up again over North, and he fired me bodily."

"Did you—did you tell him about our—"

"Yes; and that was what set off the final fireworks."

She put her hands on his shoulders and made him face her squarely.

"Stuart, did you lose your temper?"

"I—I'm afraid I did—just at the last, you know. It's simply an unspeakable state of affairs, Alicia, dear! At a moment when we should be setting the whole world afire in a superhuman effort to flog this piece of construction track into shape, your uncle paralyzes everything!"

The constraining touch of her hands became almost a caress. "What shall you do, Stuart? Is there nothing to be done?"

He took his resolution on the spur of the moment.

"Yes, thank heaven! Your uncle has got to find a printing press, or at least a telegraph wire, before he can make my discharge effective. Before he can do that, or until he does it, I'm going to pull the throttle wide open and race that discharge circular, if I go to jail for it, afterward! Who knows but I shall have time to save the day for the company after all? Good-by, dearest. In twenty minutes I shall be riding for the MacMorroghs' camp, and when I get there—"

"You are going to ride back?—alone? Oh, no, no!" she protested; and the clinging arms held him.

"Why, Alicia, girl—see here: what do you imagine could happen to me? Why, bless your loving heart, I've been tramping and riding this desert more or less for two years! What has come over you?"

"I don't know; but—but—oh, me! you will think I am miserably weak and foolish: but just as you said that, I seemed to see you lying in the road with your horse standing over you—and you were—dead!"

"Nonsense!" he comforted. "I'll be back here to-morrow, alive and well; but I mustn't lose a minute now. It's up to me to reach Horse Creek before the news of the gold strike gets there. There'll be a stampede, with every laborer on the line hoofing it for Copah. Good-by, sweetheart, and—may I?" He took her face between his hands and did it anyhow.

Five minutes later he was bargaining for a saddle horse at the one livery stable in the camp, offering and paying the selling price of the animal for the two days' hire. It was a rather sorry mount at that, and when he was dragging it out into the street, Jack Benson, the youngest member of his staff, rode up, that moment in from the tie-camp above Cow Mountain.

"Don't dismount, Jack," he ordered curtly. "You're just in time to save me eight or ten miles, when the inches are worth dollars. Ride for the end-of-track and Frisbie on a dead run. Tell Dick to hold his men, if he has to do it at the muzzle of a gun, and to come on with the track, night and day. He'll have to raise the pay, and keep on raising it—but that's all right. It's an order. Rush it!"

Benson nodded, set his horse at the path leading up to the railroad grade, and spurred up the hill. Ford gave a final tug at his saddle cinches, put up a leg and began to pick his way down the thronged street in the opposite direction.

Thirty seconds afterward a man wearing the laced trousers and broad bullion-corded sombrero of a Mexican dandy came out of his hiding-place behind the door of the livery stable office, thoughtfully twirling the cylinder of a drawn revolver.

"I take-a da mustang," he said to the boy who had held Ford's horse during the short interview with Benson. And when the bronco was brought out, the Mexican, like Ford, looked to the cinches, mounted, and rode down the street leading to the lower mesa and the river.

XXIV
RUIZ GREGORIO

He rode easily, as one born to the saddle, the leathers creaking musically under him to keep time to the shuffling fox-trot of the wiry little range pony. Once free of the mining-camp and out upon the mesa, he found a corn-husk wrapper and his bag of dry tobacco and deftly rolled a cigarette, doing it with one hand, cow-boy fashion. When the cigarette was lighted, the horseman ahead was a mere khaki-colored dot, rising and falling in the mellowing distance.

With the eye of a plainsman he measured the trail's length to the broken hill range where the Pannikin emerges from its final wrestle with the gorges. Then he glanced up at the dull crimson spot in the murky sky that marked the sun's altitude. There was time sufficient—and the trail was long enough. He did not push his horse out of the shuffling trot. At the portal hills the horseman now disappearing over the rim of the high mesa would slacken speed. In the canyon itself a dog could not go faster than a walk.

On the lower mesa the Mexican picked up the galloping dot again, holding it in view until it halted on the river bank a hundred yards below the entrance to the canyon. Since the water was low in the ford, the river bank hid the crossing, and the Mexican drew rein and waited for the dot to reappear on the opposite shore.

A slow minute was lost; then a second and a third. The man in the corded sombrero and laced buckskins touched his horse's flank with a spur and crept forward at a walk, keeping his eyes fixed upon the point where the quarry ought to come in sight again. When three more minutes passed and the farther shore was still a deserted blank, the Mexican dug both rowels into his mustang and galloped down to the river, muttering curses in the *patois* of his native Sonora.

Apparently the closing in had been delayed too long. There were fresh hoof-prints in the marl of the hither approach to the shallow ford, but none to match them on the farther side. The Mexican crossed hastily and searched for the outcoming hoof-marks. The rocky bar which formed the northern bank of the stream told him nothing.

Now it is only in the imagination of the word-smith that the villain in the play is gifted with supernatural powers of discernment. Ruiz Gregorio Maria y Alvarez Mattacheco, familiarly and less cumbrously known as "Mexican George," was a mere murderer, with a quick eye for gun-sights and a ready and itching trigger finger. But he was no Vidoeq, to know by instinct which of the two trails, the canyon passage or the longer route over the hills, Ford had chosen.

Having two guesses he made the wrong one first, urging his mustang toward the canyon trail. A stumbling half-mile up the narrow cleft of the river's path revealing nothing, he began to reconsider. Drawing a second blank of the same dimensions, he turned back to the ford and tried the hill trail. At the end of the first hundred yards on the new scent he came again upon the fresh hoof-prints, and took off the brow-cramping hat to swear the easier.

Two courses were now open to him; to press hard upon the roundabout hill trail in the hope of overtaking the engineer before he could reach the Horse Creek camp, or to pass by the shorter route to the upper ford to head him off at the river crossing. The Mexican gave another glance at the dull red spot in the western sky and played for safety. The waylaying alternative commended itself on several counts. The canyon trail was the shorter and it could be traversed leisurely and in daylight. Pressing his livery hack as he could, Ford would scarcely reach the crossing at the mouth of Horse Creek before dusk. Moreover, it would be easier to wait and to smoke than to chase the quarry over the hills, wearing one's pinto to the bone.

Ruiz Gregorio Maria set his horse once more at the task of picking a path among the canyon boulders, riding loosely in the saddle, first in one stirrup and then in the other, and smoking an unbroken succession of the corn-husk cigarettes.

One small cloud flecked the sky of satisfaction. His instructions had been explicit. If Ford should resign, quit, wash his hands of the Pacific Southwestern, he might be suffered to escape. If not—there was only one condition attached to the alternative: what was done must be done neatly, with despatch, and at a sufficient distance from any of the MacMorrogh camps to avert even the shadow of suspicion.

Now the upper crossing of waylayings was within a stone's throw of the end-of-track yards; nay, within an amateur's pistol-shot of the commissary buildings. But Ruiz Gregorio, weighing all the possibilities, found them elastic enough to serve the purpose. A well-calculated shot from behind a sheltering boulder, the heaving of the body into the swift torrent of the Pannikin, and the thing was done. What damning evidence might afterward come to the light of day, if, indeed, it should ever come to light, would be fished out of the stream far enough from any of the MacMorrogh camps.

Thus Ruiz Gregorio Maria y Alvarez, lolling lazily in his saddle while the hard-breathing mustang picked a toilsome path among the strewn boulders and through the sliding shale beds. He went even further: an alibi might not be needful, but it would be easy to provide one. Young Jack Benson, if no other, would know that Ford had taken one of the shorter trails from Copah to the camp at Horse Creek. *Bueno!* He, Ruiz Gregorio, could slip across the river in the dusk when the thing was done, skirt the headquarters camp unseen, and present himself a little later at Señor Frisbie's camp of the track-layers, coming, as it were, direct from Copah, almost upon the heels of Señor Benson. After that, who could connect him with the dead body of a man fished out of a river twenty, fifty, a hundred miles away?

There was a weak link in the chain. Ruiz Gregorio's child-like plot turned upon one pivot of hazard—hazard most likely to be ignored by so good a marksman as the "man-killer." One shot he might permit himself, with little danger of drawing a crowd from the mess tent and the sleeping shanties in the Horse Creek camp. Two would bring the men to their doors. Any greater number would be taken as the signal of a free fight needing spectators. Hence the first shot must suffice.

The Mexican bore this in mind when, arriving at his post opposite the camp in the early dusk, he chose his ambushing boulder so near the descending hill trail that a stout club might have been substituted for the pistol. The weather promise was for a starless night, but the electric arc-lights were already scintillating at their mastheads in the headquarters railroad yard across the Pannikin. Later, when the daylight was quite gone and the electrics were hollowing out a bowl of stark whiteness in the night, Ruiz Gregorio wished he had chosen otherwise. The camp lights shone full upon him and on the mustang standing with drooped head at his elbow, and the trail on the other side of the boulder was in shadow.

He was about to take the risk of moving farther up the hill-path to a less exposed lurking place, was hesitating only because his indolent soul rebelled at the thought of having to drag Ford's body so many added steps to its burial in the river, when the clink of shod hoofs upon stone warned him that the time for scene-shifting had passed. Pushing the mustang out of the line of sight from the trail, he flattened himself against the great rock and waited.

Ford rode down the last declivity cautiously, for his horse's sake. The trail came out of the hills abruptly, dropping into the rock-strewn river valley within hailing distance of the camp. Well within the sweep of the masthead lights across the stream, the boulder-strewn flat was as light as day, save where the sentinel rocks flung their shadows; and promptly at the first facing of the bright electrics, Ford's horse stumbled aside from the path and began to take short cuts between the thick-standing boulders for the river. This was how the Mexican, instead of having his victim at a complete disadvantage, found himself suddenly uncovered by the flank, exposed, recognized, and hailed in no uncertain tones.

"Hello, Mattacheco! what are you doing here?" Ford had a flash-light picture of the horse standing with his muzzle to the ground; of the man flattened against the rock. Then he saw the dull gleam of the lights upon blued metal. "You devil!" he shouted; and unarmed as he was, spurred his tired beast at the assassin.

Here, then, was the weak link in Ruiz Gregorio's chain twisted to the breaking point at the very outset. Instead of taking a deliberate pot-shot at an unsuspecting victim, he was obliged to face about, to fire hastily at a charging enemy, and to spring nimbly aside to save himself from being ridden down. The saving jump was an awkward one: it brought him into breath-taking collision with the upjerking head of the mustang. When he had recovered his feet and his presence of mind, the charging whirlwind had dashed through the shallows of the Pannikin, and a riderless horse was clattering across the tracks in the railroad yard.

The Mexican waited prudently to see what the camp would say to the single shot. It said nothing; it might have been deserted for all the indications there were of life in it. Ruiz Gregorio snapped the empty shell from his weapon, replacing it with a loaded one, and mounted and rode slowly through the ford. The riderless horse disappearing across the tracks gave him good hope that the hasty shot had accomplished all that a deliberate one might have.

There was no dead man tumbled in a heap in the railroad yard, as he had hoped to find. Silence, the silence of desertion, brooded over the masthead arcs. Painfully the Mexican searched, at the verge of the river, in the black shadows cast by the crowding material cars. Finally he crossed over to the straggling street of the camp, walking now and leading the spent mustang. Silence here, too, broken only by the sputtering sizzle of the electrics. The huge mess tent was dark; there were no lights, save in the closed commissary and in the president's car: no lights, and not a man of the camp's crowding labor army to be seen.

At a less strenuous moment the man-killer would have been puzzled by the unusual stillness and the air of desertion. As it was, he was alertly probing the far-flung shadows. The engineer, if only wounded, would doubtless try to hide in the shadows in the railroad yard.

The Mexican left his horse in the camp street and made an instant search between and under the material cars, coming out now and again to stare suspiciously at the president's private car, standing alone on the siding directly opposite the commissary. The Nadia was occupied. It was lighted within, and the window shades were drawn down. Ruiz Gregorio could never get far from the lighted car without being irresistibly drawn back to it, and finally he darted back in time to see a man rise up out of the shadow of the nearest box-car, spring to the platform of the Nadia and kick lustily at the locked door. The door was opened immediately by some one within, and the fugitive plunged to cover—but not before the Mexican's revolver had barked five times with the rapid staccato of a machine gun.

When Ruiz Gregorio, dropping the smoking weapon into its holster, would have mounted to put into instant action the plan of the well-considered alibi, a barrel-bodied figure launched itself from the commissary porch, and a vigorous hand dragged horse and man into the shadow of the stables.

"Off wid you now, you blunderin' dago divvle!" gritted the MacMorrogh savagely. "It's all av our necks ye've put into a rope, this time, damn you!"

The Mexican had dismounted and was calmly reloading his pistol.

"You t'ink-a he's not-a sufficiently kill? I go over to da car and bring-a you da proof, *si*?"

"You'll come wid me," raved the big contractor. "'Tis out av your clumsy hands, now, ye black-hearted blunderin' cross betune a Digger Indian and a Mexican naygur! Come on, I say!"

The back room of the commissary to which the MacMorrogh led the way held three men; Eckstein, and the two younger members of the contracting firm. They had heard the fusillade in the camp street and were waiting for news. Brian MacMorrogh gave it, garnished with many oaths.

"The pin-brained omadhaun av a Mexican has twishted a rope for all av us! He's let Ford come back, alive; let him get to the very dure av the prisident's car! Then, begorra! he must mades show himself under the electhrics and open fire on the man who was kicking at the dure and looking sthraight at him!"

Eckstein asked a single question.

"Did he get him? If he's dead he can't very well tell who shot him."

"That's the hell av it!" raged the big man. "Who's to know?"

Eckstein spat out the extinct cigar stump he was chewing.

"We are to know—beyond a question of doubt, this time. Who is in the Nadia, besides Ford?"

"The two naygurs."

"No one else?"

MacMorrogh shook his head. "No wan."

"You are sure Mr. Adair and Brissac are out of the way?"

"They got Gallagher to push them up to Frisbie's track camp in Misther North's car an hour before dark."

"None of your men are likely to drift in from the other way up the line?"

"Not unless somebody carries the news av the gold sthrike—and there's nobody going that way to carry it. The camp's empty but for us."

Eckstein rose and buttoned his coat.

"You have held your own strikers—the men you can depend upon: how many do we count, all told?"

"Thirteen, counting the five av us here, and the felly that runs the electhric light plant."

"H'm; it's a hell of a risk: thirteen men knowing what only one should know—and what that one should hurry to forget. But your butter-fingered Mexican has left us no choice. Ford knows enough now to send some of us over the road for life. If he got into that car alive, he must never come out of it alive."

Brian MacMorrogh had unlocked a cupboard in the corner of the room. It was a well-filled gun-rack, and he was passing the Winchesters out to his brothers.

"'Tis so," he said briefly. Then: "There's the two naygurs in the car: what av thim, Misther Eckstein?"

Eckstein took one of the guns and emptied the magazine to make sure of the loading.

"We are thirteen to one; the negroes don't count," he replied coldly. "Call in your men and we'll go and do what's got to be done."

XXV
THE SIEGE OF THE NADIA

With a horse that could have been handled Ford would not have run away when the charge upon the Mexican failed of its purpose. So far from it, he tried to wheel and charge again while the man was reeling from his collision with the rearing mustang.

But the bronco from the Copah stable, with the flash and crash of the pistol-shot to madden it, took the bit between its teeth and bolted — safely through the shallows of the stream crossing and up to the level of the railroad yard beyond, but swerving aside at the first of the car shadows to fling its rider out of the saddle. Ford gathered himself quickly and rolled under a car. His right arm had no feeling in it, whether from the shot or the fall he could not determine.

The numbness had become a prickling agony when he heard the Mexican splashing through the river to begin his search. Ford's field of vision was limited by the car trucks, but he kept the man in sight as he could. It filled him with sudden and fiery rage to be hunted thus like a defenseless animal, and more than once he was tempted to make a dash for the engineers' quarters on the hillside above the commissary—a rifle being the thing for which he hungered and thirsted.

But to show himself under the lights was to invite the fate he had so narrowly escaped. He knew Mattacheco's skill as a marksman: the Mexican would not be rattled twice in the same half-hour. Ford gripped the benumbed arm in impotent writhings.

"Now, by recognizing him, I've fixed it so that he is obliged to kill me," he muttered. "It's my life, or his neck for a halter, and he knows it. The blood-thirsty devil! If I could only get to Brissac's bunk-shanty and lay my hands on a gun ..."

There seemed to be no chance of doing that most desirable thing. The Mexican was now afoot and coursing the railroad yard like a baffled hound. Ford saw that it was only a question of minutes until his impromptu hiding-place would be discovered, and he began to look for another. The Nadia was but a short distance away, and the lighted deck transoms beckoned him.

It was instinct rather than intention that made him duck and plunge headlong through the suddenly opened door of the private car at the glimpse of his pursuer standing beside his horse in the open camp street. This was why the pistol barked harmlessly. Springing to his feet, and leaving the frightened negro who had admitted him trying to barricade the door with cushions from the smoking-room seats, Ford burst into the lighted central compartment.

It was not empty, as he had expected to find it. Two men, startled by the shots and the crash of breaking glass, were prepared to grapple him. It was Brissac, the invalided assistant, who cried, "Hold on, Mr. Adair—it's Ford, and he's hurt!"

Ford met the involuntary rush, gathered the two in his uncrippled arm and dragged them to the floor.

"That's in case my assassin takes a notion to turn loose on the windows," he panted. Then he gasped out his story while Brissac got the aching right arm out of its sleeve and looked for the injury.

Adair listened to the story of the attempted murder awe-struck, as one from the civilized East had a right to be.

"By Jove!" he commented; "I thought I had bumped into all the different varieties of deviltry since I left Denver yesterday morning, but this tops 'em. Actually tried to kill you in cold blood? But what for, Stuart?—for heaven's sake, what for?"

"Because he was hired to: because his masters, the MacMorroghs, and their master, North, have staked their roll on this last turn of the cards. I know too much, Adair. The president was sent over here to get rid of me. That failing, word was passed down the line that I was to be effaced. A few hours ago this Mexican overheard me telling your sister what I proposed to do to North and the MacMorroghs. That's why he—Ouch! Roy; that is my arm you're trying to twist out of joint, man!"

"It's all right," laughed the Louisianian; "it is only a crazy-bone bump that you got when the bronc' threw you. Say, Ford; I thought you claimed to know how to ride a horse!"

Adair was feeling in his pockets for the inevitable cigarette case.

"What he overheard you telling Alicia?" he mused. "I'm evidently two or three chapters behind. But no matter; this is the now; the very immediate now. Will your assassin keep on feeling for you?"

Ford shook his head. "Not any more just at present, I guess. He has waited too long. That fusillade of his will have turned the entire camp out by this time, and the Macs don't want any inconvenient witnesses."

"Witnesses?" echoed Adair. "Then you don't know—Say, Stuart; there isn't a white man in this camp besides us three—unless you count the MacMorroghs and their commissary garrison as white men. News of the great gold strike got here about three o'clock, and every laborer within hearing of it shouldered pick and shovel and lined out up the new track for Copah."

"What!" shouted Ford. "And these dash-*dashed* MacMorroghs didn't try to hold them?"

"I don't know about that. I had Mr. Brissac, here, over in the '01'—I came across the mountain in North's car, you know—dosing him with things out of Doctor Van Bruce's traveling case, and trying to get him in shape to show me the way to Copah. After the stampede, which took all the four-legged horses as well as the two-legged asses, I persuaded your man Gallagher to hitch his engine to our car to drag us up to Frisbie's camp at the front. I thought Frisbie would probably be in communication with you. Gallagher's intentions were good, but about three miles up Horse Creek he ditched the car so thoroughly that we couldn't inhabit it; so we got out and walked back."

"All of which brings on more talk," said Ford gravely. "From what you say, I gather that the MacMorroghs are still here. Did any one see you come back?"

"I don't know. It was after dark when we straggled in, and we didn't ring any bells or blow any whistles."

Ford stood up.

"Does either one of you happen to have anything bigger than a pocket-knife in the way of a weapon?" he asked.

"Why? what are you going to do?" Adair demanded.

"I am going to separate you two from my highly dangerous presence," said Ford definitely. "The MacMorroghs' outfit of a dozen or fifteen cutthroat scoundrels, captained, for the moment, by Eckstein, North's right-hand man, are doubtless just across the way in the back room of the commissary. You say the camp is otherwise deserted: the MacMorroghs don't know that you are here; and they do know that I am, dead or alive. Moreover, Mattacheco has doubtless told them by this time that I saw and recognized him. Wherefore, it's up to them to see that I never get a chance to go before a grand jury."

"You sit down on the floor," said Adair. He had found a cigarette and was crimping the end of it. "Have you a fraction of an idea that we are going to allow you to make a Jonah of yourself for us? Sit down, I say! Who's got a gun?"

Brissac had crept to a window and was reconnoitering the deserted camp street and the commissary through a peephole in the drawn shade. As Adair spoke, he sprang back, tripped Ford and fell with him, crying:

"Down! both of you!"

At the cry there was a shot from without, and a window on the exposed side of the Nadia fell in shivers. There were yells of terror from the cook's pantry, and the two negroes came crawling through the side vestibule, their eyes like saucers and their teeth chattering. Ford jumped up and turned off the Pintsch lights; and he was barely down again when another shot broke a second window.

"Wouldn't that jolt you?" said Adair. "They are feeling for you with both hands. What a heaven's pity it is that we haven't so much as a potato popgun among us to talk back with. What did you see, Mr. Brissac?"

"A crowd of them bunched on the commissary porch. One of them was sighting a Winchester at the car when I got busy."

Adair was again lamenting the lack of arms when the negro porter produced a pocket bulldog pistol of the cheap and uncertain sort. "Y-y-y-yah you is, Mistuh Charles," he stuttered.

"Ah, Williams—concealed weapons? That is fifty dollars fine in your native Tennessee, isn't it?" Then to Brissac: "Please go to the farther window and mark down for me, Mr. Brissac. I don't like to have those fellows do all the bluffing."

While the assistant was complying, a third bullet from the commissary porch tore high through the car, smashing one of the gas globes. Adair crawled to a broken window and the cheap revolver roared like an overloaded musket.

"Good shot!" said Brissac, from his marking post. "You got one of them: he's down and they're dragging him inside. Now they have all ducked to cover."

"That settles any notion of a palaver and the pipe of peace, I guess," said Adair, as indifferently as if he had just brought down a clay pigeon. "Prophesy, Stuart: what comes next?"

Ford shook his head.

"They can't quit now till they are sure I am permanently obliterated; they have gone too far. They'll credit me with that shot of yours, and they will take it as a pretty emphatic proof that I still live. Hence, more war."

"Well, what do we do? You are the captain."

"Picket the car and keep a sharp lookout for the next move. Brissac, you take the forward end, and I'll take the rear platform. Adair, post your Africans in here where they'll do the most good, and see that they don't go to sleep on their jobs."

The disposition of forces was quickly made, after which suspense set in. Silence and the solitude of the deserted camp reigned unbroken; yet the watchers knew that the shadows held determined enemies, alertly besieging the private car. To prove it, Adair pulled down a portière, gave it bulk with a stuffing of berth pillows, and dropped the bundle from one of the shattered windows. Three jets of fire belched from the nearest shadow, and the dummy was riddled. Adair fired at one of the flashes, resting the short-barreled pistol across the window ledge, and the retaliatory shot brought Ford hurrying in from his post.

"For heaven's sake, don't waste your ammunition!" he whispered. "One of them has gone up to the powder-house after dynamite. I heard the creaking of the iron door."

Adair whistled softly. "Dynamite! That will bring things to a focus beautifully, won't it? When they have blown us up, I wonder how they will account to Uncle Sidney for the loss of his car?"

Brissac had come running in at the sound of the firing. He missed the grim humor in Adair's query.

"Car, nothing!" he retorted. "Better say the entire camp and everything in it! There's a whole box-car load of dynamite and caps out here in the yard—sub-contractors' supplies waiting for the freighters' teams from the west end. If they smash us, the chances are ten to one that there'll be a sympathetic explosion out yonder in the yard somewhere that will leave nothing but a hole in the ground!"

"No," said Ford. "I gave orders myself to have that car set down below the junction when the Nadia came in."

"So you did; and so it was," Brissac cut in. "But afterward it got mixed in the shifting, and it's back in the yard—I don't know just where."

Adair turned to the cowering porter.

"Have you any more cartridges for this cannon of yours, Williams?" he asked.

"N-n-no, sah."

"Then we have three more chances in the hat. Much obliged for the dynamite hint, Stuart. I'll herd these three cartridges pretty carefully. Back to your sentry-boxes, you two, and make a noise if you need the artillery."

Another interval of suspense followed, thickly scored with pricklings of anxiety for the besieged. Then an attempt was made from the rear. Ford saw a dodging shadow working its way from car to car in the yard and signaled softly to Adair.

"Hold low on him," he cautioned, when the New Yorker was at his elbow, "those cheap guns jump like a scared cow-pony." Then he added: "And pray God you don't hit what he's carrying."

Adair held low and bided his time. There was another musket-like roar, and an instant though harmless reply from two rifles on the other side of the Nadia. But the dodging shadow was no longer advancing.

"I've stopped him for the time being, anyhow," said Adair, exulting like a boy. "If we only had a decent weapon we could get them all, one at a time."

"This was crude," Ford commented. "Eckstein will think up something better for the next attempt."

It was a prophecy which found its fulfilment after another sweating interval of watchfulness. This time it was Brissac who made the discovery, from the forward end of the Nadia. The nearest of the material cars was a box, lying broadside to the private car on the next side-track but one. From behind the trucks of the box-car a slender pole, headed with what appeared to be an empty oyster tin, and trailing a black line of fuse, was projecting itself along the ground by slow inchings, creeping across the lighted space between the two cars. Brissac promptly gave the alarm.

"This is where we lose out, pointedly and definitely," predicted Adair, still cheerful. "Anybody want to try a run for it?"

It was Ford who thought of the two negroes.

"Tell them, Roy," he said to Brissac. "Perhaps they would rather risk the rifles."

Brissac crept back to the central compartment, and the two watchers marked the progress of the inching pole, with its dynamite head and the ominous black thread of communication trailing like a grotesque horn behind it. At the crossing of the intervening track it paused, moving back and forth along the steel like a living thing seeking a passage. Finally the metallic head of it appeared above the rail, hesitated, and came on slowly. At that moment there was a shout, and the two negroes, hands held high, tumbled from the opposite step of the Nadia and ran toward the commissary stables. Three shots bit into the silence, and the fat cook ran on, stumbling and shrieking. But the man Williams stopped short and fell on his face, rolling over a moment later to lie with arms and legs outspread.

"God!" said Ford, between his set teeth; "they saw who they were—they couldn't help seeing! And there was no excuse for killing those poor devils!"

But there was no time for reprisals, if any could have been made. When Brissac rejoined the two in the forward vestibule, the stiff-bodied snake with its tin head and trailing horn was crossing the second rail of the intervening siding.

"We've got to think pretty swiftly," suggested Adair, still cool and unruffled. "I might be able to hit that tin thing at this short distance, but I suppose that would only precipitate matters. What do you say?"

Ford could not say, and Brissac seemed to have become suddenly petrified with horror. He was staring at the lettering on the box-car opposite—the one under whose trucks the dynamiters were hiding.

"Look!" he gasped; "it's the car of explosives, and they don't know it!" Then he darted back into the Nadia's kitchen, returning quickly with a huge carving-knife rummaged from the pantry shelves. "Stand back and give me room," he begged; and they saw him lean out to send the carving-knife whistling through the air: saw it sever the head from the stiff-bodied snake—the head and the trailing horn as well.

"Good man!" applauded Adair, dragging the assistant engineer back to safety before any of the sharpshooters had marked him down. "Where did you learn that trick?"

"It is my one little accomplishment," confessed the Louisianian. "An old Chickasaw chief taught me when I was a boy in the bayou country."

The peril was over for the moment. The severed pole was withdrawn, and for what seemed like an endless interval the attack paused. The three besieged men kept watch as they might, creeping from window to window. Out under the blue glare of the commissary arc-light the body of the negro porter lay as it had fallen. Once, Ford thought he heard groans from the black shadow where the fat cook had disappeared, but he could not be sure. On the other side of the private car, and half-way between it and the forty-thousand-pound load of high explosives, the petard oyster-tin lay undisturbed, with the carving-knife sticking in the sand beside it.

"What will they try next?" queried Adair, when the suspense was again growing intolerable.

"It is simple enough, if they happen to think of it," was Ford's rejoinder. "A few sticks of dynamite in a plugged gas-pipe: cut your fuse long enough, light it, and throw the thing under the car. That would settle it."

Adair yawned sleepily.

"Well, they've got all night for the inventive part of it. There's no rescue for us unless somebody—a good husky army of somebodies—just happens along."

"The army is less than eight miles away—over at Frisbie's camp," said Ford. "With Dick to lead them, the track-layers would sack this place in about five minutes. If I could only get to the wire!"

Brissac heard the "if."

"Let me try to run their picket line, Ford," he said eagerly. "If I can get around to our quarters and into the telegraph tent—"

"You couldn't do it, Roy. There is the proof of it," pointing to the body of the slain negro. "But I have been thinking of another scheme. The track-camp wire is bracketed across the yard on the light-poles. I have my pocket relay. I wonder if we could manage to cut in on that wire?"

"Wait a minute," Brissac interrupted. He was gone but a moment, and when he returned he brought hope with him.

"The wire is down and lying across the front vestibule," he announced excitedly. "They must have cut it up yonder by the telegraph tent and the slack has sagged down this way."

"Which gives us a dead wire without any batteries," said Ford gloomily; and then: "Hold on—aren't there electric call-bells in this car, Adair?"

"Yes, several of them; one in each state-room."

"Good! that means batteries of some sort," said Ford. "Rummage for them, Brissac, while I get that wire in here."

The wire was successfully pulled in through the front vestibule without giving the alarm. Ford twisted it in two when he had enough of it to reach the central compartment. Adair did sentry duty while the two technicians wrought swiftly. The bell battery was found, the ground connection made with a bit of copper wire stripped from one of the state-rooms, and Ford quickly adjusted the delicate spring of the tiny field relay.

What he feared most was that the few dry-cells of the bell battery would not supply the current for the eight miles of line up Horse Creek. For a time, which lengthened to dragging minutes, the anxious experimenters hung over the tiny field instrument. The sensitive magnet seemed wholly dead. Then, suddenly, it began to tick hesitantly in response to Ford's tapping of the key.

"Thank God, the battery is strong enough," he exclaimed. "Now, if there is somebody within hearing at Frisbie's end of the line ..."

He was clicking persistently and patiently, "E-T," "E-T," "E-T," alternating now and then with the Horse Creek call and his own private code letter, when Adair came up from his post at one of the rear windows. The golden youth was the bearer of tidings, but Ford held up his hand for silence: some one was breaking in to reply from Frisbie's—Frisbie, himself, as the minimized tickings speedily announced.

Ford snipped out his call for help in the fewest possible words:

Arm M'Grath's gang and bring it by train to Horse Creek, quick. MacMorroghs are trying to dynamite us in the Nadia.   FORD.

Almost without a break in the insect-like tickings the reply came:

Stand them off; help coming.

The thing done, the master workman in Ford snatched at the helm.

Did you catch and hold the pick-and-shovel men from this camp?

he clicked anxiously.

Got them all herded here and ready to go back to work—for more pay,

answered Frisbie; and Ford ticked one more word, "Hurry," and closed the key with a sigh of relief. Then, and not until then, Adair said: "Is that all, for the present? If it is, I'm sorry to have to report that the beggars outside have hit upon your gas-pipe scheme. They are rolling a round, black thing with a string attached down upon us from the commissary. The slant of the hill is just enough to keep it coming where the ground is smooth."

From sheer force of habit, Ford disconnected his field telegraph, cased and pocketed it. Then there was an instant adjournment to the rear windows on the camp side. Happily, the rolling bomb was as yet only on the way. Pebbles and roughnesses intervened here and there to stop or to turn it aside, and since it was out of reach of their longest pole, the dynamiters would start it on again by throwing stones at it.

Hereupon ensued a struggle which, under other conditions, would have figured as horse-play. One after another the three men in the car heaved cushions, pillows, obstructions of any sort, in the path of the rolling menace. And behind the commissary barricade the dynamiters patiently twitched the bomb by the firmly fastened fuse this way and that to avoid the obstacles, or sent it forward under the impact of well-directed missiles.

Ford was the first of the three to recognize the futility of the cushion barricades.

"They'll beat us—they'll drop it in the ditch right here under us in spite of fate!" he juried. "Brissac: go and break the glass in the accident tool-case and bring me the ax, quickly!" And when he had it; "Now get me a piece of that telegraph wire and bend a hook on the end of it—jump for it; you'll have to twist it off with your fingers!"

With an energy that made no account of the lamed arm, Ford tore up the carpet and fell to work fiercely, cutting a hole through the car floor; while Brissac broke a piece from the wire and bent a finger-shaped hook on the end of it. Adair, with his eye at a hole in a window shade, gave his attention to the attack.

"They are getting it here, slowly but surely," he reported. "It is going to roll under us just about where you are.... Now it has gone past my line of sight." And a moment later, in the same drawling monotone: "They have lighted the fuse, but there is a good long string of it to burn through. Take your time—" then, with a sudden failure in the monotone: "No, by Jove! you can't take your time! The fire is jumping across the road to beat the band!"

The hole was opened through the floor, and Ford was on his stomach with his face and an arm in the aperture, fishing desperately for the loop in the fuse. It was his success, his sudden drawing of the loop up into the car, that had shocked Adair out of his pose. Brissac was ready with the ax, and the instant the loop appeared it was severed, the burning end cast off, and the other end, with the bomb attached, was safely drawn up into the car.

The perspiration was running from Ford's face in streams when he had the engine of death securely in his hands.

"Take it, Roy," he gasped. "Drop it into the water-cooler. That will be the safest place for it if they fall back on the gun-play."

As if his word had evoked it, a storm of rifle bullets swept through the car, smashing windows, breaking the remaining gas globes and splintering the wood-work. Again and again the flashes leaped out of the surrounding shadows and the air was sibilant with whining missiles.

Brissac had the infernal machine: at first he fell upon it and covered it with his body; afterward he crawled with it into the nearest state-room and muffled it in a roll of berth mattresses.

When the storm ceased, as suddenly as it had begun, they crept together in the vestibule farthest from the commissary lead-hurling volcano to count the casualties.

There was none; not even a bullet score or a splinter-wound to show for the hot bombardment, though the side of the Nadia facing the commissary was riddled.

"I'm believing all I've ever read about its taking a hundred pounds of lead to kill one man in a war battle," said the New Yorker, grimly humorous to the last. "How do you two C. E.'s account for it?"

"We don't," said Ford shortly. "We're merely thankful that all humankind habitually shoots high when it's excited or in a hurry."

Then he sprang afoot, secured his ax, and sent Brissac to the pantry to rummage for other weapons. "A rush is the next thing in order," he suggested; and they prepared as they could to meet it.

But the rush did not come. Instead of it, one man, carrying what appeared to be a bundle of dripping rags, came cautiously into the open and approached the shattered car. The night wind sweeping down from the upper valley was with him, and the pungent odor of kerosene was wafted to and through the broken windows.

Brissac hurled the skillet like a clumsy discus

"Oho!" said Adair. "Having safely shot you dead or disabled, they are now going to give you Christian burial, Ford. Also, they will comfortably obliterate all the marks and scars of this pleasant evening's diversion. How near shall I let him come before I squander one of the two remaining cartridges on him?"

"Wait," said Brissac in a half-whisper. In his second pantry rummaging he had found nothing more promising than a cast-iron skillet—promising because it had weight and a handle to wield it by. The intending incendiary was no more than a few yards from his goal when Brissac rose up opposite the nearest shattered window and hurled the skillet like a clumsy discus. His aim was true to a hand's-breadth: a bullet from Adair's pistol could have done no more. With a cry that was fairly shogged out of him by the impact of the iron missile, the man flung away his burden, dropped in his tracks and lay groaning.

They looked for another storm of lead to follow this, and hugged the floor in readiness for it. When it did not come, Ford crept to the hole in the car floor and listened long and intently. Half an hour he had given Frisbie to get his track-layers together, and to cover the eight miles of rough-laid rails with the construction train. What was delaying him?

"You said Gallagher ditched your car: did it block the track?" he asked of Adair.

"It did, didn't it, Brissac?" was the answer, and the assistant confirmed it.

"Then that is why Frisbie can't get to us. Was Gallagher's engine still on the rails?"

"It was."

Ford sat up and nursed his knees. "Dick will make a way if he can't find one ready made. But it may take hours. Meanwhile, if these devils have scouts out—"

"Yes?" said Adair.

"They'll bring the warning, and there won't be much more time wasted in experiments. They can do us up, if they get right down to business."

"What are they doing now?" Adair asked of Brissac, who was on watch on the commissary side.

"I'll be hanged if I know. It looks like a young cannon, and it's pointed this way. By George! it's coming—coming by its all alone, too!"

By this time they were all watching the new menace. Brissac's description fitted it accurately; a cylindrical object mounted upon a pair of small wheels taken from the commissary store-room truck. It came toward the Nadia by curious surges—a rush forward and a pause—trailing what appeared to be a long iron rod behind it.

Ford hit upon the explanation. The cylindrical thing was another gas-pipe bomb; the iron tail was a smaller pipe containing and armoring the fuse, and serving also as the means of propulsion. They were coupling on additional lengths of the fuse-carrying pipe as they were needed; hence the jerking advances and pauses.

Adair's low laugh was as care-free as ever.

"A practical illustration of the tail wagging the dog," he remarked. "But the dog will wag us good and plenty when they get him where they want him. You can't fish that thing up through the hole with your wire—or crop the tail."

"No; it's a run for it, this time," said Ford, rising and stripping his coat.

But Brissac was pointing to three or four men dodging from shadow to shadow under the masthead lights and circling wide to tighten the line of circumvallation.

"We shan't run very far," he commented.

It seemed a hair-graying age to the watchers at the Nadia's windows before the men behind the commissary barricade got their infernal machine placed to their liking. They stared at it, all three of them, fascinated, deaf and blind to all else. A minimized shudder as of drumming wheels or escaping steam was in the air when they saw the flare of the match that betokened the firing of the fuse, but no one of the three heard it.

It was when the sputtering line of fire had buried itself in its tube that they became suddenly alive to the unbelievable fact that a locomotive was thundering down the yard on the Nadia's track. A rifle cracked; then another and a third; but the engine came on as if its driver bore a charmed life.

Surely Michael Gallagher must have prayed to the saints that night. He did not know that the very seconds had become priceless: he knew only that Frisbie had sent him on ahead to snake the president's car out of the Horse Creek yard as quickly as possible. Yet if he could have seen the bomb and the sputtering fuse, he could not have slowed more deftly to let the automatic couplers clutch each other, nor, at the touch and clamp, could he have reversed and gathered headway with greater skill.

The three occupants of the Nadia staggered to their feet as the private car lunged ahead in the grasp of the big engine, increasing speed with every wheel-turn. Mechanically, and as one man, they rushed to the rear platform. The mock cannon stood where it had been thrust; but in the camp street a handful of men were wrestling madly with the pipe fuse-carrier, breaking it, wrenching it in pieces, and stamping futilely upon the snake-like thing hissing and spitting under their feet.

"Look!" sobbed Adair. "They know—they've discovered that box-car! Oh, why in the name of the pitiful Christ don't they drop it and run?"

This from the man who had laughed, and aimed and fired and laughed again, in the heat of battle. But Ford's rejoinder was the bitter malediction of the defeated industry captain. "Damn their worthless lives!" he stormed. "In the next half-minute the Pacific Southwestern stands to lose a quarter of a million dollars!"

It was but a vanishing glimpse that they had of the handful of madmen stamping and dancing under the masthead light in front of the commissary; a glimpse withdrawing swiftly into a dim perspective as the Nadia was whisked around the curve and up the Horse Creek grade.

It was after Gallagher had picked up the lights of the waiting train of armed track-layers, and was whistling to announce his success, that the end came. For the three watchers on the rear platform of the president's car the little constellation of arc-stars in the valley below was suddenly blotted out in a skyward belching of gray flame; a huge volcano-burst of momentarily illuminated dust. Instinctively they braced themselves for the concussion that followed,—a bellowing thunderclap and a rending of earth and air that shook the surrounding hills and drowned the shriek of Gallagher's whistle.

A blast of air, down-drawn from the heights to fill the dreadful vacuum, was still rocking the stopped car when Frisbie climbed nimbly to the railed rear platform and swung his lantern to light the faces of the three men braced in the doorway.

"A close call, gentlemen," was his only comment; and then he appealed briefly to Ford for orders.

"Back us down slowly," said Ford shortly, "and follow with your train. We may need the men."

Frisbie went forward through the wrecked private car, returning presently to flag Gallagher along with the lantern swung over the railing. Down in the valley of the Pannikin the heavy, sickening fumes of the burned explosives hung in the air, and when the car swung in on the straight line the red glare of a wrecked and burning oil tank lighted the scene.

The camp site was blankly unrecognizable. Where the ten-tracked yard had been there was a vast depression, half-filled with distorted steel and débris indescribable, twisted iron and splintered wood, with the water from the river pouring into it. The commissary buildings and the surrounding bunk-shanties were gone, swept away as with the stroke of a mighty broom; and the trees on the hillsides above were scorched and shriveled as if a forest fire had blasted them.

Frisbie was the first to speak after he had flagged Gallagher to a stand on the farthermost edge of the devastation.

"Any use to turn out the crew and hunt for them?" he asked.

Ford shook his head.

"No. Leave M'Grath and a few others to stand guard and to flag the incoming steel trains, and let's get out of this. I'm sick; and so is Mr. Adair."

XXVI
THE STAR OF EMPIRE

A week, the most strenuous week in Copah's history, had passed, and still the president's party delayed its return to what Miss Priscilla Van Bruce constantly referred to as "civilization"; though the Farthest West has always been slow to admit the derogatory comparison which the word implies.

During the strenuous week much had happened, and much more was scheduled to happen. For one twenty-four-hour day the ex-speculator in Mr. Colbrith held out against the sharp attacks of the reawakened lust of conquest. Then, from Jack's Canyon on the Transcontinental, from men-clustered construction trains on the extension, over the passes from Summit Lakes, and across the brown plains from Green Butte, poured the army of gold-seekers, and the president was swept away and into the very vortex of the stock-jobbing whirlpool.

It was not until the third day of the week that Adair came ambling into Copah, riding a cart mule from Frisbie's camp. To his sister and his aunt the young man told everything; to his uncle nothing. Between gasps in the speculative frenzy Mr. Colbrith found time to complain bitterly to his nephew of Ford's defection.

"It was dastardly!" he shrilled. "We had some words; I don't deny that we had some words. But he was most unreasonable. He should have gone about his business and let me have time to consider. Here are thousands of people pouring into this place, everything at famine prices, no supplies for our miners, no railroad to bring them. What's this I hear about an accident at Horse Creek? Why isn't Ford on the ground attending to his railroad building and straightening things out? Have I got to forfeit the money-making chance of a lifetime and go and drag that track into Copah with my own hands?"

Adair seemed suddenly to have lost his tongue, which was certainly glib enough ordinarily. All he would say was that the engineering department was still at work, he believed; that the track was approaching Copah, slowly, perhaps, but pretty surely.

"But without a head!" snapped the irate president. "Ford is a traitor to the company. Tell him so from me, sir, if you know where he is skulking."

Adair did tell Ford, circumstantially, when he rode the cart mule out of town the next morning and met the young engineer at the head of a tremendously augmented track force, rushing the rails around the swelling hills on the approach to the mining-camp-city.

"Oh, he's still up in the air," laughed the director, when he had repeated the president's wrathful outburst. "Frantic because the road isn't finished; frantic because he can't get in on all the ground-floors in all the mining deals; frantic some more because he has to live in a shack hotel while he has a private car and a good cook, as he thinks, only a few miles away. Which reminds me: the '01' has a pretty good cook, and the incomparible Johnson,—don't let them escape. Have you sent the Nadia back to Denver for repairs?"

"Yes; Frisbie went over in it this morning."

"Frisbie?"

"Yes, I had to let him go. Word came from Leckhard as soon as we got the wire reestablished, which was late last night. North was taken suddenly ill the day after the explosion. He resigned at once by wire to the executive committee in New York, and two days later he took a steamer from Galveston for nobody knows where; health trip—doctor's orders—Leckhard said. I sent Frisbie over to be acting manager of the system, pending the president's—er—recovery from *his* sudden illness. Leckhard says the New York people are burning the wires trying to get word to Mr. Colbrith."

"They may go on burning them," said Adair calmly. "Uncle Sidney isn't going to quit until he owns a good half of the Copah district—or gets his armature burned out. And if he were ready to quit, we shouldn't let him. But how are things working out on the extension?—that is what interests me."

"Bully!" was the enthusiastic reply. "We're spending money like water; paying anything that's asked; and even then the men come and go like a torchlight procession. But we are keeping the surfacing gangs neck-full the entire length of the line, and Leckhard has already organized his regular train service over the first hundred miles. That puts us on an even footing with the Transcontinental at Jack's Canyon, and the tide is fairly turned our way. When we lay the rails into Copah,—which will be the day after to-morrow, if nothing pulls in two,—the first through passenger train, with the '01' in tow, will be right behind us. Does the report satisfy you?"

"Your word fits it: it's bully."

"Then I want my reward. When am I to be allowed to chase in and pay my respects to your—er—aunt, and—and Miss Alicia?"

Adair laughed.

"My—er—aunt!" he mocked. "Much you care about Aunt Hetty. And I've a thing or two to say about Alicia. Who gave you leave to fall in love with my little sister, I'd like to know?"

"She did," retorted Ford brazenly. "Don't tell me you are going to try to kick it over at this late day. You can't, you know."

Adair tilted his hat to the back of his head and thrust his hands into his pockets.

"I'm no such wild ass of the prairies," he declared. "But, my good friend, you don't come into town till you bring your railroad with you. I know how it will be: you'd linger for just one more last fond farewell, and about that time Uncle Sidney would drop in on you unexpectedly. Then there'd be a family row, after which my Pacific Southwestern stock wouldn't be worth a whoop. No; you wait till I get Uncle Sidney safely where I want him—properly in the nine-hole, and then I'll flag you in."

The chance for which the golden youth was waiting and working climaxed on the day the extension rails came down the hill-side grade above the town—a town now spreading into a wilderness of hastily built and crowding structures. It was a simple pit he had digged for an old man suddenly gone mad with the fever of mine-buying. From picking up stock in a score of prospects, Mr. Colbrith had hedged by concentrating his heavy investments in six or seven of the most promising of the partly developed properties. Then, to make assurance reasonably sure, he had sprung the modern method of combination upon his fellow stock-holders in the producing mines. The promising group was to be merged in one giant holding corporation, strong enough to control the entire Copah situation.

But there were obstacles in the way; obstructions carefully placed, if the truth must be told, by an unscrupulous young manipulator in the president's own household. The Little Alicia was in the group, was the keystone in the combination arch, as it chanced, and unhappily Grigsby had parted with a grievous block of his share of the stock—a block which could neither be recovered nor traced to its present holder. Not to make a mystery of the matter, the certificates were safely locked in a safety-deposit box in the vault of the Bank of Copah, and the key to the box rattled in Adair's pocket. And because the Little Alicia could not be included, three other necessary votes were withheld when the president tried to get action.

Mr. Colbrith was in despair. A good many of his investments were palpably bad; and they could be recouped only by the backing of the combination. And the combination obstinately refused to combine unless the Little Alicia could be gathered in. At the end of the ends Mr. Colbrith appealed to his nephew.

"You know where Ford is," he began accusingly. "You needn't deny it. I was in hopes we wouldn't have to ask him to sell us more than one share of his stock, which he couldn't decently refuse to do if we let him set his own price. But since we can't trace that block that

Grigsby let go, we must have nearly all of Ford's. Find him: get his stock if you have to pay twice par for it. If you don't, I—I shall be the heaviest loser in this camp, Charles Edward." It was gall and wormwood to the old man, but it had to be swallowed.

"So you are coming around to ask a favor of Ford?" said the young man unfeelingly. "He won't help you out. You mustn't forget that you kicked him out of the family; or rather you kicked him to prevent his getting into it."

"But think of the profit to him!" protested the president. "He paid only twenty cents for his half of the Alicia; he told me so himself. At two hundred he'd clear ninety thousand; a magnificent amount for so young a man!"

"Ford doesn't care anything about money. You can't move him that way."

"Well, then, find him for me and I'll—I'll apologize," said Mr. Colbrith, pressed now to the last extremity.

"He doesn't want your apologies, Uncle Sidney. Your little tiff was between man and man, and he'd never think of holding you accountable for anything you were foolish enough to say."

"Then what in heaven's name does he want?"—irascibly.

"Oh, a lot of things: reinstatement; your order to investigate the Denver management; a chance to build his railroad unmolested; and, as a side issue, a chance to whitewash your administration of Pacific Southwestern by conducting the house-cleaning in your name—this last because he thinks something of the family honor. He doesn't have to consider us, you know. At the next annual meeting he can elect Brewster president over your head: then you will have to stand for all the grafting and deviltry that will be unearthed."

The ground for this duel between President Colbrith and the determined young pace-setter was the lobby of the tar-paper-covered hotel, cleared now of the impromptu mining-stock exchange, which had moved into permanent quarters. The old man rose stiffly and stood grasping the chair-back.

"The same reckless charges against Mr. North and his subordinates—and now *you* are making them!" he rasped. "They are groundless; groundless, I tell you!"

Adair looked at his watch, listened a moment as for some expected sound from out-of-doors, and motioned toward the vacated chair.

"Sit down, Uncle Sidney, and let me tell you what happened at Horse Creek camp a week ago last night," he said evenly; and then he told the story of the attempt upon Ford's life, of the siege of the Nadia, of the terrible catastrophe which had involved all three of the MacMorroghs, the commissary staff, Eckstein, and the headquarters camp. When he finished, the president was shaking as if from a chill. Yet one thread of the strong strand of loyalty still held.

"It was horrible—fiendish!" he shuddered. "But it was the MacMorroghs' fight. It does not necessarily incriminate North."

"It does," said Adair, in the same even tone. "I told you that we left a few men at the wrecked camp to warn the incoming material trains. They found a single survivor of the thirteen men who tried to destroy us and the Nadia. It was Eckstein, North's secretary, and before he died he amply confirmed all of our guesses. They had plotted to have you quarrel with Ford. Ford had bought his half of the Little Alicia without any prompting, but from that as a starting point the entire scheme was worked up. The MacMorroghs' bookkeeper, a man named Merriam—who is at present in Copah, and whose deposition I have had taken before a justice of the peace—was detailed to win Frisbie over to the change of route—no difficult thing, since the change was for the better. But Merriam's part was chiefly to keep Frisbie from finding out anything about Ford's mine; which he did. Am I making it clear?"

The president bowed his head.

"Then, when you came West on your inspection trip, the trap was sprung. You were told that Ford had been doing a dishonorable thing, and you were urged to come over here and see for yourself. To make sure that there should be no slips, Penfield was sent with you, ostensibly as your acting secretary, but really as a spy—"

"Oh, no; I can't think that of young Penfield," protested the president.

"I say yes; and the proof is that Penfield has confessed. He was scared into it when I told him what had happened at Horse Creek and gave him his choice of telling me what he knew, or going to jail. Then I came on the scene at the inopportune moment, and after North had carefully issued instructions intended to delay me as much as possible, he sent Eckstein in post-haste by way of Jack's Canyon and the stage trail to get ahead of me. You see, he was afraid to trust matters to Penfield, who would most certainly have stopped short of the desperate measures Eckstein and the MacMorroghs finally took. It was decided at a council in which Penfield was present, that Ford's elimination must go through. If you didn't quarrel with him and drop him, he was to be murdered."

Mr. Colbrith was silent for a long minute after Adair ceased speaking. Then he looked up to say: "What was Ford doing at Horse Creek that night? He had left me only a few hours before; and, as I have said, we had—we had some words."

Adair smiled. "He was about to begin doing what he has been doing ever since: flogging the extension into shape night and day to get it ready to carry passengers and freight. He conceived it to be his duty—to you as well as to the other stock-holders. And he *has* flogged it into shape. Look out of that window, Uncle Sidney!"

A long passenger train, crowded to the platforms, and with the private car "01" in tow, was winding down the grade of the opposite hillside, and as they stepped to the windows the engineer woke the echoes with the engine whistle.

"The first one of many, let us hope," said the young man, standing at his uncle's elbow. Then, with quite a different note in his voice: "It's Stuart's work, all of it. He has scarcely stopped to eat or sleep since that horrible night in the Pannikin valley. And that night, Uncle Sidney, I fought shoulder to shoulder with him—as a brother should; he is a man, and—there are not many more—like him."

The president's thin lips were drawn into straight lines, and the thin goat's-beard stood out at the argumentative angle. Mr. Colbrith was chary of his emotions.

"Will he sell us that stock in the Little Alicia, Charles Edward?"

Adair smiled at the determined return to the practical.

"No," he said; "I don't think he will—I shouldn't, if I were in his place. But he will do the next best thing: he will marry Alicia and so bring it into the family. And on the railroad conditions I have named, I am quite sure he will make you his voting proxy if you want to use it in forcing the combine."

The president took a turn as far as the clerk's counter and back. The lobby was deserted, everybody having gone to welcome the first train into Copah.

"You seem to have North against the wall," he said when he came back. "Yet, for the sake of—of, well of his wife and children, he must have even-handed justice. I must insist upon that."

It was the most lovable thing in the irascible old man—his undying loyalty to a man in whom he had once believed. Adair slew the last hope with reluctance. Drawing a thick packet of undelivered telegrams from his pocket, he handed it to his uncle.

"Justice is the one thing Mr. North is most anxious to dodge," he said gravely. "When the news of the catastrophe reached him, he resigned by wire—to New York; not to you—got his physician to order him out of the country, and left Denver between two days.

Ford has sent Frisbie to Denver to hold things together, and there has been a number of removals—subject, of course, to your approval. You will find the history of all these minor happenings in those telegrams, which I have been collecting—and holding—until you had leisure to look them over."

"Where is Mr. Ford now?" asked the president crisply.

"He is not very far away; in fact, he is up-stairs in the sitting-room of our suite with Aunt Hetty and the two Van Bruce ladies and Alicia. Incidentally,—quite incidentally, you understand,—he is waiting to be asked to help you out in that mining deal."

"Fetch him," was the curt command; and Mr. Colbrith sat down to wade resignedly through the mass of delayed wire correspondence.

What remains of the story of the Pacific Southwestern is a chapter, as yet unfinished, in the commercial history of the great and growing empire of the West.

Of the rush to the Copah gold field; of the almost incredible celerity with which a stretch of one hundred and forty-odd miles of construction track was opened for the enormous traffic which was instantly poured in upon it; of the rapid extension of the line to a far western outlet; of the steady advance of P. S-W. shares to a goodly premium: these are matters which are recorded in the newspaper files of the period.

For the typically American success of the Southwestern's dramatic upward leap to the rank of a great railway system, President Colbrith has the name and the fame. Yet here and there in the newspaper record there is mention of one Stuart Ford, "our rising young railroad magnate," in the unashamed phrase of the *Copah Megaphone*, first as the president's assistant; later, as first vice-president and general manager of the system, in the Chicago headquarters, with Mr. Richard Frisbie as his second in command on the western lines, and Mr. Charles Edward Adair as comptroller and chief of finances on the executive committee in New York.

Ford's prophecies predicting the development of the new empire first traversed by the Western Extension have long since found ample fulfilment, as all the world knows. Copah gave the region its first and largest advertisement; but other mining districts, with their imperative beckonings to a food-producing population, have followed in due course.

It was early in June of the year marking the opening of the completed Western Extension for through Pacific Coast traffic that a one-car train, drawn by the smartest of passenger engines in charge of a diminutive, red-headed Irishman, stormed bravely up the glistening steel on the eastern approach to Plug Pass. The car was the rebuilt Nadia; and in obedience to a shrill blast of the cab air-whistle, Gallagher brought it to a stand on the summit of the mountain.

Alicia looked more than ever the artist's ideal of the American womanly felicities when Ford lifted her from the step of the Nadia.

"You are quite sure Mr. Gallagher won't mind?" she was saying, as they walked forward together.

"Mind? Wait till you hear what he says. Michael is an Irish diamond in the rough, and he knows when he is honored."

They discovered the red-headed little man industriously "oiling around" for the swift glide down the western declivities.

"Michael," said the first vice-president, "Mrs. Ford thinks she would like to take the Pannikin loop in the cab of the Six-eighty-eight. Can you make room for us?"

Gallagher snatched his cap from his fiery head.

"Could we make room? 'Tis by the blessing av the saints that I'm a little man, meself, Missis Foord, and don't take up much room in the c-yab. And as f'r Johnny Shovel, he'll be riding on the coal f'r the pure playsure av ut. My duty to ye, ma'am; and 'tis a pity ut isn't a black night, whin the swate face av ye would be lighting the thrack f'r us."

Ford lifted Alicia to the gangway and made her comfortable on the fireman's box, fixing a footbrace for her, and giving her his arm for a shoulder rest when Gallagher sent the steam whistling through the cylinder-cocks for the impulse needful to start the downward rush.

"'With a michnai—ghignai—'" she began; but when the engine plunged over the summit and the matchless view to the westward came suddenly into, being, the quotation lapsed in a long-drawn, ecstatic "O-o-oh!"

"You are not afraid, are you?" said the bridegroom, man-like, letting her feel the support of his arm.

"Afraid? No, indeed; I am just happy—happy! There lies the world before us, Stuart; *our* world, because, more than any other man's, yours were the brain that conceived it and the hands that brought it to pass. Let us go down quickly and possess it. Tell Mr. Gallagher that he may run as fast as ever he dares." Then with a sigh of contentment and a comfortable nestling into the hollow of the strong arm of protection: "Was there ever another wedding journey just like ours, Stuart, dear?"